ZOKU

OWARIMONOGATARI

END TALE (CONT.)

NISIOISIN

VERTICAL.

ZOKU OWARIMONOGATARI
End Tale (Cont.)

NISIOISIN

Art by VOFAN

Translated by Ko Ransom

VERTICAL.

CHAPTER FINAL KOYOMI REVERSE

ZOKU OWARIMONOGATARI

© 2014 NISIOISIN
All rights reserved.

First published in Japan in 2014 by
Kodansha Ltd., Tokyo.
Publication rights for this English edition
arranged through Kodansha Ltd., Tokyo.

Published by Vertical, an imprint of
Kodansha USA Publishing, LLC, 2020

ISBN 978-1-949980-44-8

Manufactured in the United States of America

First Edition

Kodansha USA Publishing, LLC
451 Park Avenue South, 7th Floor
New York, NY 10016

www.readvertical.com

CHAPTER FINAL
KOYOMI REVERSE

001

As you are all aware, Koyomi Araragi's tale has come to an end. There's nothing in particular to add. Much was resolved, and much wasn't. Some matters were put off, but that doesn't change the fact that a stopping point was reached. Just as every beam of light casts a shadow, every beginning has an end. And because there's an end, there's also a new beginning—though a shadow doesn't necessarily mean the presence of light. Or should we say darkness, rather than shadow? Either way, if it's dark beyond the tip of your nose, then that's already darkness.

Still, the way of the world is that endings are far harder than beginnings, and what was begun with ease calls for no small amount of effort to end. For example, as I wrestled to end the many tales that began when I casually saved a vampire on the verge of death, I thought I might die too—in fact, did die a number of times. I couldn't say I acted wisely by any means, nor that I brought it all to a tidy conclusion, but yeah, I can say with certainty that a period in Koyomi Araragi's life came to a close.

I made many mistakes, but that alone is no mistake.

I made no mistake.

And so, what'll begin here is a continuation of the end.

A worldview that wasn't supposed to be. An impossible future.

Shinobu Oshino, the husk of a vampire.

Tsubasa Hanekawa, the class president bewitched by a cat.

Hitagi Senjogahara, the girl caught in a crab's claws.

Mayoi Hachikuji, the ghost led astray by a snail.

Suruga Kanbaru, the junior who wished upon a monkey.

Nadeko Sengoku, the snake enwrapped by a snake, who swallowed a snake.

Karen Araragi, the little sister stung by a bee.

Tsukihi Araragi, the literal phoenix.

Yotsugi Ononoki, the corpse doll.

Sodachi Oikura, the returned childhood friend.

All the experts: Mèmè Oshino, the wandering older dude; Deishu Kaiki, the conman; Yozuru Kagenui, the violent *onmyoji*; Izuko Gaen, the big boss; Tadatsuru Teori, the doll-user.

And Ogi Oshino.

This is their tale—continued.

Call it a free gift if you want, but let's not make light of it— people learn more from defeat than from victory, don't they.

So.

I'll try and take it—as a teachable moment.

0 0 2

The next day, I was roused from bed—but not by my little sisters Karen and Tsukihi.

My lovable siblings had warned me:

"You're not in high school anymore. You need to wake up on your own starting tomorrow, okay?"

"Uh huh, Karen's exactly right!"

These were pronouncements that should've been made before I moved on to middle school, at the latest. I found it rather mysterious that Tsukihi was behaving like Karen's lackey, but whatever the case, the next day.

In other words this morning, I woke up on my own—I'd been up late the previous night, and I didn't need to wake up early anymore, so I'd slept in for the first time in a while.

Now, this felt strange.

Not so much because my little sisters didn't come wake me up—but that was part of it, and I knew the exact reason for my odd feeling.

"Oh…right," I muttered absentmindedly.

The words pregnant with emotion—oh, right.

Starting today, I was no longer a senior at Naoetsu High—an

evident, or self-evident fact that still felt more bizarre than any of the mysterious and unfathomable tales of aberrations I'd experienced.

So strange I almost had trouble accepting it.

Speaking of moving on to middle school, or even the time I moved on from it—from Public MS #701 to Naoetsu Private High School—I'd felt no such discomfort whatsoever. Had my time as a student at Naoetsu left that deep of an impression on me?

Especially my final year. The very last one.

It began with a hellish spring break and ended all the way in actual hell. What's more, I survived it all, came out alive, and miraculously graduated, and was ruminating on it now—no, wait, it wasn't such a pretty and emotive reaction.

If we're going to say that a lot happened, a lot happened to me during middle school too. Even elementary was no walk in the park—after recalling my past shenanigans with Oikura, so many connected traumas had come back to me that it felt like I was drowning in a sea of regret every night.

Splashing and gasping for air. Like I was going to suffocate underwater.

If I was going to feel moved about being alive today, I ought to feel moved about being alive yesterday, too—not that anyone, teens included, can live every day moved to their core.

That much sentiment would kill even a vampire.

First off, I hadn't attended the graduation ceremony held at Naoetsu High's gymnasium the day before. Boycotting a commemorative ceremony that marked the end of my high school days makes me sound like quite an anarchist, with my juniors looking up to me, but pair it with the graceful groveling I performed on all fours in the teachers' room later, and it'd be enough to throw water on the flames of a century-long love.

I don't know if I should be sharing this, but at the last moment my alma mater became a forbidden place I never wanted to visit again.

What kind of legend was I leaving behind?

Could I have wound things up in any worse of a way?

I felt like winding a rope around my neck, if anything.

It'd be odd to say that's why—it'd sound like sour grapes, but I'm still saying it—frankly that's why graduating and not being a high schooler anymore was leaving me cold. The most I felt was relief that my little sisters wouldn't be reviving me each morning.

You've served your purpose, my little sisters!

I generally tried my hardest to act cool and wasn't going to let some commencement ceremony make me tear up or gird up—I'd rather get on all fours and grovel. The one clear difference between this graduation and all the graduations before it, though, was not knowing what followed.

A total mystery.

When I graduated elementary, I knew I'd be proceeding normally to #701, and when I graduated at #701, I'd already been accepted by my (then-)dream school, Naoetsu High—in other words, my graduations so far had meant a simple change in title.

A transposition if you want, a mere transfer.

But not this time.

I'd graduated from Naoetsu High but had no idea what would become of me—honestly, at that moment, on March sixteenth, I didn't know if I'd been accepted by my first-choice college.

What came next wasn't settled. My future was uncertain.

True, the same goes for everyone, of course, but having taken these titles for granted, as naturally appearing alongside or together with my name, I was flummoxed when it vanished just as naturally.

Something was off. Stripped of my title, I was nothing. My plain self.

Not a high school student. Not someone preparing for exams.

13

Not a college student, not a rejected applicant.

Not a member of the labor force.

Plain, unbranded Koyomi Araragi—they say you only appreciate how valuable something is after it's gone, but I never imagined losing your guaranteed status in a highly developed modern society would be so disorienting.

To be blunt, I didn't even like Naoetsu High while I was enrolled there. I'd been ready to drop out. Looking back on it, I still couldn't say I led a fulfilling life as a high schooler, not even out of insincere politeness—finally losing the title was so strangely liberating.

Liberating and disorienting.

To make a Kanbaru-like comparison, I was walking down the street butt naked—like oh, I'm nothing but me now.

I should be me no matter how much I dress up, change, or grow—Koyomi Araragi should be just Koyomi Araragi, but part of you seems to be shaped by your surroundings and environment, whether you like it or not.

If a policeman stopped me now for questioning, how should I answer—nah.

My own thoughts made me snicker.

It was funny how funny I felt.

Yeah, maybe I was just getting emotional about graduating from high school—embarrassed and ashamed, loath to admit this bit of childishness, I'd begun splitting a whole head's worth of hairs, that's all. That, or the stress of waiting for my college results was too much, and I was escaping reality by focusing on something other than what was really on my mind—I guess I was able to look at myself pretty objectively these days.

It'd be so presumptuous of me to agonize over a loss of identity, anyway—consider the goddess, scratch that, Hanekawa, who gallantly ventured out into the world as her very own self the day we graduated.

Forget about police questioning, she'd be traveling where militaries might want to have a word with her (why, Hanekawa?). In the end I clung onto her and tried to stop her with tears in my eyes (not exaggerating for effect, I seriously cried) instead of seeing her off with a smile; she was the one with a beaming face as she left on her journey.

She deflected me with ease. Dodged me like it was nothing.

No point going out of my way to feel even lonelier, but eventually, the time she spent in high school with me and Hitagi would become insignificant to her.

That's how I feel. Keenly.

Meanwhile, we'll probably never meet someone as talented as Hanekawa again. *Miss Hanekawa is the real deal. She's made from different stuff than us,* Hitagi once told me, I forget when, and I was beginning to understand what she meant.

Different stuff. Or maybe different tales. In any case, different.

But I couldn't keep whining either, not when my complex about her had given the final stages of my high school life a terrible paint job—if I woke up feeling funny, I had to wipe that feeling away. Maybe I needed to wash my face.

I couldn't waste today—fortunately it was still before noon, even though my sisters hadn't woken me up and I'd let myself sleep in, (literally) unconsciously.

I understand that adults in their prime fire themselves up with the notion that if their life is a day long, they aren't even to noon. For me, it wasn't even noon in the real world—freed from exam prep or not, Koyomi Araragi was too young to be sitting around absently staring at the lawn and sipping tea (should go without saying).

Time to get active.

Why not enjoy my title-less self for a few days? It'd be over in the blink of an eye in retrospect—and if the police pulled me over for questioning, I'd tell them:

"Koyomi Araragi here. Just the man you see."

…It'd probably get me taken downtown.

Maybe they'd call for backup. Maybe they'd surround me.

Thinking such thoughts, I realized leaving the house would be a place to start—it was past breakfast time anyway, and I couldn't borrow the BMX forever, so biking with no particular destination in mind sounded like a plan—and changed out of my pajamas.

I nearly put on my uniform out of habit, please excuse my error as a cute little quirk—wearing the jeans I'd lent Hanekawa back in August, perhaps to share in the good fortunes of the *real deal* who was standing on foreign soil by now, I passed my arms through the sleeves of a shirt.

This seemed to focus my attention at once, and I left my room—my parents would have left for work at this hour, but I wondered what my little sisters were up to.

They were on vacation as well… I thought about peeking into their room before heading down the stairs but decided against it at the last moment.

I wasn't being childish and sulking because they hadn't woken me up. They weren't grade schoolers anymore, either. I was the one who needed to figure out the right distance between us.

Pulling away from them after finally settling our differences and carrying on proper conversations again was a little sad, but older brothers and little sisters are fated to grow apart.

My plan was to stay at home for a little while even if I got accepted into college, but the idea of leaving made me feel a step closer to adulthood than them. I had to encourage them to become self-reliant—or maybe self-supporting. They needed to be able to live without me.

…It did feel like that wouldn't be a problem for them.

In fact, Karen, who'd be starting high school in a month, increasingly acted like a big sister (maybe Tsukihi was behaving like a toady in response, though that was just canceling out her sister's progress). Judging that I didn't need to worry—I ignored their room and walked downstairs.

By the way, there was another person, or rather, body in my little sisters' room, an expressionless and hard-to-define doll that dared freeload there, but I ignored her on a far more fundamental level.

If I exchanged words with that tween, she might end up joining me on my bike ride—best not to offer the kid the chance. Then again, I suppose it was her job since she'd technically been tasked with observing me.

All the more reason for me to tiptoe away from home, and in fact that was the manner in which I headed to the bathroom.

Making sure no one was in the bath (Karen could totally be washing off her sweat after a morning jog), I washed my face. Getting dressed had awakened me, but splashing cold water on my face was really refreshing, a jolt signaling that something new was to come—yeah, I'm a simple man.

I hadn't cut my hair once since spring break, and it'd grown a good bit too long after a year. Wet from the collateral damage of my face-washing, it could even use a hair dryer. When you're washing your face, you gotta be bold, man.

"Phew!"

And so.

I faced forward—and looked into the bathroom sink mirror.

There I was. Koyomi Araragi.

There, laterally inverted and reflected in the mirror, was Koyomi Araragi—which might sound obvious, but until just the other day it wasn't a given.

I should've been sick and tired of seeing my face, but hadn't scrutinized it in a while.

Stuff happened—and I, Koyomi Araragi, had been left without a reflection after February. When I faced a mirror, just the

17

background was reflected, like some sort of special effect (chroma keying, was it?).

Like some vampire of legend.

I didn't appear in mirrors.

How did the story behind the word *narcissist* go, again? Wasn't a youth so enraptured by his own reflection in a spring that he fell in and drowned? Well, I fixed my eyes on that mirror like I never learned the moral.

Gazing.

They say what's essential isn't visible, but the practical thought struck me that the visible can be essential too.

"Hm?"

Still, I had all the opportunities in the world from now on to see this particular face, and whatever unavoidable circumstances may have been involved, a boy graduating from high school, barely post-adolescent, looking at his reflection forever wasn't very cool (if that doll saw me now, she'd be set for material for the rest of my life). I took my eyes off of myself.

But.

My self in the mirror—didn't take my eyes off of me.

"Um...what?"

Lo and behold. As a result of my training, did my movements now exceed the speed of light, leaving my reflection in the dust? I was flummoxed, but this wasn't the case.

I hadn't been training to begin with, and even if some dormant power in me had suddenly awakened, my reflection still didn't trace my movements on second glance.

It didn't reflect me; I wasn't reflected.

It only gazed at me, its eyes fixed on me.

I was looking at me through the mirror. The eyes almost seemed...

I reached a hand toward the surface without meaning to— what an idiot, what was I trying to check? As if the mirror might be a windowpane, and the person I took to be me was outside.

A twin brother? At this point? Were we fluffing up my backstory after all this time? Anyone would call that a stretch—far too after the fact. And anyway, that might work as a trick in a mystery novel, but people don't mistake windows for mirrors in real life.

In fact, it wasn't a windowpane installed there above the sink. Obviously enough—but after touching it, I couldn't call it a mirror, either.

Because—*bloop*.

My finger *broke into* its surface.

Broke in—or *sunk* in, maybe.

Like into some kind of spring—no.

A swamp.

"Shi-Shinobu!" I yelled down at my feet, but it was too late.

The mirror.

The face, the plane of what seemed like a mirror until moments ago, now an unknown substance, was stained purple, and—

003

Stained purple—and I was there in the bathroom.

There in the usual Araragi residence bathroom—having fallen on my butt.

"...Huh?"

Huh?

I stood right up and looked at the mirror, only to find a plain mirror, nothing particularly strange about it—reflecting nothing unusual as it reflected my usual self. I was properly mirrored, and it traced my movements.

An undeniable mirror.

I tried darting around, but it kept up with me—and naturally wasn't stained purple, either. What kind of mirror took on such a color? No matter how I much gazed at it or rubbed it, it was just a plain old mirror.

Wasn't there some phenomenon where if you keep on projecting the same photo onto a screen with an overhead projector, the kind you'd find in a school's AV room, the emitted light gets burned on and doesn't vanish even after you turn the power off? Could what just took place be similar?

Maybe I was just seeing things.

A waking dream? I might hallucinate Hanekawa, but would I really hallucinate me?

Who knew, contrary to my belief that I'd woken myself up by washing my face, maybe I was still half asleep—thinking so, I decided to finish the job and washed my face again, carefully.

Yes, with some refreshing cold water—but no.

That's what I tried to do, but I must've turned the wrong handle on the faucet because I ended up washing my face with scalding water. I accidentally put myself in a variety-show scenario, but it did even more to wake me up than if I'd used cold water, so it was an acceptable outcome.

Hm.

Looking up again, I still found nothing but a plain mirror—the mirror was a mirror, and just a mirror. I'd panicked like I'd encountered yet another aberrational phenomenon, but I suppose such dramatic occurrences aren't common.

I had to admit it felt somehow anticlimactic, or even the slightest bit disappointing, but now that I'd brought an end to my involvement with Ogi, I did want to live in peace for at least a short while.

I'd called out for Shinobu for no good reason, but it looked like I hadn't woken up the nocturnal girl, fortunately. No reaction came from my shadow.

Well, that was good to know. There was no telling how many donuts I'd have to treat the spoilt little girl to if I'd summoned her for no good reason. She was a reliable little girl but came at a high price.

Yes, I'd only seen a shadow and mistaken it for a ghost.

Actually, forget about shadows. How hopeless was I to let my own reflection scare me? While Koyomi Araragi may have spent a year fighting tooth and nail against countless aberrations, he was indeed but a shadow of his former self.

Appalled and disgusted, I picked up a towel and began drying down my hair—my self in the mirror moved in the exact same way, of course, and as he reached out for the hairdryer in the drawer with his left hand, me with my right…

"Oh, Koyomi. You're up."

A voice came from the bath—followed by the sound of the door opening.

It was Karen, the older of my two little sisters.

Huh?

I thought I'd checked before washing my face, but I guess she'd been bathing—where had she hidden that big body of hers? Our bath is of a very standard size, unlike in the anime—had she dived underwater or what?

I take back my earlier statement, she's always going to be a child. I turned to face her, but then…

"Hm?"

I was left at a loss for words—no, maybe it all made sense now. Maybe you could say in *that* case, of course she could've hidden, not just in the tub but anywhere in the room. Karen Araragi, my little sister who'd long outgrown her big brother in height, approaching six feet and still growing.

Karen Araragi's head—was far below mine.

"Hand me my towel, big bro."

While I was speechless, Karen simply had nothing special to say as she pointed at a bath towel atop a shelf—her finger hardly making it up to my face.

She could've reached it if she stood on her tiptoes, but she always knew how to make work for my idle hands—okay, it's an exaggeration that her head was far below mine, but still.

Was she even five foot tall?

She was shorter than Tsukihi… Maybe about Sengoku's height?

"What's the matter, big bro? Is there something on my face?"

Suspicious at last about the way I was sizing her up, she twisted her fresh-from-the-bath body.

"Uh, no," I said, not sure how to reply. I handed her the towel for the time being.

"Tɥɒnʞƨ!"

Karen took it and began wiping herself down but finished in no time given how little surface area she had.

"Hɒnb ɯə ɯʎ qɐnɈiɘƨ ɒnb bɹʇ."

"S-Sure," her big brother obeyed like some kind of servant.

I might have continued to if she asked me to dress her next, but I couldn't stay confused forever.

"Um, Karen...right?" I asked as I handed the girl her under-wear.

"Uɥ, ʎɐɥʔ I'ɯ Kɒɹən. Wɥo əlƨə woʋlb I bəʔ" she answered as if I was making no sense—Karen Araragi.

Yes. Of course.

I could never mistake a member of my family even after a height or size change, but fully acknowledging that fact—if I may, while teenagers get taller, it's highly uncommon for them to get shorter.

Overnight too.

"..."

Not even Karen ordered me to put the bra on her, and as I watched her do it herself, I came upon an awful possibility. Wasn't she about this height back in elementary?

An elementary-aged Karen had—no, no.

Ridiculous. Impossible.

Where was the demand for a lolita Karen?

A child forever, literally? That role belonged to someone, but not her.

As that thought went through my head, I asked, my voice non-chalant: "Karen, how old are you turning next birthday again?"

She fastened the hook of her bra and looked at me, her eyes expecting a birthday present (my aching heart).

"Sixteen," she replied.

Hm. I wasn't dealing with lolita-Karen, after all. Then again, she didn't start wearing a bra until middle school, and while her height was one thing, her legs and torso hadn't filled out like this during elementary. I'd guessed the answer to my question even before I asked, but it did away with the awful possibility of another godforsaken time warp.

Good.

You only need to experience something as absurd as time travel once in your lifetime—in fact, once is once too often. In terms of absurdities, though, my tall little sister shrinking overnight by about a foot rivalled traveling through time.

It wasn't right, no matter how you looked at it.

Oshino had warned me countless times about blaming everything on aberrations. Although I'd faced this side of myself and reflected on it not long ago, might my little sister be the victim of some urban legend? I hesitated to give voice to the thought.

"¿"

Since my perplexed look seemed to be perplexing her in turn, she wasn't seeing things the same way... Though I was no longer speechless, I realized I mustn't speak carelessly—Karen didn't know she'd suffered from an aberration even last time around with that bee. She hadn't begun to notice that the Araragi residence was quietly turning into a haunted house, and I wanted her mind and spirit to remain in good health—but did anything like that exist?

An aberration that makes you shorter...

The scariest *yokai* in the world for a short guy like me, but when you think about it, is it really so scary? I've heard of monsters that grow larger like the *mikoshi-nyudo*, but...

"Big bro, what're you planning for today? Going on a date with Miss Senjougahara?"

"N-No, it's not like I have any... I was thinking of maybe

25

going for a bike ride on my own."

"Huh. Tsukihi and I are gonna go shopping. We're preparing or celebrate the disbanding the stress trip or."

"A-Ah…you really are disbanding, then. Right, at long last you'll be a high schooler, in its full glory, huh?"

"Yeah. Well, I'm worried about whether Tsukihi's dash is a lot or think my own—smees che sah a tol ro tinhk about."

"Oh…"

I did wonder (in a bad way) about these things to *think about*, but it seemed like we were able to conduct a proper conversation.

Didn't someone say that you don't need to be too scared of aberrations if you can communicate with them?

It did also seem like Karen's voice was somehow flipped around, but maybe that was my imagination. Maybe it was echoing since we were near the bath.

How does a voice get flipped around, anyway?

How do you even express that?

"Well. Actually, you need or leave. Your little sister is in her underwear right now, though," Karen said after all this time.

Just as she finished putting on her panties.

Perhaps this was her complex, maidenly heart talking; she was fine being seen naked, but not in her underwear. I felt relieved, though—I'd started to wonder how much longer I was going to be there.

Yeah, sure—acting calm, I exited the bathroom.

I'd failed to dry my hair but was no longer in a place to be concerned about that. I climbed straight up the stairs and, without even knocking, opened the door to my little sisters' room that I'd ignored moments ago.

"Ah, big bro! So you're up."

"Do you two think I'm Sleeping Beauty or something?"

Tsukihi Araragi, who had immediately reacted in the same way as Karen—was no one but Tsukihi Araragi.

26

Tsukihi-chan.

Well, I guess Karen was also no one but Karen, but at least Tsukihi hadn't gotten any taller or shorter.

No deviations in her elevation. Normal sized. A 1:1 scale Tsukihi Araragi.

Even her hair was down to her ankles just like the day before—Karen said they were about to go shopping, but Tsukihi still had on the yukata she wore around home.

"What is it? Do you want me to praise you for waking up on your own?"

She laughed, and nothing about her struck me as unusual—if I wanted to nitpick, her voice did sound a little strange, but that had to be my paranoia. If you asked me how exactly, I didn't have a clue.

"Hey, Tsukihi? Is there something a little weird with Karen? I saw her just now in the bathroom—"

"Oh, she's bored! I'm next! You know how sweaty I get, morning dash era a must," Tsukihi said, neither listening to a word I said nor answering my question (instead answering a question I hadn't asked) as she passed by me—but no, judging by this line, she hadn't found Karen's height to be strange in the least. She couldn't have gone to bed and gotten up in the same room without noticing...so then, had my eyes fooled me?

Had the steam from the bath refracted the light to make her look shorter or something? If I wanted a logical explanation, sure, but that was such a stretch.

I couldn't come to a logical understanding. Or to any understanding at all.

"Tsu-Tsukihi?" I stopped my sister reflexively.

"Hm? What is it?"

She paused in the hallway and looked back at me, but I didn't know what to say.

Hasn't Karen gotten shorter somehow? Even shorter than you.

Maybe that's what I needed to ask, but she'd doubt my sanity if it was just a misunderstanding on my part.

And so, "You're wearing your yukata wrong again," I pointed out in my desperation.

"Oh? Am I? I always forget which side is supposed to go over the other—well, it's nice that I'm careful about it either—retro it off."

She started undoing her *obi* in spite of the distance that remained between her and the bath as she descended the stairs—how much of a tomboy was she, anyway?

There'd been a change in her attitude lately according to Karen, but I couldn't detect any kind of growth or shift given the way she acted.

Right as I had the unsettling thought that maybe it would've been nice if Ogi had done something about just her…

"Think monster, sis." a voice came from the stuffed doll adorning a corner of my little sisters' now-empty room.

Yotsugi Ononoki—it goes without saying.

The corpse doll. The parting gift left behind by the experts.

"You did off so much foreshadowing last volume and made it seem like a pretty stern topic for the series, but was Tadatsuru Teori—supposedly like destroy Big Sis even or pets or even Sis Big like destroy supposedly—Teiori Tadatsuru—just-life—all sit of tzer for the grough the or not look around walking armour—that earnist's like premiese like normal?"

"…"

Ononoki seemed the same as ever, making this meta statement the moment Tsukihi left—but something was very different about her tone.

It wasn't her usual monotone.

And—she didn't have on the blank expression she always wore.

Yotsugi Ononoki, the rigor-mortised corpse doll.

Said it with a dashing look, of all things.

004

When I tied things together by explaining that Tadatsuru walked around like normal at the shrine because we were in hell, and that was fine because what happens in the world after death is no longer the rest of your life, Ononoki said, "You're er,'uoy goob ɐɿ maintaining consistency. Fine, I won't keep botching you around. Out of pity. I'm correcting you, so keep on with that dink of educitta shte time arounda sa well." Her look remained dashing, and her appearance had changed too.

She'd always been made to wear a draped skirt that didn't suit her, but today she modeled a pair of pants that reminded me of her master (or "Big Sis" as Ononoki called her), and they fit her surprisingly well. While you could chalk this up to Tsukihi, a good dresser herself, forcing Ononoki to change clothes, the dress-up-doll explanation didn't address her tone or expression.

Don't tell me her head could be swapped out like some kind of action figure.

She wasn't getting off her high horse and continued to nitpick, "Also, I think it's a little bflliculu to figure out raht wow rou ceuglt ot cluciblu eltrli a's kniht I ,oslA..."

I walked outside, leaving her behind. Maybe I needed to be

questioning her instead, since she had as many nits to be picked as Karen, but her dashing look was kind of unbelievably irritating, and to be honest, I left home to avoid getting into a fight.

I thought an expressionless character showing an expressive expression for the first time might be charming, but real life didn't follow such dramaturgical rules.

It wasn't like my conversation with Karen had gone well either. Asking someone experiencing an irregularity to account for her situation wasn't going to yield a desirable answer—whether or not she was an expert on aberrations like Ononoki.

I went outside instead of back to my room because my shadow would be more distinct there at this hour. Shinobu didn't wake up earlier when I called for her in the bathroom, and I was glad about it then.

I had no choice but to rely on her powers now, though—on the knowledge of the aberration-slaying vampire who resided in my shadow.

More precisely, a husk of a vampire. The dregs of an iron-blooded, hot-blooded, yet cold-blooded vampire—the former Kissshot Acerolaorion Heartunderblade, whose current name, Shinobu Oshino, I called again, and loudly.

It did feel pretty contradictory to walk out under the sun to summon a vampire (another nit Ononoki would pick at viciously, I'm sure), but in any case, I called out to my shadow.

Yet no reply came—no response.

It seemed she'd fallen into a very deep sleep, though I couldn't blame her.

I'd asked the little girl for way too much the day before when I skipped graduation, and I'd constantly been relying on her until just a day before that as well—there weren't many events in my life I didn't rely on her for. I'd caused her a lot of trouble, so of course she'd be slumbering deep enough to require more than a poke to wake up since things had finally come to a stopping point, or maybe a breather today.

I had no choice but to rely on her but could only yell at my own shadow right outside my house for so long, considering how it looked... I did also want to let her, my precious partner, rest.

At the same time, when there was no guarantee that she hadn't been affected by this sudden change besetting my home, how could I wait until she woke up?

Was Shinobu not responding because something weird happened to her, just like with Karen and Ononoki? If that was why, how could I take it easy and wait until the cows came home? I'm no cattle rancher. Good things might come to those who wait, but that's not what I needed at the moment. Sure, maybe I was worrying too much, given that Tsukihi hadn't been affected at all.

In light of all this, I thought, *Then what about me?* As far as I could tell from the way I felt and what I saw in the mirror, there seemed to be nothing wrong with me, but what could be less reliable in a situation like this than a self-administered check?

Karen and Ononoki didn't seem to find their changes odd— zero reported symptoms. If anything, they all but told me they'd always been this short, that their dashing look always had pissed me off this much.

Maybe something about me changed overnight, and I just hadn't noticed. My suspicions threatened to be boundless once I got going.

Had I lost not just the title of high school student but something more important without ever noticing? Should I be taller, for instance, or more muscular or broad-shouldered, or smarter? Possible.

Quite possible.

I might even have been Tsubasa Hanekawa until yesterday... Okay, if I were her yesterday, I wouldn't have committed a huge blunder like turning into Koyomi Araragi today. I could rule that one out, at least.

There's of course Gregor Samsa, who woke up to discover he wasn't just someone else, but a bug... By the way, speaking of Franz Kafka, the author of *The Metamorphosis*, according to his bio he asked his best friend to dispose of his novels posthumously. The friend went against his wishes and released them, thanks to which the author is famous today.

Could you really call someone like that your best friend? After learning about Kafka's apparently difficult personality, though, I began thinking that "please dispose of my novels" might have also meant "but, well, you know." If this friend understood the subtext, then he was a true friend indeed.

A regular Pythias.

In any case, while there's an argument to be had about *The Metamorphosis* thematizing how wonderful and adorable little sisters are (please don't have it), this wasn't language arts class— wait, does foreign literature even go under language arts?

No good, I couldn't focus my thoughts.

Proof of my confusion—maybe I needed to go back inside and ask Ononoki, an expert, for her opinion despite everything. Between that enraging dashing look and her arrogant tone, though, I wasn't confident that me and my lack of maturity could stand her for too long.

Graduating high school hadn't made me that much of an adult.

Somehow, her expressionless face and flat tone had done a good job of neutralizing her character and let her settle into the position of *quirky girl*. Once she stepped up to operate on the same level as everyone else, the girl just had a nasty personality...

And anyway, I probably couldn't expect a satisfying answer from Ononoki when it was clear as day that something about her was off—physician, heal thyself.

That said, Oshino and Miss Gaen were no longer in town, and as for Miss Kagenui, she was at the North Pole—I couldn't rely on any experts.

Strictly speaking, I suspected the phone number Miss Gaen had given me still worked, but if the lady who "knew everything" hadn't called me, it probably meant I needed to do something about this on my own—not to mention, once you rashly asked her for help, she had a track record of demanding compensation so ridiculous you had to wonder out loud if she was being serious.

Leaning on a certain friend of mine who may not know everything but did know what she knew seemed like an option, but the thought of calling her when she was overseas gave me pause.

Not in the sense that it'd run up my phone bill. I didn't even know if whatever country Hanekawa was in right now had cell service.

In which case, I had no choice but to wait until night when Shinobu would be active again. Yup, I needed to wait for the aberration-slaying girl, to whom Oshino had imparted some amount of expert knowledge through special tutoring sessions, unless I was going to turn to the gods.

"Hm? Oh, right," I realized at this late stage. She was no expert, nor did I expect her to have any expert knowledge, but there was a god in this town now, wasn't there?

Yes, the grand deity known as Mayoi Hachikuji—okay, maybe not a grand deity, but the young ghost girl who'd been newly deified at Kita-Shirahebi Shrine to quell the strange happenings in town. She must've received some schooling from Miss Gaen before being placed atop that mountain to watch over us all.

Maybe she knew something.

Actually, these abnormalities could be a kind of side effect of turning her into a god half by force—an accidental solution owing to an impulsive act on my part, it had seemed like a sharp idea. Thinking about it with a calmer head though, deifying a young girl who'd been sent to hell sounded like a stretch even for an empty shrine.

Hachikuji becoming a god and Karen getting shorter, or Ononoki starting to have expressions, had no clear causal link. The reason might be entirely different, but since I had no clues at the moment, talking to her was worth the trouble.

Abnormalities aside, I wanted to tease the young girl at Kita-Shirahebi for her divine antics. And scold her if she was getting carried away.

As a friend, of course!

Oddly enough, I now had a destination for my bike ride—and no sooner than I'd decided, I straddled the BMX I still had on loan from Ogi and began pedaling toward the mountain that the shrine presides over. While I wouldn't be able to go up it on a bike (well, maybe on a BMX, since they say it can climb stairs, but not with my skills…), I'd still get to the entrance faster despite the slopes.

Or so I thought, but either I got flustered or wasn't used to a BMX, not to mention the several-month gap in my riding career—because it took me longer than I expected. Was it a lie that you never forget how to ride a bike?

I nearly tipped over again and again and got lost too. I hadn't heard about any barrier being placed on the mountain, but maybe, as someone with an aberrational nature, I was being prevented from approaching the shrine, holy ground where a god had alighted.

If that was the case, I couldn't just drop by casually. Since a vampire dwelled in my shadow, maybe it was to be expected, but being kept out of holy ground is pretty depressing…

I thought this as I chained up the now-parked bike (who knew how gleefully Ogi would browbeat me if I let it get stolen) and began up the familiar mountain path, which I could honestly say was much easier than half a year ago thanks to my trips up and down it. Not a game trail, but a me trail. By the time I finished my hike and passed through the *torii* gate, the sun was directly overhead.

In other words, it was noon—the time of day when aberrations seemed least likely to appear, but then not every aberration is nocturnal.

No one was on the well-kept grounds of Kita-Shirahebi, rebuilt last year. Not many people would visit a location as secluded as this, god or no. We needed to come up with something for the shrine to be worshiped again... There was probably nothing I could do, but given the events that led to Hachikuji becoming a god, I wanted to help in some way.

Maybe they could try selling *omikuji* fortunes.

Hachikuji omikuji—I liked how that sounded.

So what if it sounds good, you may ask, but it'd matter to Hachikuji.

I ought to broach the subject with her after discussing my issue—but then the all-important factor, Mayoi Hachikuji, wasn't even around... Maybe she was inside the hall? I'd met her in town only yesterday, so maybe she was out there observing, or just talking a walk? Something about a god who liked going out on the town seemed to lack gravitas, or to be too footloose...

"Hachikujiii? Hello-o-o?" I called out from in front of the offering box. Even if she was inside, I couldn't just barge in. Maybe I shouldn't be scared when I had an aberration living in my shadow, but I still hesitated, fearing the divine punishment that would surely come. If Hachikuji was delivering it, not only would she not go easy on me, she'd be merciless.

Ah, right—how about putting some money in the offering box? Thinking back to when we first met, her reaction to hard cash was anything but cold... Heheh, it's not every day you come up with a novel idea like summoning a god with an offering.

How I've grown. Apparently, an unpleasant conman had visited this shrine on a regular basis since New Year's, but what set us apart was that only I had these dazzlingly original ideas...

With that pleasing thought, I took out my wallet. Having grabbed it as I left home and stuffed it in my pocket, I didn't know how much money I had...but yeah, this was a shrine.

The standard good-luck offering of a five-yen coin ought to do.

Alas, I happened to be out of five-yen coins—but did find four one-yen coins, which might serve as a suitable substitute. Four or *shi* is considered unlucky, given that it's homophonous with the word for death in Japanese, but maybe it was fine because it also alliterated with *shojo*, girl? The greater number of coins made you feel like you're getting more, yes?

I felt for a moment like I might be messing up, but pluckily refusing to be distracted by any figment of the imagination, I tossed the four coins into the offering box—then gave two bows, two claps, and one bow, or whatever. I'd been taught what to do but couldn't remember, so I bowed my own way to get across at least the sentiment and rang the bell extra hard.

Nothing in particular happened.

Nothing like the shrine's door opening and a god storming out—I almost wanted a refund but didn't even have anyone to complain to.

Was she really taking a walk? She wasn't the type to sit still, whether she'd ascended to godhood or descended to hell—my only option now would be to climb down the mountain and wander aimlessly around town.

Mildly despondent, I thought maybe I ought to see it as a good thing that she was being her active self even after becoming a god, and began to turn back when—

"Awɛwɛgiiiii!"

Someone grabbed me from behind, tackling me. Not remotely ready for this full-body attack, I fell to the ground and panicked, only to be locked in a submission hold.

"Eeeek!" I shrieked, but the maneuver was in place before I knew it—what were these moves, military combatives? Every joint in my body had been locked into place.

I could neither resist nor run.

My opponent seemed to be about my size but was on a different level in terms of proficiency. I couldn't find any opening I could use to move—the submission hold affected my entire body as though I'd been vacuum-packed.

"You came to visit me! I'm so happy!!"

"Eeeek!"

No, forget about the joint lock. It was just creepy how my assailant didn't hold back and glued fast until our cheeks rubbed, which is why I screamed. I felt like a slug was crawling along my body.

Wh-Who was it? What was it? What exactly was going on?

Paying no mind to my utter confusion, the criminal—I see nothing wrong with using that word here—pressed our bodies together even more tightly.

"I'm so happy, I'm so happy, I'm so happy!! Aww, I was so lonely! I don't mind a rub, dog, but I don't get any visitors and might dog clothe the up on giving up! I left all! I'd left giving up on the whole dog thing and climbing down the mountain or emcee a regular lady! C'mon, emmel, dloh you more and love you more and kick you more!"

"Eeeek! Eeeek!"

"Here their lady eoin died violent! Just let the pots gied violent! Yeah, take care of everything! I'll be gentle when I take it all away from you!"

"Eeeek!"

Wait... Lady?

My ears picked up this scrap of a word, and I tried to look behind me—only my eyes moved since my neck was locked too—but indeed, the perp who'd shoved me onto these holy grounds, and who was wound around my body, was a woman.

She had to be pretty muscular to have the strength, but actually, I did sense a kind of smoothness and softness as well—even if I was in pain more than anything else.

...Hold on, I knew this person.

"Graaah!"

"Aiə!"

Biting the earlobe in front of my face finally made her get away with a (feminine) cry—and stand slim and tall.

Her hair gathered together in the back, her balanced features betraying none of the perversion she'd been guilty of—yes.

I'd met this person before.

I'd met her before—in a different timeline.

"M-Miss...Mayoi Hachikuji?"

"Yes," she replied with a smile, her arms crossed as if to emphasize her developed bust. "Miss Mayoi Hachikuji, twenty-one years old."

I think this goes without saying.

But the Mayoi I knew was a ten-year-old little girl, not a twenty-one-year-old pervert—excuse me, lady.

Yet the young woman standing in front of me was Mayoi Hachikuji—and I knew this to be true.

She'd lost her life in a traffic accident nearly a dozen years ago, *but if she'd avoided that accident*—she'd have turned out like this lady.

I'd seen her thriving and surviving even in a world that had fallen into ruin—though her airs then seemed a little different (or rather, her personality had undergone a total change). But if we were to go by simple appearances, this was exactly how she looked.

"What is it, Awawagi? Why're you looking at me with so much passion in your eyes? Sorry, but you know I'm everyone's big sister. I'm not going to be yours and yours alone, okay?"

"First off, please stop calling me Awawagi."

Umm.

I put my mind to work—or at least put my hands to my head.

I'd started to get an idea of what was going on but was having trouble making sense of it all… The change to Karen's body, the change in Ononoki's personality, and now Hachikuji... In other words, this problem extended beyond the Araragi residence, to *the entire world*... But then what about Tsukihi?

Nothing had changed about her. Or maybe I just didn't notice?

"Araragi," Hachikuji...no, Miss Hachikuji spoke my name, this time in a slightly different tone. "You seem kind of serious today. You know I'm always here to listen if anything's worrying you."

"..."

This made me certain I was dealing with Hachikuji—as soon as she treated me with kindness, I felt like relying on her.

But just as I couldn't rely on Ononoki, I doubted I could get anything useful out of Hachikuji, given that she herself had changed...

At the same time, if a change had come upon the entire world, it didn't matter who I talked to, it'd be true of everyone—maybe that even included Shinobu, once she woke up at night.

In that case, I needed to ratchet up my readiness another notch.

"There's something I was hoping to check with you, if that's all right," I said. It did feel a little odd to be speaking politely to Hachikuji, but what choice did I have? I had to mind my tone with a twenty-one year old. "You're a...god, yes? Miss Mayoi."

"Of course, I'm a god. Why was that now? You made me into a god, haven't you already forgotten—yaderesey tsul!"

"..."

We were on the same page there. The details didn't seem to have changed much, either.

Which meant that this Miss Hachikuji was an aberration, and not alive—come to think of it, the parallel world where she survived to twenty-one instead of dying at ten was in exchange for a world in ruins.

Judging from the scenery as I rode toward this mountain, my town was fine—I'd had the same fear facing the shortened Karen, but it seemed I could count out a scenario where I was back in that other timeline.

But even if she was divine, there was the precedent set by Sengoku. Miss Hachikuji could be a god incarnate, or a living god, and not necessarily dead.

Hmmm.

I couldn't just ask her to her face if she was alive… She seemed to be, going by how her body felt as she held me (not to mention having bitten her earlobe), but even when she was a little ghost girl, I could touch her like normal, so that wasn't a valid criterion.

"*Really, Araragi. What's the matter? Did you grab your own ear—rest-taking and realize that you bombed your exams? There, there. In that case, your big sis will do everything she can to make you feel better.*"

"No, that's not it… Um…"

Then, after all my hesitation.

I ended up revealing everything to Miss Hachikuji, everything being all the abnormalities since the morning: Karen's body, Ononoki's expression and tone (also, I keep forgetting, but her clothes were a little different too)—and her own transformation from the Hachikuji I knew.

The fact that Shinobu didn't wake up even when I called.

Though perhaps unrelated, I also threw in the weird sense I got from my reflection in the mirror when I washed my face— I thought it might help gauge my mental state.

…The whole situation seemed kind of serious to me, but when I talked about it out loud, it sounded so comical, or just all in my head.

If I were told such a frivolous story, at least, I might dismiss it as "the sort of thing that happens when you're a teen"—what was it called again, jamais vu? The feeling that you're learning about something for the first time when in fact you've long known it to be true. Maybe Karen was always that tall, and Ononoki always that kind of character.

Even with Hachikuji, was I just under the impression she was ten, when she was actually twenty-one? Well, that was true, in a sense.

What about Shinobu? Once, she didn't come out of my shadow no matter how many times I called, but our link had been severed by the Darkness. Did it stay severed ever since or something?

That definitely made me too careless for my own good and also counted as its own kind of bad news. But even if it wasn't déjà vu or jamais vu, there remained a logical explanation for my predicament.

A way to make sense of the nonsensical situation.

The hypothesis was no less hard for me to accept—or believe, but nonetheless.

"Huh. Araragi..."

Nonetheless, having heard me out, Miss Hachikuji began speaking with a troubled expression (which made her look surprisingly intelligent).

"Let me make sure, erm. Karen, your tall little sister's got shorter. Expressionless Ononoki turned expressive—and the former Kissshot Acerola-Orion Heart-under-blade now won't come out, while little I'll... Hachikuji turned into big sis Mayoi?"

"Y-Yes... That's it."

"So—everyone's been reversed in some way. Can we say—right?"

"Reversed... Um."

Could we?

No—putting aside Shinobu (who could just be asleep), it wasn't *everyone* when nothing had changed about Tsukihi, who wasn't "reversed" or anything. That bit made the situation that

42

much trickier…

"You're right. We can think about that later, but wasn't Tsu-kihi wearing her yukata backwards?"

"Backwards? Oh."

The left side of her yukata over the right.

That's how it looked—and I let her know, because that's how you dress the dead.

I'd sort of sneered, thinking that she didn't know how to wear traditional clothes despite loving them so much, but if that was the change that overtook her…

It was the easiest to understand, in a way.

Reversed, or maybe inverted?

Inverted—*as if I'd seen her in a mirror.*

Not a delusion, but a reflection.

Left switched places with right. It also explained Shinobu's stubborn silence—*vampires aren't reflected in mirrors*, after all.

Something that I'd experienced myself recently—in other words.

"In other words, Araragi. It's not that everyone changes, or... that's to say... because it did—it's not as if you've changed. It's just that you made it over or visible," Miss Hachikuji declared.

A divine revelation.

"You're inside a mirror now."

"…!"

Faced head-on with a conclusion I'd quietly arrived at a while ago, I couldn't help but blurt out—

"A-Are we sure that lukewarm of a setup will do?!"

006

Lukewarm or not, whether it did it or not, this setup—or rather fact was something I needed to accept.

Having been told this, I took a look at the gate to find that it said "ꓘiɾɒ-Ƨdiɿɒʜɔɘdi Ƨdɔiɿɘ." Left and right were indeed inverted. I wasn't going to fish them out to check, but when I'd thrown my offering into the box, something had felt wrong—I suspected that left and right had been flipped for the number on the coins.

As for my difficulties riding the BMX to the mountain, the bike's structure had been mirrored—the left brake controlling the front wheel and the right brake controlling the rear more than sufficed to make it a new experience, and if the town had been flipped around as well, that explained how I'd gotten lost. Of course, hearing it from Mayoi Hachikuji, the once-lost girl, felt backwards in its own way.

I confused hot for cold when I washed my face because the handles had switched places... And everyone's voice sounded somehow reverberant—or reversed, for the same reason.

Right. In hindsight there'd been hints all over the place, and as a professed fan of *Doraemon: Nobita and the Steel Troops*, about a mirror world, I should've noticed sooner.

An upside-down world.

Karen, Ononoki, Hachikuji—were inverted here.

I also needed to accept that Shinobu wasn't in my shadow. Vampires, who aren't reflected in mirrors, didn't exist in this world.

It was a world with a different worldview.

I still didn't get what was up with Tsukihi. She'd only worn her yukata in the wrong order.

"B-But," I objected, "going from my big all-out fight with Ogi, which had me going to hell and back, to something this lukewarm…"

"I think it's fine," Miss Hachikuji answered with an encouraging smile. "Chilled-out mascot characters have been all the rage, so what's wrong with a chilled-out world? A churld."

She was trying to encourage me…but "churld"?

It sounded so lame.

If you're curious, Miss Hachikuji's line here and the ones that follow were all still reversed. I concede that it's hard to read, so I'm using my narrator privileges to translate them.

"Ogi, huh," she muttered meaningfully but continued with a shrug. "I got carried away and said you're 'inside a mirror'—but I don't know. For us, *this* is the normal world, and *that* side is in a mirror, to match your perception. If you'll allow me to spin this, I don't think it's as lukewarm as you think. Aren't you in a pretty bad spot?"

Her assurance that it wasn't lukewarm freaked me out just as much. "Wh-What do you mean?"

"There's no way for you to return to what you'd call your original world, is there?"

"…"

A way to return?

Ah. Distracted by the lukewarm setup, I hadn't gotten around to wondering about that. If I was in another world, then I had to go on to return to my world—how?

The Araragi residence's bathroom mirror.

If I'd been pulled into "this side" when I touched it, returning from there seemed like a possibility. But right after I sensed something was off, I checked it myself—and found it to be a plain mirror.

Or found it had returned to being a plain mirror—I couldn't come and go between worlds simply by touching its surface.

Had a temporarily opened gate been closed, or was it a one-way path? I started to fret.

I was no Hanekawa, but I'd been stranded alone in a foreign country—even at a sunny tourist destination, being in another culture can be unsettling.

Yes, this reminded me of how I'd been sent to different realms, whether by traveling through time or by going to hell. The very rules of the world were different...

A world with different rules.

People I was familiar with becoming different made this more than a matter of, say, just trying to stay calm. The fact that Karen was shorter than me, for example, scrambled one of the factors that defined me (my complex over being outgrown by my sister) and messed with my ability to maintain my ego and sense of self.

...I guess I wasn't unhappy about getting to meet the grown-up Mayoi Hachikuji again, even if it was under these circumstances—then.

"Hup."

Then Miss Hachikuji pulled me close, not with another rough hug, but gently, as if to embrace my head.

"It's okay, it's okay. No need for you to be so scared. You're okay, Araragi, I promise."

Based on nothing, but it's also a divine pronouncement, assured Miss Hachikuji, patting my head repeatedly.

I felt embarrassed, almost as if I was being nursed, and wanted to pull myself free—I was too old to be comforted like this, I'd just graduated from high school a day ago—but reconsidered and let her have her way with me.

This was another world, even a kind of illusion reflected in a mirror, but that's how much seeing a grown Hachikuji meant to me. I was like a kid brother for this twenty-one year old, but having known her ten-year-old self best, it felt like seeing a daughter grow up.

In that sense, we were on totally different emotional pages, but even the ten-year-old Hachikuji had always comforted me, saved me. This wasn't much of a change.

"Still, what to do?" Miss Hachikuji freed me at last and began wandering around the shrine grounds—a little too restlessly for a goddess. Circling around with me as her focal point, she asked without slowing her pace: "You traveled back in time by eleven years once, to rescue me from my traffic accident. Remind me, how did you go there, and how did you get back?"

Her history, the tragedy eleven years ago and such, seemed not to have changed—I guess this Miss Hachikuji died back then, too?

By the way, if we're being precise, traveling eleven years into the past to rescue her was a reason we made up after the fact, after we ended up in the wrong year by accident. We were just trying to go back by about a day so I could do my summer homework—but I saw no need to go out of my way to correct her.

"How? Well, we used this shrine's torii as a gate…not that there was any deep meaning to it…"

Shinobu had used the spiritual energy gathered at the then-abandoned Kita-Shirahebi to open a gate—precipitating a major incident that would ensnare the whole town, but that had nothing to do with time travel.

"Hmm…" Miss Mayoi said, looking pensive.

Given my first impression, I couldn't help but see her as a

mischievous young woman. Sinking into thought like this for my sake, however, did quite a lot to affect me and win my trust—so there was a connection between her and the Hachikuji that I met in a ruined world.

"In that case, couldn't you go home if you made another one of those gates? I'm not sure the same logic applies, of course."

"Er, that's not really…" I started to convey the obvious fact that Shinobu, not I, had summoned the gate, and that we were now in a mirror.

But did Shinobu Oshino, or the former Kissshot Acerolaorion Heartunderblade, ever exist here in the first place? Even if I mentioned her to Miss Hachikuji, wouldn't her reaction be, *Who're you talking about?*

But then, she'd brought up Shinobu a moment ago: *the former Kissshot Acerolaorion Heartunderblade,* though it was a little stand-offish of Miss Hachikuji to call her that.

Hm—the more I thought about it, the more it threatened to turn into a wholesale rejection of the life I'd been living. This was hardly a lukewarm twist.

If Shinobu didn't exist, though, would I have met Hachikuji at that park? How were those loose ends tied up?

"*The loose ends,*" Miss Hachikuji said as if she'd read my mind, "*must not matter—in this case.*"

"…"

"In this case—which is to say, this world. There are no paradoxes in a mirror world—or maybe I should say everything is a paradox here. That's how logic works, right?"

The word *logic* coming from Hachikuji's mouth felt like its own paradox, but she continued.

"Just as taking a true statement like 'Araragi is a pedophile' and flipping it around makes it false—'pedophiles are Araragi,' or 'you aren't a pedophile if you're not Araragi'—paradoxes and contradictions can exist here. There must be some propositions that hold up even if you turn them on their head, so 'everything is a paradox' is an overstatement, but I'd imagine a great number of things here will feel 'inconsistent' to you since you came from a world that acts as the standard."

For instance, I don't realize it myself, but don't you see me as a pretty contradictory presence to begin with? asked Miss Hachikuji.

And I had to agree.

If she'd grown to be twenty-one, she'd lived until that age, but the accident eleven years ago also seemed to have happened. Even if she was a living god, we shouldn't have ever met, but she knew who I was.

The young woman was a walking mess of contradictions.

She was all loose ends.

And yet—her existence was undeniable.

Still, what kind of an example was that?

You aren't a pedophile if you're not Araragi—really?

"A world where loose ends are just fine," she said. "Considering how you've solved many cases by making ends meet by hook or by crook… Sounds like a cruel world for you—far from lukewarm. Haha!"

"…"

Perhaps she meant to buck me up with that cheerful laugh, but her analysis was plenty cruel on its own.

Given how little information I still had, I didn't know how meaningful it'd be to piece together a hypothesis, but if I were to: I looked at that mirror in the morning—and the "world" reflected at that point, when my movements didn't match up, got reversed, but not all of history up until then?

"Maybe. After all, I know about Miss Shinobu Oshino, the former Kissshot Acerolaorion Heartunderblade. *At the same time, I know that vampires don't exist in this world.* I don't find it strange that I'm talking about her and seem to be familiar with the name of a non-existent aberration. I accept the contradiction without a second thought, like how I might claim that life should be trea-sured and still eat meat every day—neither is a lie."

"…"

A world where contradictions were fine.

A dream scenario for a novelist. Not being needled with points like the ones Ononoki raised—but it also seemed tough.

What was it called again? The Ozma Problem?

How explaining the difference between left and right to an alien would be difficult, verbally, or something—but just as per-fect spheres don't exist, probably nothing has perfect bilateral symmetry, so the world I knew and the mirrored land I now in-habited would conflict at every turn…

"No, Araragi, I don't think that's necessarily true. It's not that everything is upside down—though you could also say that makes the situation all the more troublesome."

"What do you mean?"

"Take Karen. If everything about her was reversed, she wouldn't be your little sister, she'd be your big sister or your little brother—she may have appeared from the bath when she shouldn't have been there because that part of her had been reversed, but getting out of the bath and wiping your body dry with a towel is the most proper thing in the world. If we were to be strict about it and reverse even that, she'd need to soak herself in a towel before splashing herself with water."

"I don't know if she'd need to…"

That'd be beyond bizarre.

Even I wouldn't have been able to keep my cool in that case—and would've questioned Karen's sanity.

Not everything had been reversed. So then, *what* had been?

I couldn't comprehend the standard when it came to things getting flipped around—considering the reversal of the bicycle's structure, the placement of the faucet handles, and letters in this world, the scenery did all seem to be reversed. Its denizens, on the other hand…

"The fact that there's been no change to your other little sister, Tsukihi, does seem key—I wonder about knowledge. Hey, Araragi, what's one plus one?"

"Should I answer using the decimal system? Or in binary?"

"Stop being clever and just answer me, kid," threatened Miss Hachikuji. A lady who was my senior—but she followed up with a gentle admonishment: "It's a serious question, so could you give me a serious reply?"

The emotional turbulence made me queasy.

With the ten-year-old Hachikuji, my light jab would have kicked off a three-hour conversation, but I guess it was natural for this lady to have left behind what you might call the Hachikuji-ness of the Hachikuji I knew, now that she was eleven years older—she didn't mangle my name even once.

If anything, I'd tried to mangle her earlobe.

While I felt a tinge of sadness, I'd be worried if she was still acting that way at twenty-one, so I accepted it.

"…"

But no, maybe this was a part of her personality that had been flipped around—the more I thought about it, the deeper I sank into the quicksand.

"Two. One plus one is two," I gave a straightforward answer anyway, as embarrassing as it was.

"Hm. Okay, then what's 100 minus 50?"

"50."

"What's 9 times 7, and 9 divided by 3?"

"63 and 3."

She tested me on the four basic arithmetical operations, one at a time.

Those laws were the same wherever you were, though… At least, they seemed to be in this mirrored land. And so—

"Okay. I'll ask non-arithmetic questions too," Big Sis Mayoi said.

"Bring it on."

"Maybe I should start with science."

"Sure thing."

"What is the biological species name of a seahorse?"

"Why would I know that?" Something a little more general, please?

"What's the largest star in the solar system?"

"Saturn."

"Is that so. Here, it's the Sun."

"Don't ask me trick questions!"

"Excuse me? Is that how you speak to an older person? This is for your sake, you know."

"…"

Awkward…

I actually knew that trick question and the correct answer. I'd replied with the ten-year-old Hachikuji in mind, but our banter wasn't going anywhere. It made me realize just how important age differences are when you're conversing.

"Also," she said, "if you're going to fall for it, the answer in this world is Jupiter."

"Oh, right!"

I'd fallen for it on purpose but mistaken it wrong. I didn't need to wait for my test results at this point, I knew my fate. It sapped my motivation to return to my world—not that I wanted to make this realm of contradictions my final resting place.

That said, as I confirmed more things with Hachikuji, this world didn't seem too different, in terms of knowledge and common sense—even idioms like *right-hand man* and *out of left field* weren't flipped around.

Even if most people were left-handed from my point of view, the logic here meant that they were called *right-handed*—hmm, this really was the Ozma Problem.

"Well," I said, "I guess I'm lucky that causality, or the over-all laws of nature, aren't flipped around. How would I plan any course of action if my predictions and reasoning of X causing Y to happen had been turned upside down too?"

"Don't let your guard down. It's only true for what we talked about just now—but then, being too cautious might be *counter-productive* in its own way," Big Sis Mayoi warned, touching my hair.

She didn't know how to keep her hands to herself. As a healthy young man, I was sort of tickled.

"Well, to summarize, it looks like there's only one way for you to get back to your world."

"Just one? You sure narrowed that down quick."

I wished she'd range a little further when it came to my options, but you can only ask a god for so much.

In fact, I was shamelessly receiving her divine favor for an offering of just four yen. I'd best shut up and listen with humility.

While I was perplexed after getting lost in another world all of a sudden, I was also enjoying this, improperly enough. Another world or not, it was Hachikuji's first job as a freshly appointed (freshly anointed?) god. Listen with humility, humbly watch her work her magic.

So…how's Miss Hachikuji gonna save me here?!

Perhaps to punish my mindset—Mèmè Oshino, who held that people just went and got saved on their own, would have sneered at me—the deity said, "Just get the former Kissshot Acerolaorion Heartunderblade to open up a gate."

"…"

"What's with the dissatisfied look? Wasn't that Aberration Slayer a broken, anything-goes character? She should at least be able to create an opening in and out of this mirrored land."

"Er, when you put it that way, I guess she could, but…"

I wasn't sure.

There are theories that time travel is physically possible with a massive amount of energy…or so I've heard, but traveling between entire worlds fell outside the purview of physics classes.

I suppose it was possible, if time travel were a type of travel between worlds, or for that noble king of aberrations, the exceptional aberrational existence—at her peak.

Practically Majin Buu, the way she could do anything.

But not now, when she was a little girl—and even if we could address that, "Shinobu doesn't exist in this world, though," I reiterated—stating her absence. "Vampires can't in a land of mirrors. Maybe you're assuming that a thrall might do the same, but I'm telling you, I can't. My being here means our link is as close to severed as it can get. Think of me as a plain human now that I've been separated from Shinobu, just like back in hell."

"I'd never expect something so unreasonable—only the former Kissshot Acerolaorion Heartunderblade could open a gate."

Her tongue really didn't slip, did it? Even when she was saying that whole name. "B-But like I've been trying to tell you, Shinobu's not on this side of—"

"Even if she's not on *this side*, she can open it from the *other side*," the god suggested. "If she's not here, it means she's there. And if you've been separated, isn't the legendary lady free from her bindings and back in peak form?"

"…"

A brilliant, unimpeachable plan—would be going too far.

There were details that needed filling in, but it was indeed a neat and clearheaded approach that I hadn't thought of myself. She'd responded solidly to my plea.

Geez, look at her.

I didn't have anything to worry about. She was doing just fine as a god.

"Ha ha ha, call it *The Only Neat Thing to Do*. One of science fiction's three greatest cool titles."

Not that I've read it, she added flippantly—in a faint echo of the eleven-year-younger Hachikuji.

"…Can I ask what the other two are?"

"*The Moon Is a Harsh Mistress* and *Do Androids Dream of Electric Sheep?* Neither of which I've read."

"You haven't read any of them…"

Read them already.

Putting aside whether this setup was more science fiction or fantasy, there was now a ray of hope—I'd get Shinobu to open a gate from the other side.

Having been left behind, she'd figure out in no time that I'd gotten wrapped up in some sort of anomaly. Even if a vampire couldn't enter this land of mirrors, she'd be able to open a gate if she'd returned to her peak condition.

I'd been causing her nothing but trouble lately, forcing her to become big, then small, then big all over again—but the question was how I might convey the plan when she inhabited a different world.

Maybe I needed to go home and start banging on that mirror? Did I just have to knock?

No, it had gone back to being a regular surface, and even if there were something to the mirror, Shinobu might not be standing in front of it… If she'd regained her full powers, she wouldn't show in it and wouldn't go out of her way to look in any—unless she'd heard my voice calling out to her right before I was sucked in.

Still, she was tired from all this getting bigger and smaller lately…so I might not have done enough to wake her up. If she'd woken up to find me missing all of a sudden, she'd simply be confused. She wouldn't possibly imagine that I'd become Araragi Through the Looking-Glass (doesn't roll off the tongue, does it).

Having been too powerful, she wasn't the intellectual type, and living for centuries had worn down her mind. This state of affairs would only make her panic, and she might not be able to trace my steps—this was bad.

"If you wrote a letter and left it on your desk, wouldn't it show up on the other side?"

"No, it doesn't seem like acts in the other world and this one are linked. Just a single moment got sliced out..."

In that case—why did the Araragi residence's bathroom mirror turn into a gate to another world at that moment? Was there some kind of reason?

There's a reason for every aberration, the experts say, but it happened so abruptly that I couldn't see the need. It seemed more like a random supernatural phenomenon—I'd been spirited away, if you would.

It did seem ironic that I was asking a god for help if they spirited me away... So, how to contact Shinobu. If only I could communicate with her telepathically as her thrall.

"Well, relax, Araragi, it's not as if your life is in immediate danger. If your little sister looking a bit different is too hard on you, you're welcome to stay the night here," Miss Hachikuji offered considerately—while it wasn't exactly hard on me to see small Karen (amusing, more like), I didn't relish this turning into a drawn-out battle.

If I was getting accepted to college, I needed to go through the actual matriculation process... I had to return within the next few days at the latest.

"Oh, right... Yes, you did study hard. In that case, hmm, maybe forget about counting on Shinobu, and just wait stubbornly in the bathroom you came through, until the gate opens again?"

"..."

While the plan wasn't neat, it would certainly do—assuming that what happened once would happen again.

But there was no guarantee it would in the next few days—it might just take another thousand years was the issue here, and that issue was a dealbreaker. Little wonder Miss Hachikuji had discounted it at first.

Also, realistically speaking, I couldn't stand on guard forever in front of the sink. I mean, that space connected to the bath, which my parents and sisters used.

They'd chase me out of there every time they wanted to take a bath, like in the morning—I might somehow stand my ground against my little sisters, but I'd have to leave when it came to my parents. The gate could open during one of those intervals, which put that many holes in the plan.

Moreover, it'd be impossible to keep watch over my bathroom for twenty-four hours a day with dinner-plate eyes. Disconnected from Shinobu, I was nothing more than a regular human, and I needed to eat and sleep—how could I even live in a bathroom to begin with?

I'd be able to soak in the tub the moment I felt tired, of course, but really, what kind of benefit was—

"Oh!"

"Ahh!"

When I shouted as inspiration hit, Miss Hachikuji let out a super-cute scream of surprise—so cute I nearly lost my hold on the new idea (come to think of it, her scream during her young-girl days was "Graaah!"), but I just barely kept one pinky around its tail.

"Wh-What? Yelling like that all of a sudden."

"Kanbaru's home," I began to explain without preamble, but with a lot of gusto. "I think their cypress bathtub—"

007

In essence, you could call it a magic charm.

A trifling one that an elementary school girl might use—Kanbaru's home clearly has a lot of history to it, so it'd be odd for there not to be a tradition or two of the sort.

A year had already passed since I first heard of it, so I couldn't describe the specifics. I want to say it went something like this, though: the surface of the water in her home's cypress-wood bath reflected, on occasion, the image of the person you'd marry one day.

The legend is so cute even I hesitate to make any uncouth jokes or jabs about it, and I had to wonder if I should really be looking to it for help—but it was a different story when I considered that Toé Gaen, mother to Suruga Kanbaru, and older sister to Izuko Gaen, was tied to this legend.

It took on a very different complexion.

Though she'd passed away, her involvement in our storyline would utterly change the course of the tale—in fact, it's not an overstatement to say that she had something to do with the majority of the aberrations I'd experienced as a high school student.

Even if the legend came straight from the Kanbarus, to hear

that Kanbaru's father once saw a vision of Toé Gaen in that water's surface assured there was *something* about the wood bath.

Something.

It was worth a try, at least.

This was like *Nobita and the Steel Troops*, where he uses the bath in Shizuka's home to travel to another world. Hoping that it connected back to my world was expecting too much—but couldn't it work as a communication tool?

If I looked at the surface and saw someone other than me, wouldn't I be able to leave a message?

If you saw whoever you were going to marry in the future, I absolutely wanted it to be Hitagi there in the water, but if it just meant a lifelong partner, maybe I'd rather it be Shinobu—it'd be quicker that way.

I might not see anyone, of course.

I might just see my own stupid face reflected—but it did seem far more productive than staring into the bathroom mirror at my own home.

"Okay, then you go visit Suruga's—I'll go searching for other possibilities, just in case. I don't have any ideas left, but maybe other gods will have other ideas," Miss Hachikuji said, approving my plan. I had to admit, she might have matured, and we may have been in another world, but she was still such a good person, offering even to use her divine network.

Though…it did give me pause that Hachikuji simply called her "Suruga" in this mirrored land. Given their respective ages, it was appropriate—I really shouldn't be worrying myself over consistency.

In any case, I climbed down the mountain alone and began pedaling the BMX to Kanbaru's—and arrived in no time, as it wasn't far.

Once I knew that left and right were reversed, I had an easy enough time riding the bike. I'd also grown accustomed to seeing the flipped-around world. Humans can adapt to anything.

If I got too used to this world, though, it'd be a hassle once I returned—I'd end up only being able to write backwards, and soon my nickname would be Leonardo da Vinci.

People might start touting me as a universal genius.

I'd feel so self-conscious.

The Kanbaru residence—or rather, estate was so grand I almost felt like calling it the Kanbaru mansion. Some said it contained eleven TV sets.

I entered the "residence" about twice a month to clean up Kanbaru's room (and borrowed their cypress tub a number of times—the reason I was just barely able to recall it) but still shrink every time I stand in front of its gates.

Perhaps there were some things humans don't adapt to—and the gate had been flipped around as well, with even the doorphone on the opposite side.

Opposite.

The world fully mirrored.

It'd be hard to explain, but you can't just barge into someone else's bath (no matter how well you know the person). I needed to get Kanbaru's permission first…but was having trouble summoning the nerve to hit the call button.

I needed her permission, but come to think of it, in this mirrored world Kanbaru might be a completely different character from the junior I knew…

Going by the stats I'd compiled, cases like Tsukihi's, where someone hadn't changed, were in the minority. In the past I hadn't felt too reserved about relying on my close friend Kanbaru (what kind of a senior was I?), but nothing guaranteed she'd be the candid, gallant person who never failed to lend a helping hand.

I may respect you as a senior, Araragi-senpai, but letting you use my bath is out of the question, she might say, without any feeling even.

I'd never recover if I heard that from Kanbaru, in a different world or not. I'd carry the baggage for the rest of my life.

It kept my finger from hitting the button, but then…

"Pfft," I laughed—why was I worried?

Aside from Tsukihi, all the girls—whether it was Karen or Ononoki or Hachikuji—differed from the versions I knew but hadn't changed fundamentally as people.

Grownup Hachikuji was still helping me out. Ononoki's expressiveness exposed her nasty personality to the world, but you could say she was the same as ever.

Flipped around or reversed, they were still them—and Kanbaru would be too.

We had a relationship of trust, didn't we?

Why be so negative, anyway? In fact, the trait that always gave me pause might be turned around and canceled out.

A Kanbaru who isn't sex-obsessed.

A Kanbaru who isn't a masochist.

A Kanbaru who isn't shameless.

A Suruga Kanbaru who fancies just literature, always has her underwear on, and quietly walks along the sidewalk; considerate to the untalented, not prying when speaking to the timid, and ever-prudent—okay, she'd be unrecognizable at that point.

While I loved her boyish ways, I'd have no other chance of seeing her act gracefully. I felt excited when I thought about it that way.

Just what kind of Kanbaru would she be—yeah, why overthink this?

Maybe I'd find that I guessed exactly right. I'm not bad at reasoning.

After all the serious battles I'd recently faced, it didn't hurt to have the emotional wherewithal to enjoy laidback twists.

True, being transported to another world was unbelievably huge, but why not be a big man who welcomed such a crisis? The kind who quipped as bullets flew by.

I'd be like Space Pirate Cobra.

I made up my mind and used my Psychogun, or actually just my plain finger, to press the button—I think I pressed it.

But.

Something pressed back.

"...?!"

A fleeting moment.

I had no idea what had happened—of course not. Who, in modern-day Japan, ever pressed a button that pressed back? In any age or world, as a matter of fact, but I hadn't survived so many battles for nothing.

I'd been to hell and back, I played with fire without getting burned.

Even with what you might call zero fighting abilities, I could go toe-to-toe with anyone thanks to my first-rate danger avoidance—which is to say, skill at running away.

Well, I wasn't going toe-to-toe with anyone if I ran, but anyway, I had the presence of mind to spring back. I'd have sprained my right index finger otherwise.

If I were lucky, actually. My finger could've broken—into multiple pieces.

Because what pushed back wasn't strictly speaking the button, but rather the gatepost behind it—no, not even the gatepost. The doorphone and the gatepost were simply destroyed by the pressure applied to the other side.

And sure enough, what came sticking out of the pulverized post—was a fist.

"Ah..."

It flew too fast for the human eye to perceive it as such, and I must have recognized it only because I was familiar with it.

A fist—a paw. Because I knew about that Monkey's Paw...

"Aaaaaaaaaaaaaaaaaaaaaaaaaaaaaaaaaaaaaaaaaaaaaaaaaaaaaaaaaaaaa aaaaaah!"

I'd like you to know that the scream wasn't mine.

Honestly, I was so dumbstruck I couldn't even scream—in other words, the cry belonged to the girl who appeared from the other side of the gate along with the Monkey's Paw.

A cry—be it a girl's, or a beast's.

"R..."

I finally began to speak.

It wasn't raining, or the least bit cloudy—but a figure in a hooded raincoat and rubber boots came crashing through where the gate once stood, and I spoke *her* name.

"Rainy Devil!"

No. Should I still have called *her* Suruga Kanbaru?

"A...aaaaaaaaaaaaaaaaaaaaaaaaaaaaaaaaaaaaaaaaaaaaaaaaaaaaa aah!" roared the Rainy Devil—or Suruga Kanbaru.

Before saying, just as before:

"I—I hate you I hate you—"

"...!"

Baths were the least of my worries.

If anything, I needed to avoid a bloodbath, but too stunned even to mumble that quip, I straddled the BMX—I couldn't believe it.

A lukewarm setup? Give me a break.

A highly hazardous aberration had shown up in the middle of the day—how much of a beatdown had I received at the hands of this demon monkey last May?

I also lost one of my favorite rides back then—I began to pedal, swearing I wouldn't lose the borrowed BMX and let history repeat itself to that degree.

Pedaling for dear life, dammit!

What kind of a world was this?!

Of all the things to happen, for the Rainy Devil to reappear because Kanbaru got mirrored...

"I—"

At my back, a voice that should've been distant...

"I hate you I hate you I hate you I hate you I hate you I hate you I hate you!"

Grew closer.

I knew I shouldn't look back. I needed to focus only on moving forward, but my fear got the better of me and I turned my head—I really shouldn't have.

Wall-running.

The Rainy Devil ran perpendicular to the wall surrounding the Kanbaru residence as she chased after me. Each step she took crushed and demolished the white surface, turning it into flour-like dust.

What a terrifying musclehead.

If there was any saving grace, she wore boots—and couldn't gather the kind of speed she could in running shoes.

Still, she seemed faster than the flipped BMX's top speed, and the distance between us continued to shrink—this was bad. Since my link to Shinobu had been cut and nothing about me was vampiric, I hadn't the durability to withstand a blow from the Monkey's Paw.

At this rate, I'd die in this nonsensical world before ever finding out if I'd gotten into college—come on, this inconsistency went too far! How could she have lived until now as the Rainy Devil? This was who Miss Hachikuji chummily called "Suruga"?!

I cursed and complained as I turned the handlebars—steering at this velocity was all but impossible, but I might earn myself some time if I veered away from the wall-running Kanbaru.

Fortunately, BMX bikes were made for acrobatic tricks, and I needed to resort to stunts if she beat me on speed.

But no, I soon learned how shortsighted my idea was.

A misconception.

I should've known that her legs' true power lay not in their speed, but in their jumping skills. The Rainy Devil kicked off the Kanbaru residence to leap parallel to the ground—thereby following my turn and still chasing straight after me.

Depending on how you looked at it, it was a vertical jump.

She caught up to me—passed me.

"I hate you I hate—!"

Her hatred only grew.

Packing it into her balled left fist, she descended in front of me and, still midair, swung it in my direction—wait, her left fist?

Huh? I forgot to hit the brakes, or even to take my hands off the handlebars to guard my vitals—*her left hand*?

No, that was how it went.

The paw Kanbaru once wished upon was a left hand. The original and authentic item had been a right hand, but the memento bequeathed to her by Toé Gaen, her mother, was a southpaw.

Kanbaru had kept her left arm wrapped up in bandages every day at all hours—because underneath was the furry limb of a beast, the price she'd paid for wishing upon an aberration.

As the Rainy Devil too—it was her left arm, as she wore a raincoat and tall rubber boots, that wrecked my body and my mountain bike.

The impression had been so strong that I hadn't noticed, but…it didn't make sense, did it? Even if you accepted that she'd become the Rainy Devil in this mirrored land—wouldn't her paw be her right hand?

Right hand, left hand.

Because mirrors—flip left and right.

If the original was a left hand.

Then it needed to be a right hand.

"—I! Hate! Youuuu! Ihateyouihateyouihateyouihateyouihateyouihateyou—!"

That was as far as my thoughts got.

As Kanbaru's howls gradually collapsed in on themselves, perhaps due to the Doppler effect, I rode right into the incomprehensible left hand—its destructive power had smashed a gate into dust and would surely reduce my body to putty.

"Heh…" I had to laugh.

I couldn't believe it. Despite Ogi's lectures, I was still hopeless—after all this time.

Suruga Kanbaru.

I don't want to die, but maybe it's not so bad if it's you, I found myself thinking—Koyomi Araragi is such a lost cause that it made me want to laugh, and to weep.

You were right, Ogi. But you know, even this late in the game, even in another world, my junior Kanbaru—is someone I just can't bring myself to hate.

"ihateyouihateyouihateyouihateyouihateyouihateyouihateyouihateyouihateyouihateyouihateyouihateyouihateyouihateyouihateyouihate—" "—myaaaahahahahahaha!"

Then.

The monkey's cry was joined by a cat's.

And I—was scooped up, bicycle and all.

008

Like a predator snatching prey in the savanna—is probably what it was. From my perspective as the prey, I'd been scooped away a split second before Kanbaru's left hand could sink into my heart. The predator, however, took me like it was nothing and might as well have been humming to herself.

The action centered around her—I should be treating her as the protagonist. Or maybe just as a cat.

In any case, once my eyes stopped spinning from the impact to my flank, I found myself completely elsewhere.

My self, completely elsewhere.

Kidnapped and taken someplace else—but also familiar. That is, if you accounted for the mirroring—this.

This was Shirohebi Park. Familiar to me even if I had only learned its true name the other day.

I was splayed out on the ground in its plaza.

Next to me was the BMX, its wheels klacking as they spun—thank goodness, it looked like Ogi's ride was fine for now.

The bike was one thing, but I'd have trouble saying I was. No, Kanbaru's fist hadn't grazed me or anything, I had no injuries—but this incredible fatigue coated every inch of my body.

I'd pedaled with all my strength to elude the Rainy Devil's pursuit, but that wasn't why. Even I'm not that feeble. No, I'd been sucked dry as I was abducted—yes, by the cat.

The special ability of the aberration known as the Afflicting Cat: energy drain.

"Myahahaha."

And then.

Opposite the bicycle, which was on either its left or right side, its right at least from my perspective—sat, on all fours with an amused look on her face…well, no need to put on airs now.

It was Black Hanekawa.

"…"

Though exhausted, I could at least move my eyes, so I looked her over—to find her with white snowy hair stretching to her back and large cat ears.

Also, she was in her underwear.

A polka-dot-patterned bra—something whose existence in the world is surprisingly difficult to confirm, a strapless one at that—along with black-and-white panties made out of a thick material and adorned with large frills on both the front and back. The clash between top and bottom gave off a different feeling from when they'd matched… No, this wasn't the time to be contemplating her underwear.

How should I describe this Black Hanekawa? Was this the initial design? Not Black Hanekawa from before the culture festival or after summer break, but during that nightmare of a Golden Week, when she was at her most feral and untouchable…

Then it was extremely dangerous for me to be splayed out in front of her like a fish on the chopping block—or maybe a mouse being toyed with by a cat. I may have escaped from the Rainy Devil, but my life was still under threat.

"And taking a catnap after being kidnapped by a cat. Lame, even as a pun…"

"Myaaahahahaha!"

But Black Hanekawa, with her low laughter threshold, cackled with glee as I muttered to myself. Please, could you not use Hanekawa's body to double over in hysterics in nothing but underwear?

"You really are an amewsing one, human—what a sharp wit you've got."

After cachinnating for a little while, she stood up to look down at me where I lay. Wasn't she aware that when she did that with breasts as large as Hanekawa's, I couldn't see her face?

"You nyoh, I haven't heard any thanks from you yet. Can't you at least try?"

"…"

I hesitated for a moment.

"Thank you," I then complied—it was true that she'd saved me, whatever her intentions had been and whatever she planned on doing to me next.

Of course, from my perspective, I was thanking her pair of breasts…

"Myahahaha. Nyo nyeed," Black Hanekawa said with delight after demanding my gratitude—the issue here wasn't her character, but her brains.

It seemed her intelligence level hadn't improved, and I was unsure of how to take the fact. Her idiocy was less a chink in her armor than a natural fort that made asking her for explanations pointless…

I didn't know how to approach her.

"Nyactually, how long are you planning on nyapping anyway, human? I myight've energy drained you when we touched, but it was only for a split second. It shouldn't have done too much damage."

"…"

Seriously, cat? You're far from the mark—I'm not staying

down to get you to lower your guard or anything, I literally can't move a finger…

Hanekawa liked to downplay herself as an innocent kitty and overestimate my abilities, and Black Hanekawa seemed to share that trait.

Despite my awful physical state, my mental state—my mind had started to clear. Perhaps thanks to having Tsubasa Hanekawa stand near me in her underwear even if it was in Black form.

Not an energy drain, but an energy injection—but now that my mind was clear, I found it full not of exclamation but question marks.

Not "Black Hanekawa! What are you doing here!"

But "Black Hanekawa? What are you doing here?"

?????

I mean, it didn't make sense, did it?

Black Hanekawa had been accepted into Tsubasa Hanekawa's heart back then, at the end of summer break, and should have disappeared forever.

Umm, hold on a second… That made it hard for me to stay calm for more reasons than one, but maybe the proper way to look at it was that Hanekawa's mirrored form is Black Hanekawa, just as Suruga Kanbaru's is the Rainy Devil?

Still. Hadn't Hanekawa gone on a trip overseas?

Was even that fact flipped around in this mirrored land? Yes, it was possible. A world where anything goes, where anything is conceivable, where contradictions are fine—

"Myaahaha. Looks like a lot's going through your head right nyow, human—but you're nyoverthinking it. You just nyeed to accept things as they are and as they appear, nyohkay?"

"As they appear…" Echoing her for no reason in particular, I looked up at her—or meant to, but as I should've known, all I saw was a massive amount of underboob. What good did it do me to accept its appearance?

I was going to have trouble taking any of this seriously unless she stood a little farther back, but that's when I noticed—and once I did, it almost felt strange that I hadn't until now.

Her bra and its unusual design were no excuse, I needed to feel ashamed as a Tsubasa Hanekawa devotee.

Well, given that this was how things should be, it was quite pointless to reflect too much on my error after the fact—but her chest.

It was her chest. Black Hanekawa, or Tsubasa Hanekawa's mammaries, taken not as a whole but divided into a left and right breast and observed thusly, revealed the right breast to be ever-so-slightly larger.

They say the left one is more likely to grow larger because of the heart's placement on that side of the body, but in Hanekawa's case, her right one is just a bit larger—probably because of all the use she gets out of her dominant hand while studying. The difference is minute, but my sharp eyes can't be deceived.

Putting aside the fact that she would put something sharp in said eyes if I told her—the difference was *the same* despite us being in a mirrored land.

Just like Kanbaru's "left hand."

It wasn't flipped around—hadn't been reversed.

"Wait, relax... Vision can only get me so far. I can't be sure and address this unease until I feel its root cause, those breasts, with my own hands."

"I'm nyot joking when I say you'd die if you touched my breasts in your condition. It'd be your chest nyeeding emyergency attention, nyot mine," quipped Black Hanekawa, taking a step back—allowing me to see her face at last.

"..."

I felt a little relieved.

Because her expression looked peaceful.

Although her design was the most ferocious and brutal one

from Golden Week, her mood seemed closest to Black Hanekawa at the end of summer break.

I guess that didn't match up, either... It felt inconsistent.

In that case, could I just think of this as a straightforward rescue?

"Hey, Black Hanekawa," I said, able to talk clearly at last. "Can I ask you just one question?"

"Sure. If it's something I can nyanswer."

"Yeah, literally true in your case... Anyway. I just wanted to check, we're in the land of mirrors now, right?"

To which Black Hanekawa responded, "Who nyohs," with a self-effacing smile. "It's nyot that I can't give you a nyanswer to that one—but as someone who lives in this world, I can't give you the one you want. Nyo matter what I say, it's nyot going to purrove anything."

"..."

"So I can't nyanswer your question, but I can give you a piece of advice. Don't go nyeer that monkey's home—I can imyagine why you'd visit it, but you're nyot going to get past that Monkey's Paw."

I didn't need to be told. But now that I had been, the number of question marks in my head only grew. She could "imyagine" why I'd visit Kanbaru's home? If anything, that's what I wanted to ask this world's Black Hanekawa...

"I'm going to reject that advice."

"Who knew advice is something you can reject?"

"I have to get in Kanbaru's bath, no matter what it takes."

"That'd be quite a puzzling line nyout of context."

"So let me change the question. *Who exactly asked you* to save me?"

"Wait a myanute, what makes you so certain that someone asked me to?"

"..."

Faced with this reply, I had no grounds to stand on and felt like I'd said something off the mark.

It was just that Black Hanekawa, this generation or any other, wouldn't go out of her way to help me—if she did, I assumed someone else's will had been involved.

"Nyahaha. I'll take a pass on that question too—and give you anyother piece of advice to replace the one you rejected. I nyoh you'll accept this one. If you have to go inside that home nyo myatter what, don't go alone. Go with a partnyer."

"A partner?"

"Hey, nyow, don't expect anything from me—as you've guessed, I hate you, Koyomi Araragi," Black Hanekawa said.

Using my name.

As far as I could recall, as an aberration she'd never spoken my, a human's, name—though maybe it was natural for her in this world.

"Cat—no, Hanekawa, tell me. What exactly…do you know?"

"I don't nyoh everything—I only nyoh what I nyoh."

Nyahahaha.

In the end, she'd answered none of my questions—nor did she wait for me to recover.

Because with that, Black Hanekawa left Shirohebi Park—slipping away like a stray cat whose eyes had met mine for just a brief moment.

009

I needed to rethink this all through.

To readjust my understanding.

Black Hanekawa might laugh again and tell me I was over-thinking things, but I wasn't capable of doing as little thinking as her—I needed to think. Bereft of my vampire skills, it was all I could do.

As shocked as I was when the great and holy Mayoi Hachikuji informed me that we were inside a mirror, I accepted it—but maybe it wasn't that simple.

Kanbaru's left hand. Hanekawa's right breast.

Nor was that all—the duo I encountered in quick succession had been flipped around in a way that seemed distinct from what I'd seen until then.

I mean, they'd turned into aberrations.

They'd aberrated. How did that make any sense?

A monkey and a cat. The Rainy Devil and Black Hanekawa—and you know, Tsukihi still bothered me too. Why had there been no change to her and her alone among everyone I'd met?

Dammit. It was times like these that made me regret how anti-social I was, or maybe just how few people I knew. There were passersby, but since I didn't know them to begin with, I didn't know how they'd changed, if they'd changed at all.

They say a friend in need is a friend indeed, and I was learning just how true that is by having so few... Pathetic.

As I thought this (and was finally able to move again), I settled on my next course of action—pride aside, taking Black Hanekawa's advice uncritically seemed risky, but sauntering back to Kanbaru's home unarmed went past reckless and straight into foolish territory.

I didn't know what she meant by finding a partner before heading to Kanbaru's. If I could call anyone that, it was Shinobu Oshino, but I needed to reach the Kanbarus' cypress bath precisely in order to contact my partner.

The reasoning already felt flimsy enough. Land of mirrors or not, it wasn't as if I could ignore moment-to-moment continuity.

So, the advice aside, I was going to head to the bookstore to grasp the situation, or maybe to reassess my strategic position. I decided on the location because, naturally, the sight of Black Hanekawa's body had ignited my passions, and I could use some dirty magazines—no, of course not.

While I had few real-world friends, I knew more than a little about historical figures from studying for my entrance exams. If I leafed through books that described them, I ought to be able to gauge how people had been flipped around in this world. A way to increase my sample size.

I wouldn't need to unfurl any massive historical tomes; reference books for grade schoolers should do. Descriptions of Nobunaga Oda and Ieyasu Tokugawa, of Napoleon and Lincoln, would show me how they'd changed from the figures I knew and aid me in understanding how this world worked.

When Miss Hachikuji and I had compared notes, we'd focused on nothing but scientific matters, so that'd been a blind spot. If personalities and bodies were flipped around, characters throughout the ages should've changed as well, even if history itself stayed the same. Maybe some people even differed the way Kanbaru and Hanekawa did... All right, I was probably expecting too much (though some historical figures turned into aberrations, didn't they?).

I might discover yet another pattern of transformations nonetheless. With that thought, I picked up the bicycle, made sure once more that it wasn't broken, and began pedaling toward the one large bookstore in town. Unsteadily—it'd taken a few hours for me to recover from Black Hanekawa's energy drain, so I did try to hurry to make up for lost time.

To cut to the chase, though, it was utterly fruitless, or rather, I ended up conducting a meaningless survey.

Well, the idea of looking into great historical figures wasn't meaningless in itself, but the failure came from looking to the written word for answers. I entered the store and immediately started deliberating on what book to buy only to find that I couldn't read all the flipped-around characters.

They were only mirrored, of course, so it wasn't too hard to decipher each character on its own, but when it came to the meaning of the passages, none of it stuck in my mind.

As if reading a book drained my energy—it was extremely wearying. I soon gave up on the approach. Not that I had any other plans if I gave up...

Return to Kita-Shirahebi Shrine? No, Miss Hachikuji probably wouldn't be back yet. In which case, I wanted to try something before meeting up with her.

Well... I was reluctant, or it was pretty much the last thing I wanted, but the only option seemed to be to go home and pay my respects to the tween doll plopped brazenly down in my little sisters' room. What I should've done at the very start...

Her dashing look and tone pissing me off had blotted out everything else, and asking someone who was experiencing these abnormalities hadn't seemed like a good idea. But why use that criterion to pick who to talk to if almost everyone in the world had been flipped around?

Whatever. If her dashing look pissed me off, I should just avert my gaze—come to think of it, her nasty personality wasn't new by any stretch.

I'd try to see her as conceited, not malicious. I steered toward my home—my sisters, Karen and Tsukihi, must have gone shopping, so now was a better opportunity than this morning to have an open conversation with Ononoki. Even if things took a turn for the worse and we ended up brawling, I could keep the damage to a minimum, or so I thought, but my plans always having a hitch in them held just as true in this mirrored land as it did in my original world. Maybe I should just call it nothing ever going the way I wanted.

No, even then, what happened next was too inconsistent a twist, or not to mince words, in bad taste—when I got home, parked the BMX, and entered from the front entrance, there in the house that should've been empty except for a doll, now that my sisters had left...

Stood a girl I didn't know—coming down from the second floor at the sound of the front door opening. I really had no idea who she was.

Shorts and a camisole with no bra.

A girl with shaggy short hair—not exactly in her underwear, but in an outfit that came close in terms of exposure.

Her attire seemed far too at-home for any guest my sisters might've invited over. Not even homewear but roomwear, like an open statement that she lived here. What, did I have a third little sister in this world? A bigger little sister, a littler little sister, and a middlish little sister? Things were already complicated enough now that my bigger little sister was littler than my littler little sister, so for a third little sister to appear—but wait, wasn't she coming across like the oldest of the three?

As I blinked in the grip of confusion, the girl looked at me and expressed her relief.

"Oh, it's just you, Koyomi. You scared me there."

For a moment I couldn't fathom why she'd feel relieved, but since my little sisters' shoes weren't by the front door (a pair of sandals I was seeing for the first time, not having noticed them in the morning, sat in their place—were they hers?), I realized she was afraid a burglar had come in while she was home alone. But hold on, home alone?

That really made her a third little sister... Her dismissive tone, though? Was she my big sister? Miss Hachikuji did theorize about Karen flipping around and turning into my older sister...

No, wait a sec. I'd thought I'd never seen this girl, but her voice sounded familiar...

While I wasn't the best at distinguishing between girls' voices, I'd heard this one before, only the tone was different—it used to berate me.

"Hm? What's the matter, Koyomi? Why're you just standing there?" asked the girl in the shorts, puzzled, as she descended the stairs rhythmically and closed the distance between us. She grabbed my hand and pulled me into my home.

I'd considered leaving, timidly enough, but instead hurried up and took off my shoes, forced to by her assertive attitude—I say forced, but she hadn't tugged my arm with all that much force, I'm just easily persuaded.

This overbearingness... I'd experienced it before...

"Hmmm? Huh? I thought you might've gone out, Koyomi, was it to the bookstore?" interrogated the girl in the shorts, keenly spotting the plastic bag in my other hand. She grinned. "You bought another dirty book? Ah, you're hopeless."

How did she know?! I omitted that whole bit—how did she know I'd purchased a photo collection where the mirrored characters didn't matter, and brought home *Cat-Eared Class Presidents of the World*?!

Only a little sister had that kind of intuition!

"Talk about rude. After living under the same roof with this cute a girl for almost a decade, you prefer books? Come on! But I guess we're like family at this point. Maybe I can't blame you."

"...Like family?"

In other words, not family?

Huh? Then seriously, who was she? Another freeloader, like Ononoki? But this girl was clearly human, not an aberration or a doll...right?

Almost a decade, though?

"C'mon, Koyomi. I know you want to enjoy that dirty book, but at least join me for a cup of tea. I was so bored holding the fort, I didn't know what to do! Listen, I have some sweets for the tea, and the perfect math puzzles," the girl in the shorts said, hauling me along into the living room.

Dammit, why couldn't I resist her?

I couldn't, at all. Partly because I was recovering from that energy drain, but I also couldn't disobey her on some instinctual level, her familiar voice enfeebling me—math puzzles?

...

......

....

"Wait, you're Sodachi Oikura?!"

"Whoa! Geez, don't scare me like that!" the girl in the shorts exclaimed in a familiar voice—that once showered me with abuse.

She sounded even more surprised than me.

"You're saying that now, Koyomi?! I've been living with you ever since elementary!"

010

Her impression was so different that I had no clue—but once I realized the truth, it seemed obvious. Of course she was *that* Oikura.

Sodachi Oikura.

Her hairstyle was different, and the Oikura I knew never exposed her limbs this much—most of all, the look in her eyes was just so different.

Once, they were so clouded that you worried she was afflicted with some kind of curse and was casting it on you with her gaze. Now, she was nothing but jovial.

"Hey! Hey! Isn't this puzzle amazing? This puzzle is amazing, and I'm amazing for figuring it out, don't you think?! It seems really hard, but look, the answer's obvious once you diagram it out! Don't you love this feeling? It's like a haze of mystery over the whole thing clearing up all at once!"

Oikura, who used to never come within three feet of me, as if she were dealing with some sort of waste product, now sat by my side on the sofa, her shoulder jostling against mine, not just dealing with me but sounding giddy. How was I supposed to recognize her?

She was a different individual, plain and simple.

This different, shorts-wearing Oikura, as far as I could tell from the fragments of information I gleaned from her words, had been in the Araragis' custody for eight years now—and we'd grown up on friendly terms, like brother and sister, though I'm not sure who was the older sibling in this case.

"Y-Yeah, sure, Sodachi…" Although nothing about it felt right, I called her by her first name. It was unnatural to use her family name if we weren't just childhood friends but living under the same roof—though it was going to be awkward whatever I called her given how weird the situation was. "You never fail to impress me. I've got to take my hat off to you for solving such a difficult problem."

The trauma carved into me during my first year of high school was so deep that I was trying to stay on her good side and pacify her with words even though her personality had been flipped. Of course, the Oikura I knew would have snapped at my obvious fawning, but this version was different.

"Hahaa! Koyomi praised me! Hooray!" she rejoiced like a good girl.

If the Oikura I knew, the difficult girl who wanted to be called Euler, saw herself acting this bright, cheerful, and merry, she might go on a rampage…

In fact, to be honest, I almost felt like running around and breaking things myself—it didn't make sense for me to be embarrassed, but I'd never imagined I'd be able to communicate with her like this. It felt like an impossible delusion, which made me blush.

"Hm? What's the matter, Koyomi? Your face is red. Could you be sick or something?"

Plop.

Oikura touched her forehead, already so close, to mine—like it was the most natural thing in the world. Stop! I wasn't the least bit happy, but she was going to make me start grinning!

"Hmm. Less hot than I thought," she said, her hand already working to solve the puzzle. She was writing down numbers with her left hand, but this didn't help me since I couldn't recall her dominant hand.

Then I had an idea.

"Hey, Sodachi... I forget, who's that mathematician you worship again? Euler?"

"Huh? What're you talking about? Euler is great, of course, but the mathematician I respect the most is Gauss. You know that!"

"..."

The difference was so minor that I didn't know what it signified. Did that count as being flipped around? Or rather, she was so fundamentally different that it was like being introduced to someone for the first time. Seriously, it made zero sense.

What was with this world? How did you flip that Oikura around to get this character?

Enjoying a placid, familial relationship with someone who was once on bad terms with me, or who hated me unilaterally with a vengeance, I should say, was yet another lukewarm, laid-back twist. Even so, I was too unaccustomed to all of this to know how to react.

I just couldn't accept the lack of tension.

I'd never met a female lead like this one.

"Okay, Koyomi, let's solve this problem together. I've gotten pretty far on it myself, or actually I do have an answer, but it feels like such a brute-force solution. There's nothing beautiful about trying every possibility, you know? There must be a cleaner way to solve it."

"Y-Yeah, sure, Sodachi..."

Even the numbers she wrote were mirrored, making the problem pointlessly hard, but I couldn't ignore her if I was her friendly older (younger?) brother—my plan of going to the second floor and asking Ononoki for help had been thwarted.

In fact, I was painting the perfect target on my back if the *shikigami* saw me like this—with that dashing look you couldn't even draw. But no, maybe not if this was the norm in this world? If this was Koyomi Araragi's usual behavior...

"Hm?"

Huh? Something gave me pause there.

It felt odd for a moment...like the closest I'd gotten to putting my finger on a hint for a clean solution—

"Lemme have some of your tea, Koyomi."

Oikura, who seemed to have finished off hers, took the teacup in front of me and elegantly sipped its contents. Not a problem on its own...

"Heheh! Second-hand kiss with Koyomi!"

When she didn't think twice about saying stuff like that, though, I didn't have any idea how to respond. This intimate, jokey Oikura sent my mind into the clouds, and I couldn't gather my thoughts.

I guess I was a noob at flirting because every relationship I'd managed to build involved arguing.

And so, I lost my train of thought.

"Phew," I sighed—well, maybe it was fine.

Why not just one Oikura like this, even if this wasn't an all-out parallel world but an inconsistent world full of contradictions—it might not lend a helping hand to the Oikura I knew, but family time with a girl who wasn't blessed in that department wasn't so terrible.

It resembled resignation, but I did at last reach such a state—could feel that way about a childhood friend who was still striving to find happiness.

"Hey...Sodachi. I have a question about Tsukihi."

That notion must have provided me with solid ground because

I put my concerns behind and launched into the matter at hand. Well, I ought to have been bringing it to Ononoki, but if this girl was saying we'd lived together for nearly a decade, she'd have to know my littler little sister better than the shikigami, who when it came down to it had started living with us only recently.

"Hmm? Tsukihi? She went shopping with Karen. They invited me too, but I wanted to tell you about this puzzle asap."

The point of my question didn't get across to her, and I should've known. She simply informed me of Tsukihi's current location—so I continued, "Has anything about her changed lately?"

No, that wouldn't work, either. Even if there'd been a change—some kind of reversal that I didn't notice, it'd be her natural state in this mirrored land.

"What kind of person was she, again?" I rephrased my question.

"Kind of person? What a weird thing to ask, Koyomi. Well, I see why you're worried about her. I am too. How's she going to make it in the world with that personality of hers?"

Forcing a smile, Oikura began conveying her impressions of Tsukihi Araragi as she understood her. As a girl talking about another girl, she went easier on her in some ways and harder in others, but on the whole none of it gainsaid my own impression of Tsukihi.

In which case, she really hadn't changed... Did some people change but not others, or was Tsukihi the sole exception?

If she was, I supposed I understood... If the formidable Oikura was this much of a mess (sorry), I ought to assume that most people were reversed in some way.

The existence of one such Oikura did no harm, but on the flip side, I couldn't deny also feeling that I didn't want to see her like this.

"..."

The flip side.

Right?

"Wow. Amazing, Koyomi, you figured it out. I know I get better grades than you, but I'm no match for you when it comes to this sort of thing. I don't mind, though, somehow it doesn't annoy me... Phew."

And then.

Once I finished solving the math puzzles she'd prepared, she plopped her head down on my shoulder—and something about it felt like a slight departure from the sisterly, familial vibe she'd been setting off.

"Hey, Sodachi—"

"I wonder what it is. It's strange," she interrupted me before I could chide her, not moving. "It's been like this since forever, right? But I find myself wanting it to be. Isn't that weird?"

"..."

"Is something wrong with me? You're here, Karen's here, Tsukihi's here... Uncle and Auntie are here, and you're all so nice to me, and we get along so well, like a real family, and I'm so happy, but—"

Suddenly, Sodachi Oikura...

Spoke like Sodachi Oikura: *I wonder why*—

"This all seems like a lie."

011

I ended up going back to Kita-Shirahebi Shrine without speaking to Ononoki—no, it's not like Oikura refused to free me from the living room even after I solved all her puzzles.

If anything, I had an opening.

She'd headed to the bathroom, saying she'd take a shower to freshen up and shake off her strange mood—and I used it as my cue to visit my little sisters' room.

Incidentally, she'd also issued a joking invitation: *You don't seem too well either, wanna join me?*

I firmly declined. There are some lines that even I won't cross. Too scary.

This entire emergency owed to washing my face to freshen up in the first place—I did take a casual glance at the bathroom mirror during our exchange, but it was nothing more than a mirror, as you might expect.

So then, to my little sisters' room.

Where Yotsugi Ononoki—wasn't present.

There were plenty of explanations for this—a variety of interpretations, but the most standard hypothesis was that she'd gone outside on her own for a walk.

But I didn't adopt the hypothesis.

Out of the variety of interpretations, I didn't choose it.

Even if her dashing look pissed me off, even if she spoke in a haughty tone, Ononoki was still Ononoki, an expert, regardless of her flaws.

An expert disappearing in this situation seemed like cause for alarm—I'd never admit it to her, even with a gun to my head, but I admired her brisk work and sense of responsibility.

Which meant there had been *something*, that *something* had occurred and urged her to take action—dammit.

If I'd known, I'd have put a lid on my irritation and heard her out in the morning, no matter what it took—I thought as I left home.

"I'm going out for a bit, Sodachi," I returned to the bathroom and told her from the other side of the frosted glass as she (judging by her silhouette) washed her hair, before taking off to Kita-Shi-rahebi on the BMX.

Miss Hachikuji should have returned by now; I needed to update my understanding of the situation and rethink my strategy.

A sudden plunge.

I'd been wrong to call this a lukewarm setup—I still didn't get what was going on, but I was possibly in a worse fix than ever before.

This reality was unsettling and improper.

Maybe it entailed actual risk.

Right, this wasn't some benign mirror country.

I'd asked if it was science fiction or fantasy, but come to think of it, weren't there also lots of ghost stories that involved mirrors?

Urban legends.

Street gossip.

Tall tales.

For instance—hadn't the mirror turned purple?

Agh, with my twentieth birthday not far away, I'd remembered the words: purple mirror.

How did the urban legend go again, were they cursed words that killed you if you still remembered them when you were twenty? I wanted to say there was another phrase to undo the curse, but I'd forgotten it.

Was it saying "Bloody Mary" three times?

No, that was a different mirror-related curse.

Not that any of this seemed relevant—it's just that there's no shortage of mirror-related aberrations. Even an ignorant fool like me could easily start listing them off.

In which case this world might be no land of mirrors, simply irrational and incoherent, but rather an aberrational phenomenon with a proper reason to it.

I returned to the foot of the mountain crowned by Kita-Shira-hebi Shrine with the sense that I'd been sent back to the starting tile in a board game—not a good outcome in a game, but honestly? I wished I could start all over.

I all but dashed up the mountain as soon as I chained up the bike, a regular trail run. Sprinting up and down the stairs in such a short period of time reminded me of just the other day—not that those were the best memories.

Why would they be? Back then, the god enshrined at the shrine wasn't Hachikuji—and so.

I walked through the shrine's gate, indeed feeling like I'd returned to the very start—okay, that's an exaggeration, but like I'd been sent back about five squares.

"Heya, Araragi! It's Missy Mayoi! Looks to me like things haven't been going so good for you, huh? But don't worry! I thought that might happen, so just for you, just for you, just for you, Araragi! Your friend here used all her connections to bring over a super reliable helper!"

The great god Hachikuji pushily, and I really mean pushily, said this from her position in front of the shrine, to introduce a "god"—of all the people.

A girl I thought I'd never meet again, of all the people.

Someone I'd personally wounded, of all the people.

Of all the people, Nadeko Sengok—

"Hsshh hsshh hsshh! What's up, Big Brother Koyomi? That's right, it's me! Been a while, huh? So? You been doing good all this time? Hmmmm?!"

"…"

Nadeko Sengok-who?

012

I know, a character intro this late in the story is silly, but just in case, Nadeko Sengoku—whom Miss Hachikuji brought over after making use of all her connections—had been friends with Tsukihi Araragi, my little sister, since elementary school.

They did fall out of touch at one point but recently started seeing each other again—a resumption that began with my reunion with her, but thanks to a certain conman's schemes, I'd fallen out of touch with her myself, ironically.

Because around last New Year's she, an average middle school girl, became the shrine's god—a snake god.

Well, to get to the real root of the problem, it was probably karmic retribution for my actions, but let me omit that part if I may—none of that could be undone at this point.

I can think about what I've done on my own.

But Sengoku, with whom I'd cut ties, now stood before me—we weren't supposed to ever be in such close proximity. Do you have any idea what you've done, Big Sis?

Making a fool out of me even in another world, Hachikuji—I wanted to say, but I swallowed the words at the last second because this really was a different world.

Whoever this Sengok-who was, with her gaping maw and mocking "Hsshh hsshh hsshh!" (what was so funny?), a snake in more ways than one, it wasn't the Nadeko Sengoku that I knew. Nope, I didn't know of a Nadeko Sengoku like this.

There were, at absolute most, two types of Sengokus—an easy set to complete if she were made into trading cards.

First off was what I guess you'd call her basic form? The girl I crossed paths with on the stairs to this shrine—the introverted middle school version with a face covered in bangs and a tendency to look at the ground as she muttered. There were some changes in her hairstyle and clothing, but that was normal for anyone living a normal life.

The other type was the aforementioned snake god version— who took on a dreadful form, each of her hundred-thousand-plus strands of hair a white snake, like some kind of Medusa, her expressions so unleashed you could never imagine them coming from her basic self. The Sengoku that tried to kill me countless times, and in fact did, but let me omit that part as well.

It'd be long, and I don't want to talk about it.

Meanwhile, the audacious Sengoku standing next to Miss Hachikuji seemed like neither—sure, she was wearing Middle School #701's trademark dress uniform, but her hair was cropped short and entirely white, yet not made out of snakes. Her fearless, carefree, and savage expression did seem poised, at the same time, to bear down on me from on high and gobble me up.

How do I explain it? It felt like she'd placed herself in some kind of middle, that she was immature, even incomplete—in the middle of trying to change something about herself. Right, like an organism stirring to life from within an egg…

"I think you know who she is, Araragi, but let me introduce her in case you don't, having come from another world. This is my senior—or rather, my predecessor as a god. This is Miss Serpent."

"…I see."

Miss Serpent.

I nodded in understanding at Miss Hachikuji's words, but they weren't entering my brain—yes, partly because I was baffled by this sudden encounter with a girl that I thought I'd cut ties with.

But since we were in this land of mirrors, you could also say that it didn't count, even if it wasn't a good thing by any means. What baffled me the most was that I seemed to be wrong.

Given my experiences after climbing down the mountain, I'd started to suspect that this world consisted of my delusions.

Delusions might be too harsh.

To put it differently, I thought I might be dreaming—I may not have pinched my own cheek, but I'd considered the line of reasoning as I returned to the mountain.

A dubious dream—if Oikura found out about her utterly different iteration, which was in such bad taste, she'd kill me—but wasn't I still snoring away under the covers, despite thinking that I was awake, because my little sisters never came to wake me up?

It'd explain the lack of consistency and coherence—and make sense of nothing making sense.

A dream.

In other words, one of those it-was-all-just-a-dream stories.

A bit of a foul as a narrative technique, but using it just once didn't seem so bad? They do say that rules are made to be broken. In any case, by any reckoning, *...and that was my dream* was more convincing than *...and that was the land of mirrors I visited*.

Story quality aside.

Kanbaru being the Rainy Devil... Hanekawa, who should have been overseas, being Black Hanekawa, who should have vanished... I'd observed multiple examples of things that couldn't be explained as a simple reversal in some kind of mirrored land—yet my hypothesis of this all being a dream was its own convenient delusion.

Almost a piece of wishful thinking.

I mean, I at least knew about the Rainy Devil and Black Hanekawa…and if you insisted that I wanted Oikura to act that way, I'd have trouble arguing with you.

But—I didn't know. Did not know.

This Nadeko Sengoku, I did not know—neither god nor human, something in between, but also looking ahead to what was to be. I didn't know her, didn't even have the right to.

In other words.

If dreams are made of the thoughts and memories stored in your mind, I'd never dream of this Sengoku.

Nadeko Sengoku with her hair cropped short? Unthinkable, which meant this being a dream was unthinkable too.

"…"

Then what the hell was this world?

I was already at peak confusion, but now they were trying to set a new record? Miss Serpent? Didn't that name ring a bell, at least?

"Hsshh hsshh! I see."

Amused, Nadeko Sengok-who laughed—the timbre of her voice was Sengoku's, but the tone seemed rough or maybe vulgar, all wrong, making her feel so different I thought she had to be a twin sister.

Though I've yet to meet any real-life twins…

"Listen, you're overthinking things—just like the cat said."

"Huh?"

The cat? As in…Black Hanekawa? She did say I was overthinking things…but as far as I knew, Sengoku and Black Hanekawa never interacted?

I glanced over at Miss Hachikuji.

Who returned a wink.

That's not what I wanted from you… Also, you're awful at winking.

I gave up on her and faced Nadeko Sengok-who again—though communicating with her seemed challenging in its own way.

"Hmmmm? What is it, Big Brother Koyomi? You saying you don't understand? My point's not getting across? Well, I'd imagine as much. Hsshh hsshh!"

"…"

"Don't glare at me like that. It's not like I'm messing with you, okay? Listen here, I may not look it, but I was once the god of this shrine. I'm going to be more cooperative than the cat, at least."

Come here, Nadeko Sengok-who—Miss Serpent—beckoned me over.

There was something serpentine about both her gesture and her tongue, so I hesitated, but being scared wouldn't do me any good. I began approaching Miss Serpent and Miss Hachikuji, cautiously, step by step—

"Hup!"

Once I was within several feet of the young ladies, the more big-sisterly of the two leapt at me—and pushed me to the ground for no reason.

How many times was she planning on shoving me over in a shrine?

Or maybe a poisonous spider was about to attack me—I began to look around in shock, only for Miss Hachikuji to smile and speak.

"C'mon. What're you being all serious for? Isn't that exactly why everyone's saying you're overthinking things? It's not every day you get to come to a mirrored land, so you ought to relax and even try to enjoy it, kid."

"All right."

What a selfish lady, telling me to be serious when I was being silly, then telling me to lighten up once I turned cautious—but actually, she was right.

Imposing my image of Sengoku, from my original world, onto this one was unnecessary, and while caution usually paid off, I mustn't overdo it—*relax. Even try to enjoy it.*

True.

Getting straddled by a twenty-one-year-old Hachikuji would surely be a great story once I returned—and so I turned to Miss Serpent while still in that position.

"I appreciate your help," I thanked her belatedly.

"Hmmm? Eh, sure, if it's help you're seeking, that's what you'll get. I'm a god, after all—but that's not what I meant when I said you're overthinking this."

Continuing to pin me to the ground (why wouldn't she move?), and unfazed by Miss Serpent's denial, Miss Hachikuji said, "Oh, I see. Still, Araragi, lean on Miss Serpent here. Of all the gods and buddhas out there, she's the one you ought to count on the most!"

"Of all the gods... How?"

It sounded like hyperbole, but Miss Hachikuji didn't retract her overblown promotional statement. "Well, snakes are experts when it comes to mirrors," she said.

"Huh? Snakes are experts when it comes to mirrors?" I echoed, looking at Miss Serpent—and catching a glimpse under her dress from my position on the ground.

"Hm? Yeah, sure. What, you couldn't figure it out the moment you saw me? Why else would Big Sis Mayoi call me out here, Big Brother Koyomi?"

"Why?"

Wasn't it because she didn't know too many gods, having just become one herself? She'd gone to her senior—her predecessor—for help with this quandary...or was it something more?

"Listen, Araragi," Miss Hachikuji told me.

Proud of what she was about to say.

"The Japanese word for mirror originally comes from 'snake eyes'—*kaga-mi.* You didn't know?"

013

Of course I didn't.

Snakes being called *kaka* in old Japanese hadn't been required knowledge for my entrance exams—as much as the idea resisted being put to rest, this too was proof that I wasn't experiencing a dream.

Maybe the fact that Shinobu Oshino, someone previously compared to a sea serpent, laughed with a distinctive "Kakak!" sat deep in my mind, and theoretically you could connect the dots to arrive at a dream, but that was far too forced a payoff as far as foreshadowing goes—in any case, I hadn't even considered hoping for an expert on mirrors, but her appearance now, whether goddess or middle school student, was appreciated.

"Aren't you hungry, Araragi? It sounds like you haven't eaten anything all day. Let's eat and talk. C'mon, Miss Serpent, you too."

Now that she mentioned it, the tea Oikura made me was just about the only thing I'd consumed—I hadn't really noticed because the sight of her had filled me up on its own. Having lost all of my vampiric qualities, however, I needed proper nutrition if I didn't want to collapse.

And so, I was invited inside Kita-Shirahebi's main shrine for the first time and sat down to eat a meal prepared by Miss Hachikuji.

"Hold on, aren't these offerings?"

"That's right, they are."

"..."

I should've been the only person paying visits, so maybe they were Miss Serpent's offerings? And wait, was it okay to eat them?

As I sat there hesitating, Miss Hachikuji and Miss Serpent dug straight in. To avoid any awkwardness, I humbly joined them.

I doubt this bears repeating, but what a situation—I was sitting in a circle with two gods and having a meal.

Who exactly was I?

In the world I'd been living in until that morning, Mayoi Hachikuji was a god as a result of Nadeko Sengoku no longer being one—in other words, the two never reigned concurrently, but this was another point of incoherence, or maybe inconsistency in this world.

"Gulg glug glug glug." "Glug glug glug glug."

The two gods drank straight from sake bottles that also seemed to be offerings—Miss Mayoi, twenty-one years old, was one thing, but Miss Serpent, outwardly a middle school girl, was a sight to behold.

"Big Brother Koyomi—could you be thinking that mirrors show the world with left and right reversed?"

Miss Serpent got to no warning with the matter at hand—sorry, Miss Serpent got to the matter at hand with no warning.

So suddenly that I stumbled over my narration... How embarrassing for my tongue to slip in Hachikuji's presence, though hers didn't anymore.

"Ah, um, what? Could you repeat that?"

"Could you be thinking that mirrors show the world with left and right reversed—I'm asking you a question, hmmm?"

She spoke like she was trying to pick a fight with me. Was this some kind of stress interview? That wasn't why, but I couldn't make out her question's meaning even if I understood it.

Mirrors show the world with left and right reversed—yes, that's what I thought. The kind of common knowledge possessed even by an elementary schooler.

Why do you think mirrors show the world with left and right reversed? would have some kind of philosophical edge to it, so I wouldn't have minded it. Her question, though, seemed less philosophy and more Zen koan—was she going to tell me that it's in fact us who are reversed, that our mirrored forms are the truth?

No, wait.

Elementary schoolers probably didn't know about this property of mirrors, but honors-roll students like Hitagi and Oikura would point out that it's not left and right that are reversed, but front and back, strictly speaking... Is that what she meant? That was just semantics, though. The way we see it—the "mirror image"—remains the same.

"I've heard that if you take multiple mirrors, like on a vanity mirror," I offered, "and put them at a right angle and look at where they meet, left and right are where they should be... Is that what you want to say?"

Wasn't there some mirror that shows left and right correctly even as a flat surface, by making good use of reflections? I didn't know about this world's Rainy Devil, but Kanbaru did love new and unusual things, and I remembered seeing one as I cleaned her room.

"No, no—hsshh hsshh. That's not what I mean, I'm asking if, just looking into a mirror, *you think left and right are reversed.*"

"Well...yeah, I do. When I raise my right hand, my reflection raises its left, and if I raise my left leg, my reflection raises its right, doesn't it?"

"Huh. You do ballet stretches in front of the mirror? What a weirdo."

"It's just an example. Why would I?"

It's Karen who does them, not me. Did she in this world too?

"In any case, my reflection moves in the opposite way as me."

"Do you really think that?"

Relentlessly.

Miss Serpent closed in on me—my image of snakes was that they were persistent, and that's exactly how this situation was playing out.

"Don't you just think that because it's what everyone says?"

"D-Don't be ridiculous. Do I look like the type to be bound by common sense?"

True, mirrors reversing left and right—or front and back—was a piece of common knowledge, which is to say a preconception. If I were asked to explain a mirror as an object, that'd be how. I don't remember who, but someone must've explained a mirror to me that way, and I must've understood it that way: *Oh, so it's a board that shows reality, but with left and right flipped around.*

"Miss Serpent, are you saying that's not the case? What do you think, Miss Hachikuji?"

"I'll chime in with my opinion at the end. Keep going for now," the young lady replied.

With dignity. She sounded so authoritative.

Since I knew her back when she was ten, it was hard to tell if she was being serious, silly, or just glossing over the fact that she didn't have an opinion.

"You know the mirror test, don't you? To see if an animal— for example, a snake—recognizes itself in a mirror," Miss Serpent said. "But doesn't the animal recognize the reflection as itself precisely because left and right are flipped, and the image is its *counterpart*? If left and right moved exactly the same in the mirror, the animal would think it's moving in a different way, that it's a different creature—maybe. Hsshh hsshh."

102

"Well, the reflections do move with left and right reversed, so…"

"In any case, snakes don't have limbs, so your phrasing isn't convincing me—and anyway, mirrors don't give off any light. They just reflect the light that enters them, and the viewer just assumes that it's 'showing' an image. When you think of it that way, that's not the function of a mirror at all, is it?"

"Miss Serpent…" It felt like I was being toyed with—or straight-up being teased, so I replied in a somewhat stern tone, even though I was speaking to a god. "If a mirror doesn't show you the world with left and right reversed, then what exactly does it show?"

"The truth," Miss Serpent declared. "And no, Big Brother Koyomi, I'm not saying that there's a 'true' left and right. It's how mirrors were treated in ancient times—they were holy items."

"Oh… Yeah, magical mirrors and the like crop up all the time."

"Like Cinderella's mother's," Miss Hachikuji chimed in knowingly, when she'd confused Cinderella for Snow White. Still, it was a good example.

We have an unromantic explanation nowadays, but images in mirrors seemed quite wondrous in the past, so people naturally granted them some sort of meaning—hence all the aberrations revolving around mirrors.

They show the truth, huh?

"Shown the truth, Medusa turned to stone—but who wouldn't be petrified by someone with snakes for hair? Hsshh hsshh!" laughed Miss Serpent. Maybe I didn't get snake humor, but having witnessed a serpent-god Sengoku looking just that way, I didn't find it funny at all… Did that version of her never exist in this world?

"They show the truth? Okay, I admit that's suggestive, but so what? What kind of lesson am I supposed to take home here?"

Going on about lessons made me sound like that conman, but my only impression so far was that looking back on history could sure be edifying.

You call it the truth, but it's still facing the wrong way around, I almost wanted to say in a salty mood. While I'd made a four-yen offering to Miss Hachikuji, I couldn't take that attitude with Miss Serpent, who'd made a cameo appearance free of charge.

In hindsight, my donation to Miss Hachikuji was so meager I'd be better off not having paid anything. I suddenly felt like apologizing—sorry for my callous quips, even if I kept them to myself.

"Do you still not get it, Big Brother Koyomi? Listen here, I'm just trying to tell you that the same goes for this world. Viewed head-on, it might seem like left and right are flipped, but that doesn't mean it's reversed—it's not about deciding which one is correct, both of them are, okay?"

"What?" Both—were correct? The truth?

"This world might look like an inconsistent mess from where you stand, but just like your world, that all depends on if you lewd in the right way."

"Lewd in the right way..." I took her seriously, but wait, my world wasn't that lewd.

"Pardon me, view it in the right way."

"How do you make a mistake like that? How do you confuse those two phrases? They're practically opposites."

"Opposites, eh—hsshh hsshh."

Miss Serpent echoed my vacuous quip as if it were profound—hm?

"All right, fine, let me recap," she continued. "All the nice people you know who you've met in this world, whether your sisters or your friends or your juniors or your childhood acquaintances—along with me and Miss Mayoi. It's not like our left and right have been flipped around. You've started to figure that out by now, haven't you?"

"…"

"Yes. It's not that we're flipped around—we're out here as our honest selves, in our own way. We might be reflections, but we're not illusions—hsshh hsshh! Judging by the way you've been looking at me, I'm nothing like the me you know, to the point where you can't believe that we're the same people—but I'm sorry to say, this is also who I am."

I'm Nadeko Sengoku, Miss Serpent said.

Nadeko Sengoku said, in other words.

Even my dull self was beginning to see her point—but something about it wasn't sinking in. Was it some visceral reaction?

The logic that the reflection in the mirror is identical, is the same person, made sense for Tsubasa Hanekawa and Black Hanekawa, but I couldn't bring myself to accept it for anyone else.

Take the first person I met. If Karen got shorter, didn't her entire identity crumble away?

"People who're tall don't always wish it was that way—just as some people develop a complex over being short, others can about being tall. Your cute little sister only just graduated middle school, right? Do you think she's grown up enough on the inside—to catch up to her height?"

"On the inside…"

Well, when you put it that way, yes, her body had done all the growing but the person inside of it had yet to fill it out. She was still a child—it seemed to me, at least.

"…"

And?

If you adopted that approach with Tsukihi—Ononoki—Hachikuji—Kanbaru—Hanekawa—Oikura—Sengoku—the jumbled way they'd been flipped around finally started to line up along a common theme. But what did it mean?

"Hsshh hsshh. It's starting to come together now, so why don't we jump back a bit. You said that mirrors flip around left and right because when you raise your right arm, your left arm moves—but that example doesn't apply to a snake with no limbs. What would you say is flipped around in the case of a snake? How would you—how do you explain left and right being 'flipped around' to me?"

"I'd, um, use the shape of your scales, or the way they're lined up…"

"Don't picture literally explaining it to a snake. What are you, stupid? I'm asking how you'd explain left and right being flipped around to someone who lacks those concepts."

"Well…"

It was like a variation on the Ozma Problem. It might seem easy, but it's harder than you think. For example, moving your body to the right would make your counterpart move left—but the key is to explain left and right being reversed without using the words.

"The Ozma Problem reminds me of the Wizard of Oz," Miss Hachikuji chimed in with a comment that I could safely ignore (not quipping even silently at her expense now just made me seem cold). But as I continued to agonize over the question, I arrived at a very simple answer.

"That's it. You could just show them reflected letters."

"Hsshh hsshh. Letters?"

"Yeah. Well, there are a lot of symmetrical letters depending on the way you write them, so maybe use full words? Put that in a mirror and it'll be reflected with left and right switched around, which should let you explain a mirror's properties, right?"

Koyomi Araragi would be reflected as Ӄoγomi Aɿɒɿɒǫi. Miss Serpent would be reflected as Miƨƨ ƧɘɿqǝnɈ—the "mirrored letters" that made me give up at the bookstore.

Seeing them, it was immediately obvious that you weren't looking at a simple piece of glass, and that reality isn't being shown to you as it is.

"Yes."

That's it, Miss Serpent said.

Her facial expression was less of a *Right! You're smarter than I thought, Big Brother Koyomi!* and more of a *So you finally managed to put together the answer I wanted—look at all the work you made me do.* Well, then maybe you should've just given it to me up front in an itemized list.

Maybe gods had some kind of rule where they couldn't deliver messages too directly from on high, but I'd heard enough about mirrors; I was even reminded of that abandoned cram school and Oshino force-feeding me his extensive knowledge on aberrations. For her to look disappointed on top of it all was too much to handle.

Speaking of which, what became of that cram school in this world? It didn't exist in mine anymore. The designs of buildings and other sights around town were flipped around, but that was all I'd noticed...

"Okay, Big Brother Koyomi. Time for the next step."

"You weren't done yet?"

"Don't you worry, this is the last of it—we'll ask Miss Mayoi for her opinion after this."

"Huh?" Mayoi Hachikuji seemed honestly surprised to hear Miss Serpent mention her—she must've forgotten her own earlier statement.

I was right, it was just an excuse and she didn't have an opinion...

"If, out of the blue, someone showed you the words Ʞoγomi Ʌɹɐɹɐǥi, not in a mirror but on a piece of paper—what would you do?" asked Miss Serpent.

"...So I'm playing the snake now? Do I also need to pretend that I have the brain of a reptile?"

"No, even yours should be up to it."

What a mean thing to say—well, of course Miss Serpent

would be partial to reptiles, she was a snake god.

Umm.

"Well, I'd probably just think of them as mirrored letters."

"But you don't know what a mirror is. Nor do you know what mirrored letters are."

"Okay, then I wouldn't think of them as mirrored letters, but that just means I don't know how to read. I'd still think of them as flipped—"

Hm? No, that wasn't it. I'd normally only think of mirrored letters as "flipped around" if I were in front of a mirror. Try to remember, what did I do when I struggled to read those history books?

Right.

I tried to read the pages from the opposite side, through the paper—an attempt that failed, but that meant if I saw mirrored letters on a piece of paper...

I'd probably turn the page to look at it from the inside out.

Yes. Mirrors didn't turn left and right around—

"They turn people—*inside out.*"

Now I understood.

For the first time since coming to this world, I finally got it—this was no mirrored land. Well, it was a totally correct understanding, but—the girls I'd seen hadn't been flipped around.

They were turned—inside out.

What was hidden inside of them was now on the outside.

Ah... That's why Tsukihi was the only one who hadn't changed, aside from her clothes—actually, even the clothes were a regular mistake by her standards, but in any case, that's the kind of person she is.

Someone with only one face—Tsukihi Araragi had no inner self that could appear, even in a mirror.

Yes.

Here, on the other side of that mirror, was an inner world.

014

To start with a discussion of terminology, the world you're placed in after completing a videogame used to be called a *secret world*— this might not be common knowledge since games these days tend not to have endings at all, but think of it as an especially hard stage, or maybe a bonus stage.

In my case, it meant the world on the other side of the surface, like the opposite side of a coin—you could also take it to mean an inside-out world.

I'd spent almost an entire day up to this point getting it all wrong. Of course, *a world where left and right are flipped around* and *an inside-out world* might not seem that different, and you might be thinking that they're the same thing at the end of the day. While that's true of the world as I saw it, it wasn't of the personalities that it contained.

I suppose Hanekawa's example is the easiest to understand. Black Hanekawa might not be Tsubasa Hanekawa, but it's not true either that they're two different people—nor is Black Hanekawa a fabrication who doesn't exist in the real world.

The aberration that appeared during Golden Week was both the *yokai* known as the Afflicting Cat and Tsubasa Hanekawa herself.

Something that saintly woman had repressed.

Her self and her long-suppressed pain.

That—was Tsubasa Hanekawa's inner self.

Oshino may have named it Black Hanekawa, but in truth, you could call the cat "Tsubasa Hanekawa" and Hanekawa "White Hanekawa"—and if we looked at this world from an inside-out perspective, the same applied to the others.

Seeing small Karen was so unconventional and novel that I felt a shock on the level of the discovery of a new continent—but as Miss Serpent said, Karen really was concerned about her height. The gap between her lack of growth as a person and her growing body existed in her mind.

It must've been there. If that inner part of her came to the surface—it'd take that form.

The way she looked wasn't at all new. It was a manifestation of her poor balance as a person.

In Ononoki's case, being a shikigami meant taking the form of an inexpressive, affectless doll lacking any intonation in her voice, but she'd told me in the past that she simply wasn't able to surface those qualities—couldn't display them on the outside, and that she wasn't inexpressive or affectless at all.

Taking into account Tadatsuru Teori's testimony, we might say that her interior in contrast to her exterior, who she was on the inside in contrast to on the outside, had been made visible.

In fact, my impression of Ononoki wasn't that her personality had changed but that her nasty personality had been exposed—and Mayoi Hachikuji's case was even easier.

Hachikuji, who previously appeared before me as a ten-year-old girl, was in fact a ghost who'd died ten-plus years ago. She'd be twenty-one if she'd aged normally.

She looked like a young girl on the outside but had the temperament of an adult woman on the inside. On the one hand, ghosts don't mature, time doesn't accumulate for aberrations, and you can't just tally up her mental age; on the other hand, even being sent to hell and becoming a god didn't annul her history of wandering the streets for eleven straight years.

I didn't understand it too well myself, but she had an inner side that was invisible to people like Kanbaru, who praised her to the skies and went on about cute young girls—and what I saw was what you got if you turned that inside out.

Speaking of Kanbaru, Suruga Kanbaru, her case was a little complicated—it was intertwined with her mother, Toé Kanbaru, and her aunt, Izuko Gaen. But if you looked at her on her own and spoke of her just in terms of inside and outside, her left hand—the Monkey's Paw—read the inner wishes of its owner from the start and granted them. Its very existence as an aberration was like a cheat code.

She wore a raincoat and tall rubber boots.

Her form as the Rainy Devil was the hidden, interior Suruga Kanbaru—while her attachment to me as her senior was genuine, she couldn't ever fully rid herself of the hatred she bore me.

It's not like something that never existed appeared.

It always existed there, always was there.

The distinctions make it sound like I was dealing with mathematical definitions, but you can simplify the problem by saying that the Rainy Devil was none other than Suruga Kanbaru—and speaking of math, there was Sodachi Oikura and her unwatchable version.

Honestly, I had yet to process what I'd witnessed. That open and free personality she'd never given a glimpse of, and the way she acted like one of the Araragis, might be something I'd daydreamed, but it was more for her sake, more than she'd ever ask for—so I'd like to think.

That happiness, too good to be true.

I wanted to believe from the bottom of my heart that Sodachi

Oikura hoped for that kind of thing—a girl like that on the other side of her prickly personality and hostile behavior did feel like some sort of saving grace.

Maybe I'm being too self-serving, but it's impossible for me to speak about her, a childhood friend, logically.

Compared to that, my evidence for Nadeko Sengoku's case might be slightly more convincing—because the god known as Miss Serpent, the indigenous god worshipped at Kita-Shirahebi Shrine, was something she'd hatched within her.

Maybe not quite a case of split personalities, but Shinobu and I had seen Sengoku speak with this serpent god once—a snake that had nested inside her, invisible to both of us.

That rough way of speaking, that rude, carefree behavior.

That too was Nadeko Sengoku—one and the same, as she said herself.

As hard as it was for me to accept, having only ever seen her as my little sister's friend, there was no Nadeko Sengoku who was simply reserved, introverted, and cute—something I had no choice but to accept with remorse.

Beneath the reserve was a childishness.

Beneath the introversion was aggression.

Beneath the cuteness was audacity, all there.

A Nadeko Sengoku who could explode, who could burst at any moment resided in Nadeko Sengoku—that's how it was.

I went back over my adventures through this world I saw as strange to find that it wasn't so at all. I'd simply been seeing these girls turned inside out.

This world allowed inconsistency and contradiction—not because it was a land of mirrors, but because the girls appeared as the characters they were in their own hearts and minds.

Freedom of thought.

Is that what you'd call it? It did center this world, which had felt so unstable and uncertain to me. It even changed the way I saw the sights, which simply seemed mirrored until then.

By the by, regarding what Miss Hachikuji told me about the etymology of "mirror" in Japanese, *kagami*, and how it's derived from "snake eyes," *kaga-mi*—there are of course many competing theories, one apparently being that it comes from "seeing shadows," or *kage-mi*. A device to see people's shadows.

Wherever there is light, there are shadows.

Whenever you see a surface, something exists underneath—everyone has another side to them.

Miss Serpent explained it to me in manga terms—out of nowhere, but I assumed it was for my own ease of understanding.

"I've heard you pick up certain bad habits when you're drawing faces looking left or right, depending on which hand you draw with—so when you draw a face looking in your weak direction, you check it later in a mirror, or even draw a face looking the other way on the back side and trace it over on the front. Yes, obverse and reverse are also about strengths and weaknesses—the same essence expressed in completely different manners."

The manga metaphor was easy for me to understand, but it was from an artist's perspective for some reason…

Hm. Okay, there were many types of reversals, and lazily, I'd harbored a major misunderstanding until now. Miss Serpent had been worth my time, and she'd just worked a miracle—still, hearing her interpretation made me wonder, *So what?*

Being in another world, in a place I saw as a foreign land, and not having the first clue as to how to return plagued me just the same as before.

This expert on mirrors had enlightened me with the knowledge that mirrors pierce a person's truth from the inside out, but there was no *Which is why you need to do this!* along with it.

Even if they weren't the girls I knew, they were still one side of them, so I'd resolved not to treat them with disdain—but I'd gained no answer or solution to the question of how to get back to my original world and why this had happened.

No, strictly speaking, she made a fairly sharp point about the why, even if it wasn't a full hypothesis—*she* in this case being not Miss Serpent, but Miss Hachikuji.

Lo and behold, she hadn't been bluffing about giving her opinion at the end—she did have one doubt, unrelated to Miss Serpent's take. A question she'd found herself with after we'd parted ways earlier that day.

"Well, putting aside this place being inside a mirror, or a mirrored land, or another world, or another dimension, whatever—there are people you know here, right? Like your family and friends, your juniors and childhood acquaintances?"

"Yup... In that sense, I haven't been tossed into a completely unfamiliar realm, but your point?"

"What about you? Where are you, Araragi?"

Me?

"You haven't met you, Araragi—isn't that strange? Everyone knows you, me and Miss Serpent included—we each have a relationship with you. Some of us, like Suruga, might try to attack you, but that's still a kind of relationship. But doesn't that mean you've existed in this world long before you ever came here?"

"..."

"In that case, where did that Araragi go? Your personality and behavior seem familiar to us...but you're not this world's Koyomi Araragi, are you? Shouldn't another Araragi aside from you—shouldn't your inner self be in this world?"

There we go. The idea, or maybe clue that slipped away from me when I was talking to Oikura...

The normal Koyomi Araragi.

Traveling through time with Shinobu, we'd talked about there being two patterns: "you" existing in the time traveled to, and "you" being absent. In this case, though, there was only one possibility.

114

If the girls here knew me, it didn't make sense for me not to exist—even if I wasn't here now, I had to be before now.

When I looked in the mirror this morning.

That mirror image that didn't line up with my movements.

Those eyes that seemed to glare at me—

"Could Araragi have gone to the other world, switching places with you, Araragi? And now he's confused by 'a nonsensical world where everything is consistent'… Heh, I think they'd be having a tougher time over there than we're having here."

"…That still makes things tough for us, too. We'd have to sync up perfectly with the other side when both of us return to our original worlds."

Oh—actually, if the me who wasn't me was in a world with Shinobu, things could get settled faster. We might be able to communicate with that world without using the Kanbarus' wooden bath.

No.

Even if that were true—even if the me from this world had gotten sucked into the other world to take my place, it still wouldn't go that well.

How would we pull off a perfectly synchronized two-man play? There was no guarantee that we thought the same way just because we were two sides of the same coin, the same person.

Twins can share the same genes but have different fingerprints. Why would the timing of our actions line up—this was the bigger issue.

Because.

Because thinking this through—judging by the examples of Black Hanekawa and the Rainy Devil, even if Koyomi Araragi existed in this world.

The flip side of Koyomi Araragi—was my nemesis.

It would have to be Ogi Oshino.

015

I wanted to complain if all of this was Ogi's plot. This is way too fast for you to be coming for revenge, how obsessed with retaliation are you, I know it's not on the heels of yesterday but this is still on the heels of the day before yesterday, I'd say, but what good would it do to make speculative comments to a person who wasn't even present—though the fact that the girl known for appearing at the most unexpected of times had yet to show herself for once did make me feel very uneasy. If this world's Ogi had been sent to the other world to take my place, that meant there were two Ogis over there, and well, just the thought was scary. The world I needed to return to would be enveloped in darkness. Two Ogis... I couldn't think of any way to deal with that. I nearly felt glad I wasn't present for it.

"True, Araragi, it doesn't change what we have to do—somehow sneak over to the bath in Suruga's place and communicate with the other world. I don't imagine avoiding the Rainy Devil's watchful eye would be easy, though."

"Yeah...I guess," I sighed.

"I know I'm repeating myself, but there's no point in panicking... Go to bed for today. You only have a regular human's stamina now, so resting is an important step in achieving your goals. What do you want to do? Wanna stay here at this shrine?"

"I appreciate the offer, but no, I think I'll go home… There's something I want to check there, anyway."

"Oh. Well, Miss Serpent and I will keep on going, so come by again tomorrow, maybe in the evening. If you do get the chance to go back to the other side, though, you of course shouldn't let it get away. Leave a letter behind or something if that happens."

"Okay… I'm sorry for causing you all this trouble."

"You haven't caused any trouble at all—and it's my job now to keep this town under control," Miss Hachikuji said, with dignity. She only recently became a god in this world too, but seeing her so in her element was somehow very reassuring.

So this was what divine favor felt like—even if Miss Serpent added, "Well, you're causing trouble for me, pulling me back in like this when I've retired." Although she spat this venom at me (in keeping with her nature as a poisonous snake), she also said, "Eh. I'm curious about what that cat is up to," hinting at something before going quiet.

Come to think of it, we'd never gotten to Miss Serpent and Black Hanekawa's relationship, and the snake god started heading back before I could ask… Maybe she'd never meant to tell me—not that it seemed important. Logic suggested that a third party had gotten involved if I'd been saved by Black Hanekawa, who hated me, but logic had no meaning in this world.

"This might be turning into a drawn-out campaign, but I can't stay here for too long," I griped. "There's paperwork I'll need to do to enroll if I passed my entrance exams."

"In the worst case, just have Shinobu take you back to the past once you've returned."

"That's the kind of obviously flawed solution from an episode of *Doraemon*…"

"By the way. In *Doraemon*, Nobita ends up getting married to

Shizuka because he changed his own future. But that means Shizuka has to get married to someone she used to look down on, when she should've married Dekisugi, a way better guy who's almost too good to be true. How are we supposed to feel about that?"

"…"

A view befitting a young woman. As a boy, I didn't know what to say.

In any case, I walked down the mountain, got on the BMX, and headed back home—where was the owner of the bike?

The BMX existing in this world implied that Ogi existed in it until at least the day before yesterday, but I couldn't say for sure… It was hard to live in a world that allowed for inconsistency.

It defanged all of my theories and reasoning.

I'm not clever by any stretch, but in my own way, I'd used my wits to get myself out of every situation thus far—so it felt like I'd lost a weapon here in a world with no use for wisdom. Even if that wisdom wasn't much to speak of.

Even my line of thought that a Nadeko Sengoku unlike any Nadeko I knew proved this wasn't a dream might be an instance of overthinking things—there was no rule saying that knowledge you didn't possess couldn't appear in a dream.

And even if this wasn't my dream, it might be someone else's— though that gave this story an SF tinge all over again.

…I suddenly wondered what Hitagi Senjogahara was like in this world. Oikura showed that you could be the complete opposite, and while I didn't have the bad taste to desire it, what was Hitagi Senjogahara like in a world where your inner self came to the surface?

I'd be lying if I said I wasn't curious.

Still, I had to admit it'd be in bad taste—even if it provided me with a hint on how to escape this world, it was only a pretext for sneaking a look at my girlfriend's heart.

Anything that'd make me unable to look her in the eyes after

I got back home was off limits—and as I swore this to myself, I arrived at the Araragi residence.

Half as a joke, I tried imagining how things might be for her. No harm in that, right? Maybe it was fine if a Hitagi still lived in the palatial estate that once stood, supposedly, near Shirohebi Park, where Black Hanekawa had taken me after kidnapping me.

The Valhalla Duo might be going strong, too, with no rupture between their time together in middle school and high school—it didn't link up with the Rainy Devil's existence, but consistency wasn't a thing in this mirrored land.

While this world was nothing but trouble for me, that made me wonder if it wasn't so bad after all—this place could even allow for a future where everyone's happy, that idea mocked by Oshino.

Well, it was nothing more than wishful thinking, and things naturally didn't turn out as I wanted—the detail I wanted to check at home ended up being a swing and a miss. I thought meeting my parents once they came back from their jobs might strengthen Miss Serpent's divine hypothesis (hy-apotheosis?) about this being an inside-out world, but their work was going late, and neither would be returning tonight.

Talk about bad timing... I did get what info I could from my little sisters and Oikura, but my parents, like Tsukihi, weren't too different from the people I knew.

I couldn't say for certain until I saw them, but then again, even if it wasn't at Tsukihi's level, neither was the type to have a hidden side... Of course, I'm sure part of it was the fact they were adults, and my parents.

You could turn their personalities inside out, but if you covered it all up with "adulthood," they wouldn't seem any different... I had to admit, I was a bit relieved. The feeling wasn't as strong as with Hitagi, but I didn't particularly want to see who my parents were on the inside.

120

I began to regret not taking Miss Hachikuji up on her kind offer if this was the outcome. In addition to not wanting to impose too much, I'd refused because my good sense told me that while a ten-year-young girl was one thing, staying the night with a twenty-one-year-old Hachikuji was out of the question.

The wall between minor and adult wasn't nothing, but if you just looked at the numbers, only three years separated us—seeing Mayoi Hachikuji as a woman didn't come easily at this point, but I still needed to draw a line.

Yes, I knew how to behave myself.

Or so I thought, but after I got out of the bath and saw there indeed wasn't anything strange about my bathroom mirror and felt dejected; after I put on an optimistic mask and decided to go to bed because everything might be back to normal when I woke up in the morning; once I entered my flipped-around room—

"Koyomi! Oh, you. You're gonna catch a cold if you don't dry off your hair. Not that it'd make you any less hot! Haha," Oikura said from her top bunk. She was wearing heart-patterned pajamas and reading a book of sample math questions.

…Come to think of it, I hadn't entered my room in this world, but I should've seen it coming.

Since Oikura lived with us and we only had a limited number of rooms, the kids—me, Karen, Tsukihi, and Oikura—had to form two pairs. Apparently, I was with Oikura.

Not spending the night with the older Miss Hachikuji was making me use the same bunk bed as Oikura, who was my age… I began putting together a sneaky escape to the sofa on the first floor, but it ended in failure.

"Whaaat? Why, why, why? Did I do something wrong?! Are you mad, Koyomi? Stop it, don't act so distant! What, are you seeing me as a girl now?!" asked Oikura, or someone else I didn't recognize, squashing my plan. As much as I dreaded an extended war, I didn't have a solid idea of when I'd be returning to my world, so I had to be careful not to act too suspicious.

Witnessing Oikura in such high spirits was probably insulting to her, but this Oikura didn't totally satisfy the theory that I was in an inside-out world where the internal was made external. There was the very practical matter of having to observe her... Talking to her made it clear that we did indeed live in the same room, but we at least respected each other's privacy when changing and the like, so I gave up resisting and got into the lower bunk bed.

As sad as it is to admit, I felt a little excited about getting in a bunk bed for the first time in so long... Back when I was little and sharing a room with my sisters, I'd insist on the top bunk (Karen, Tsukihi, and I rotated each night between a bunk bed and a single bed), but the bottom bunk was interesting in its own way. Knowing that someone was sleeping right above me felt odd— even apart from the said person being Oikura.

"Hey, Oiku—Sodachi. Do you know anything about mirrors?" I asked upwards after turning off the lights. I wouldn't say I was going all-in, but I should make effective use of anyone as smart as her.

With so much I couldn't say, my question had become pretty straightforward. Despite the complete change in her, Oikura's answer wasn't perfunctory and went beyond flipping things around.

"I guess I remember hearing that they never reflect an image accurately," she replied sleepily. "Because while mirrors reflect the light that hits them, it's impossible to reflect all the light. How did it go again? Normal mirrors are only about eighty percent reflective? They always end up absorbing some amount of light. So—mirrored images look blurrier than the real thing."

"..."

"We might look at ourselves in the mirror, but we only ever see a blurred image...can only know a blurry version of ourselves. Inaccurately, with a dim outline..."

I was intrigued and wanted to hear more, but it seemed Oikura had fallen asleep.

Mirrors aren't precise with their reflections.

Info that could turn into the first step of a solution, or maybe not—perhaps it was a careless question if my goal was to keep up appearances.

It also felt like I was hitting some kind of limit… Relying too much on gods like Miss Hachikuji and Miss Serpent didn't seem right, maybe I should take this opportunity to visit Kanbaru's home tomorrow with Oikura? No, probably not.

Find a partner.

That's what Black Hanekawa said—but that partner didn't exist in this world.

Someone I could rely on in a situation like this, without fore-thought…not even about the trouble I might cause. She really was the only one for me in the end, I thought, and before long I fell asleep too.

As I did, a dreamy notion went through my mind: I'd forgot-ten and couldn't remember, but maybe, back when I was a grade schooler and the Araragis had taken her in for a time, I'd drifted off to sleep with Oikura like this.

016

Someone woke me up right away.

Like they were waiting for me to fall asleep.

For a moment, I was in that state where I didn't know if I was asleep or awake, in a dream or in a daze, but even after that moment passed and I woke up, I didn't know what was going on.

"Shh."

There, standing by the bed with her index finger up against her mouth, the lights still off, was none other than the shikigami tween of unknown whereabouts, Yotsugi Ononoki.

It was Ononoki.

No, that wouldn't have been so confusing on its own—it was the usual level of eccentric (and harassing) behavior for her. Normally I'd have the mental composure to feel nice and relieved that she'd made it back home safe—but.

There was a reason that didn't happen.

"Kind monster sir, you need to get up without making a sound. Without waking up Big Sis Sodachi. Put on clothes so that you can go outside," Ononoki said, her tone uninflected, unfeeling, and flat—spoken with such little expression on her face that I knew exactly how she looked even in the dark, unlit room. That was why.

No expression, no emotion, just words, just standing there.

She did have that outfit on with the pants, but I was certain that she was the Yotsugi Ononoki I knew.

"…?"

What was going on? Why?

Why did yet another exception have to pop up just as I'd gotten used to this world and started doing my best to analyze it—where was the emotive Ononoki?

Then, this Ononoki said something to exacerbate my confusion.

In, of course, a flat tone.

There was no feeling behind her words, but they were as shocking as could be.

"Stay quiet and just follow me, monstieur. If you do, I'll take you to Shinobu—to the Kissshot Acerolaorion Heartunderblade who exists in this world."

017

"I should let you know in advance…not to get your hopes up too high. I've barely figured any of this out myself, and I'm far from being able to say I understand it all," Ononoki warned as we plodded along the streets at night. Wherever it was we were heading, the Unlimited Rulebook could have gotten us there in no time with a single hop, but I wasn't up to it in my current form.

A method of transportation that violent would kill any flesh-and-blood human.

So I was on foot, and not on the BMX, either—Ononoki could probably keep up with me even if I biked at full speed, but I didn't feel like trying. Though not as bad as the Unlimited Rulebook, riding that altered bike in the middle of the night was far too dangerous.

"Ononoki."

"What is it, monstieur?"

"Er, well…"

She'd replied in a flat tone, at her own leisure, not so much as looking in my direction—indeed the Ononoki I knew.

After assaulting me in my sleep…or just rousing me from it, she'd led me out of my home, careful not to wake Oikura or my sisters, and made me walk for quite some distance now. Yet I hadn't gotten used to her.

Okay, in terms of what I am and am not used to, this was the Ononoki I was used to and felt comfortable around—but why had she "flipped around" to being this way all of a sudden?

I had no idea what had caused the inside-out her to turn inside out again—not explaining a thing was also very much like her. I hesitated to ask her any direct questions and was tamely following her through town.

That makes me sound so passive, but I just couldn't ignore the name she'd spoken—Kissshot Acerolaorion Heartunderblade.

A vampire, who shouldn't exist in this mirrored land—no, wait. If this was more than a world "inside a mirror," then maybe it wasn't too strange for a vampire to exist here?

That seemed like a stretch—but if Ononoki really was going to take me to Shinobu (excuse the cautious wording, but the Ononoki I knew wouldn't think twice about telling that malicious of a lie), we'd move toward a solution in no time at all, wouldn't we? It'd save us the trouble of having to contact Shinobu on the other side.

If this side's Shinobu opened up a gate on this side, I'd be able to return to my original world—an immediate simplification of the plan.

The thought was exciting enough that being roused in the middle of the night felt fair. Sadly, I also realized that at no time in my whole career had a twist been so convenient.

My natural reaction was to brace myself.

It was like watching a movie and knowing, given how long it'd gone so far, that a certain twist could only be the middle act and not the climax—not that I should let my guard down, since my story could get lopped off, cut short before its finale.

In any case, I couldn't stay silent forever. The change in Ononoki intimidated me, and I was losing my motivation after all these dizzying twists and turns, but better to be the boy who cried wolf than the one who jumped at his own shadow.

I made my move.

"That outfit looks good on you."

Made my move, starting from a distance.

Hey, even the most talented boxer starts off with a few jabs.

"Thank you," Ononoki said, surprising me by taking the compliment—she wasn't the type, so her words, even if they were flat, stunned me. "Though this does feel wrong in its own way—I feel like I was wearing cuter clothes. Not that there's any point in complaining about such a trivial matter... In any case, they're not to my taste. No, maybe this is my taste... My taste, as well as my bad taste."

"..."

"Oh, you want me to explain, don't you? All right, I get it. I know what you're like, kind monster sir, from the way you like little girls to the way you like tween girls."

"Know me less narrowly, please. And that's not what I'm like, that's what I like... Not that those are my likes!"

"I am a professional, you know," Ononoki objected. "When you saw me and spoke to me this morning, you seemed sure that there was something off about this world... And the way you were acting, I started to feel like something was off too."

When you gaze into the abyss, the abyss gazes into you, Ononoki pulled out an awfully pretentious quote.

Put simply, she'd been surprised to see me surprised. I'd thought I'd managed to get out of that situation, even if I hadn't kept a cool head through it all. Her keen professional eyes drove home that I was just an amateur.

"What? Monsieur leaving without even trying to pull down my pants? Impossible, I thought. That doubt is where it all started."

"Please don't use that as a starting point. And when you say that, do you mean just take off your pants, or your underwear too?"

"Well, peer into your own bosom for the answer… Speaking of chests, it was also suspicious that the man who always used my chest, didn't."

"What do you even mean by that? How am I a man who's always using your chest?"

"It's my curse to be unable to let any grounds for concern go, you see. Once you left, I performed a self-check—what about my condition surprised you? I wondered what had us make out."

"Make out? I'm pretty sure we didn't."

"Sorry. I meant to say, *what had you creeped out.*"

"Those are nothing like each other. How do you make a mistake like that?"

Of course, anyone would feel creeped out if we really did make out…

"My maintenance couldn't pinpoint why you felt creeped out, but at least I realized that I was not currently in a state to perform at full capacity. I was defective as a monster, as a shikigami who serves Big Sis—and so."

I rebuilt my personality, she said—Yotsugi Ononoki did.

If ever she'd spoken in a monotone, it was as she said this line. The casual way she passed it off made it easier for me to digest. Oh, of course, yes, no, hold on, what did she just say? She rebuilt her personality?

"In other words, I *scrubbed* my character—polished it up. I'm not sure if I did a good job of it, but it seems to have gone well for the most part, judging by your reaction."

"…"

This was a bombshell…but she was right.

Now that she mentioned it, she was right.

As an artificial aberration, Yotsugi Ononoki didn't have a consistent character. She was always influenced by her surroundings, ever *shifting*—indeed like a mirror, always influenced by those

130

around her, always reflecting them.

It seemed more like a flaw than a characteristic, but to think it'd end up working this way...

While her ever-changing, kaleidoscopic personality had thrown me for multiple, painful loops, putting up with it had paid off. A smug expression and tone did hamper Ononoki's ability to do her job, so it made sense for her self-check to catch them.

It did...but having experienced for myself just how big of an ask it was for something to "make sense" in this world, I couldn't help but be impressed by Ononoki, who'd done it all on her own.

"Oh, it's hardly commendable. I couldn't have done it without your help. That's why I thanked you. Thank you, monsieur, for not taking off my pants."

"C'mon, it was nothing. I just didn't do what comes naturally to me."

Nope—just don't.

Let *that* come naturally.

But thinking too hard about it brought up a new set of questions—because if the Koyomi Araragi who existed in this world was Ogi Oshino, I couldn't see her ever doing such a thing.

I wouldn't, but she was even less likely to—Ogi stripping a doll naked and playing with it every morning betrayed who she was as a character more than anything I'd seen.

Too painful a sight.

All of this hinted at unexplained mysteries...but in any case, I felt encouraged that Ononoki had returned to being the character I knew.

"Of course, only someone like you who changes personalities like a dress-up doll changes clothes could do that."

She was the polar opposite of Tsukihi, who was herself because she only had one side to her. Ononoki's duality was so excessive that she could change even her inside-out self.

To use Oikura's mirror reflectivity analogy, her outlines were fuzzy from the beginning, so her image never got set in place.

"Like I said, it's not like I understand what's going on either—in fact, I'm really pushing it here. Changing who I am as a character to this degree is deviating pretty far from what's allowed of an aberration... I wouldn't be surprised if the Darkness showed up."

"!"

The word sent a shiver down my spine—a visceral reaction.

Oh. So that concept existed in this world too.

The very embodiment of darkness seemed even less tenable than vampires in a mirrored land consisting of reflections of light, but I guess it didn't matter because it was non-existent from the outset.

It traumatized me even more than that snake god, but Ononoki remained serene—because she'd remade her personality to be that way, but still...

"And so, monsieur, there's only so much I can do. It'll threaten my existence if I go too wild," she said. "I can't vanish before fulfilling my promise to you, that we'd go and see the ocean together one day."

"..."

I'd made that cool-sounding of a promise?

While also pulling down her pants every morning?

Whatever the case, I now understood why Ononoki had turned back into the character I knew. It was news to me that she was best able to perform, in peak condition, when she was stone-faced and flat-toned, but maybe it was called being unaffected.

Even in martial arts, they do say that the ultimate stance is having no stance at all—being a doll with no personality meant she could play any role she wanted.

I'd learned once again that in spite of her freewheeling ways, Ononoki was surprisingly professional at all times.

"So, what did you do after that?" I asked her. "Are you saying that you went off to investigate this strange state of affairs, just like I went to Kita-Shirahebi Shrine to ask for help?"

"You went to Kita-Shirahebi Shrine... Huh. Tell me about that later, will you?"

"Oh, so you don't know what I've been doing." The offhanded way she'd brought up Shinobu's name made it feel like she knew every last thing I'd done today.

"Hey, don't be holding such high hopes for me. My head's pretty messed up right now because I put too much into reforming my personality—I assumed you were off doing something, monstieur, but it was just about as likely that you were off buying a present for Sodachi."

"How likely is that? Zero percent?"

"Well, she kept asking you. 'Koyomiii, you have to buy me one, buy it for me! Please! I'm not letting you go until you say yes!'"

"I've really been spoiling her, huh..."

What had she begged me for?

And just what kind of person was I in this world, trying to take off Ononoki's pants and indulging Oikura when it wasn't even her birthday (I felt pretty certain it wasn't)?

"Ah. Sodachi's going to feel so let down."

"Stop, don't pressure me like that," I said. "Any idea of letting her down is painful to me. Don't pile more tasks on top of what I already have on my plate... So, after surveying the town...you decided to have me and Shinobu meet?"

"Right. Of course, the former Heartunderblade is different from the former Heartunderblade you know. I'm not giving you the details yet, I want to enjoy seeing your reaction when you meet in person... Just be ready for it."

"Yeah, okay... Wait, you just want to see my reaction? That's your reason?"

"Yup. What're you gonna do about it?"

"Why are you even doubling down?"

Hmph.

While we didn't have a particularly good relationship back in my original world—let's just call it a long and bumpy ride—going back and forth with Ononoki "like usual" did help soothe my nerves.

Only, I had to think about Shinobu being different, as Ononoki put it. Maybe I needed to be not just ready, but on alert—because I couldn't begin to imagine what the other side of Shinobu was like, who her inner self was.

If she existed in this world, we could solve everything just by getting her to open a gate from this side—my line of thought went, but it was an optimistic one that ignored such issues.

Though it wasn't in this mirrored land, I'd met another iteration of Shinobu in another timeline—I'd encountered the aberration known as Kissshot Acerolaorion Heartunderblade.

She resented and abhorred me.

Enough to destroy the world.

That probably wasn't the exact form of Shinobu's other side, but no one could deny the possibility existed in her.

She'd lived for around six hundred years. There had to be many "other sides" to her—and to be frank, I wasn't confident I could accept them all.

This was no time for pathetic whining, though... So long as that monkey demon protected the Kanbarus' wood bath, we needed to try a different approach, if any existed.

"I know nothing," Ononoki said, "about the circumstances on your side... Do I get along with Big Sis *over there*?"

"Hm? Er, well," I stammered. I didn't really know the answer to that one. When I'd asked Miss Kagenui about their relationship—for whatever reason, she'd deflected the question.

"Hm. Well, I'd imagine as much."

Ononoki shrugged, taking my silence for an answer—her face showed no expression, so I couldn't tell if she felt any way about that.

It wouldn't have been Ononoki any other way, of course.

I felt a little bad—when I thought about it, I'd taken this world's Ononoki, who'd been living a peaceful, expressive life as a doll, and turned her into a flat, emotionless, doll-like doll. Maybe I needed to reflect on what I'd done.

It may have been her professionalism, but she didn't need to act just because she noticed this land of mirrors wasn't logically consistent.

"So, monstieur. Where did you go today, and whose pants did you take off?"

"Can't I get at least a little sentimental over you? If you want to know, ask me like a normal person."

"What was it? You went to Kita-Shirahebi first thing to take off Miss Mayoi's pants?"

"Imagine the kind of divine punishment that'd get me. Instant karma."

Bantering like this, I gave Ononoki a rough outline of my day. I was afraid it'd take a while—we might arrive at our destination before I was done (she still wouldn't tell me where we were going. Did she want to see my reaction to that, too?), but my fears proved groundless.

Then again, only two things had happened: I'd failed to enter the Kanbaru estate, and Black Hanekawa had saved me. My surprise over the personality differences I witnessed today was a subjective matter.

"Hm. So you met Miss Mayoi, Big Sis Monkey, Big Sis Cat, Big Sis Snake, and Big Sis Sodachi today, and took off their pants."

"At this point, you obviously mean their underwear too?"

"Oops. I forgot to include the Fire Sisters."

"No need for that."

"Wow, monstieur, impressive. Your little sisters' pants don't even count."

"Am I not impressing you in any other way? If that's what you took from everything I just said, even I'm gonna be depressed."

"Well, to me it just sounds like the regulars I know in the regular way I know them—but I do agree with you about one thing."

"Huh, what's that?"

"Looks like we're on the same page for once…"

"We're not in some kind of buddy-cop movie. We've agreed plenty of times before. What is it?" I asked again.

"Black Hanekawa saving you—is almost impossible if we went by my understanding of her."

Oh… I'd wondered if an "inside-out" Black Hanekawa also felt differently about me, but if that was the professional opinion of this world's Ononoki…

Then was my initial guess correct? She'd saved me on someone's request? I'd suspected it was Ononoki, but that seemed unlikely after this exchange.

"Who could it be, though? Who'd ask Black Hanekawa to save me?"

"Indeed. Who would ever want to save you? Certainly not me."

"That's not what I meant—the kind of person who'd go to Black Hanekawa with that request. Certainly not you? How about you stop being so hurtful? You're helping me right now, aren't you?"

"I want you to think that, just so I can abandon you at the last possible moment and enjoy the look on your face."

"How unbelievably nasty are you? Start over and remake your character again."

In any case, I'd hoped to glean some kind of clue from Ononoki, but she didn't seem to have any idea either. The mystery persisted.

Not that it had deepened—I was now able to talk to Ononoki like this, and it was by pushing forward that we'd make progress.

"Does Shinobu know I'm coming? I won't pepper you with questions if you don't want me to, but I'm just curious. Did you, uh, make an appointment?"

"I did. Don't worry, I'm not sure how it is in your world, but that woman and I are friends in this one."

"That absolutely can't be true. Even the phrase *that woman and I* sounds hostile... Hm?"

And then.

After coming this far, I knew where we were headed. Normally I'd realize sooner, but between it being nighttime and the streets being flipped around, it took me a little longer. I'd visited the location countless times over the past year.

The ruins that the vagrant expert known as Mèmè Oshino once treated as his castle and keep—the building beyond us was that former cram school.

In the world I knew, it had caught fire last summer and burned to the ground, but it still had to be fine here if that's where Ononoki was taking me.

Maybe in this world, instead of dwelling in my shadow, Shinobu continued to live in that classroom ever since she was there together with Oshino?

In that case, she might not be too amicable towards me...or rather, *Koyomi Araragi*.

I didn't think my life was in danger, especially with Ononoki around, but maybe I needed to get my guard up a little higher.

"What's wrong, monstieur? You suddenly went quiet. Did you die?"

"No, why'd I die? I was just thinking. Maybe I shouldn't be, since everyone keeps telling me I'm overthinking things, but I just can't help it."

"Teal, don't mink, as they like to say."

"You mean feel, don't think."

"It's the same thing—reach for the skies and don't stay too grounded. Your thoughts need to be free. As an outsider, you might find the right balance that I can't as someone who's always lived in this world…or you might feel sorry that you got me involved in this and get on all fours to lick my boot."

"I do feel bad, but not that bad."

"Works for me. I don't want you licking my boot."

"Now it sounds like something else."

"Don't mind. I knew this day would come."

"…"

Huh? Another one of those cool lines you'd expect from an unlikely duo of crime-fighters? As in, it was clear we'd fight side by side eventually—but when I tried to ask her what she meant, it was a bit late for such questions.

We'd arrived at our destination.

My prediction turned out to be half right, half wrong—no, I'm grading myself too easily.

Objectively speaking, I was ninety percent wrong. I'd only gotten the location right.

Of course, it was sort of impressive that I'd gotten the location right at least: where the abandoned cram school Mèmè Oshino once treated as his castle and keep *used to stand*.

That much was right.

In my world, it'd caught fire and turned into a burnt-out field, leaving no traces behind. The same wasn't true in this world.

In fact—a completely *different building* stood there.

"Daze…"

I was so dazed that I actually said the word. I mean, I wouldn't be this surprised if I'd seen an office complex, a house, a store— simply another building.

Actually, it didn't matter where. I'd be just as surprised if *this* stood anywhere in town, former cram-school site or not.

"…"

There, on the real estate Mèmè Oshino once treated as his castle and keep, was an actual castle for goodness' sake.

018

I call it a castle, but it wasn't the domestic kind found in Nagoya or Kumamoto. Western style—a massive edifice atop plenty of square footage towering over all.

It shot into the sky.

Grand enough to qualify as a certified cultural asset, in my amateur opinion—soaring high in a Japanese suburb in the middle of nowhere, it seemed too surreal to be true.

Like a poorly faked photo.

It was hard to accept, easier to buy as some sort of 3D graphics—its style and its ancient, austere mood suggested that it hadn't been built on the site of that abandoned building but had stood there for many centuries—for six hundred years, so to speak.

"…"

This was a new one.

Over the course of the day I'd seen many humans, as well as aberrations, existing in a different way, but this was the first time any building or piece of scenery had transformed beyond being flipped around.

Did I need to gather something from this? It did tell me that my journey was entering the next stage.

"Shinobu…is here, right? She lives in this castle, doesn't she, Ononoki?"

"Yes, kind monster sir. She's here—she lives here. Heartunderblade, the former Kissshot Acerolaorion Heartunderblade. Now they call her Keepshot Castleorion Fortunderblade."

"Liar…what a blatant lie. You're not pulling that one on me."

"Well, you'd have found a castle this fantastic even if I didn't bring you here, but I thought I'd mediate between you two… Now, shall we?"

"G-Go in? This isn't the sort of place you just stroll into."

"A castle's not going to have an intercom, okay?"

True, it'd be such a letdown—the solemn structure felt like it might have sentries on guard, but they didn't seem to be around either.

It really was like a cultural asset in that sense, not a domicile. Then again, that seemed to suit a vampire.

I knew surprisingly little about vampires despite having turned into one and wasn't too familiar with their types of castles. Still, I'd believe it if you told me a legendary vampire lived here.

Its presence in our Podunk town felt as wrong as could be—but I followed after Ononoki.

The castle's halls and stairs were dark, and an eeriness overwhelmed any sense of majesty—did it not have electricity? To make it seem like the Middle Ages? This was more like actually from them…

"Speaking of which, Ononoki."

"What is it, kind monster sir?"

"About my adventures that I just told you about… I'd been convinced that Shinobu didn't exist in this world. Since vampires don't appear in mirrors, there wouldn't be any inside one, either. Miss Hachikuji thought so, too… Well, she didn't out and say it, but seemed to imply it. So why is Shinobu here? Why's she living in a castle she built?"

"There seems to be a bit of a misunderstanding…on your part, and on Miss Mayoi's. She only became a god recently and isn't perfect. Of course, as immature as she is, and despite how it may look, she's doing her absolute best."

"How condescending… How high of a pedestal are you putting yourself on to look down on her that hard?"

"Hey, that's part of what's inconsistent about this world. Kind monster sir, I call you kind monster sir, don't I?"

"Yep. That's been your name for me for some time."

"Do you know why I call you that?"

"Why? Well, yeah, I guess I do?"

"Oh. *Because I don't*," Ononoki said, making no sense at all.

"What's that supposed to—"

"A mirror world, or the flip side… It falls into place when you explain it that way. From my perspective, of course, your world seems narrow and constricted. The reverse reversed is the obverse—you might say, but really, it's still reversed," Ononoki intoned. Our dark surroundings didn't seem to affect an aberration like her, and she walked just as steadily as when we were outside. "Every coin has two sides…but you can also have a record with two A-sides. Don't you feel this world is a lot fairer and squarer than a world where you have to put on a happy face to hide what's underneath?"

"That's, er, um."

Don't be ridiculous. Like I'd ever feel that way.

Or so I began to say, but my judgment kicked in and I thought better of dissing the ways of this world too harshly. I was talking to one of its inhabitants—but this itself was an example of the "happy face" she mentioned, a surface at odds with my inner self.

A surface, and what lurks below.

Discussing them as opposites tends to give off the impression that the surface is good, while what lurks below is bad, but that's not always the case—smoothing over a mistake isn't fixing it, and we shouldn't judge a book by its cover.

But going on to argue that authenticity lies beneath the surface, or that surface appearances are always false, doesn't seem right either—take Miss Serpent's gruff, disheveled attitude. That might be Sengoku's inner self, the real her, but the Sengoku I knew, who always had her eyes to the ground, was the real her too.

Inside, outside, both sides are you.

The quickest way to lose sight of yourself is actually to start going on about *your true self*—there's nothing wrong with going on a journey of self-discovery, but how do you even take the first step if you lack a self to begin with?

I did wonder about Shinobu. I'd been focusing on her relationship with me, but I was curious about the "inner side" of her other facets...

"This way. The former Heartunderblade is waiting for you in her bedchamber—not that that's what you should call her. She might not be Keepshot Castleorion Fortunderblade, but I don't know about Shinobu Oshino either."

"What do you mean? There's nothing *former* about her?"

"You're a sharp one. What a shame—one less thing for me to enjoy seeing."

Stop trying to enjoy this. Keep your enjoyment quota at zero.

But hold on, it meant that right now—that in this world, Shinobu hadn't lost what made her special as a vampire and was at the height of her powers.

Not the former Kissshot Acerolaorion Heartunderblade, not Shinobu Oshino, but the genuine Kissshot Acerolaorion Heartunderblade?

I suspected she wouldn't be in her little-girl form, but still... it forced me think of the Shinobu who destroyed the world in a different timeline. I needed to be even more on my toes than I was already.

Or so I thought, but when Ononoki finally led me to the bedchamber—a word that doesn't do justice to how big it was—and I saw her there, waiting for me on her luxurious and magnificent bed, I realized that my resolve fell short.

This world wasn't going to abide by my expectations—that said, while I didn't expect this, it wasn't an unbelievable, unfathomable twist either.

Seeing it, I could believe it.

Technically, I saw nothing. The bed was enveloped by a thin curtain, and I only saw dimly through it, but the silhouette was all I needed to figure out the rest.

I figured it all out.

"Thank you for venturing all this way, Sir Araragi, and well met. It is a pleasure to meet you—I suppose I should say. I am Kissshot Acerolaorion Heartunderblade."

Her cordial greeting sounded like something from another time.

But this elegant lady was no vampire.

She was human.

019

Ah, well—in that case, sure.

In that case.

Vampires aren't reflected in mirrors and therefore can't enter them—that was my logic for why Shinobu wasn't in my shadow. I'd accepted that my partner didn't exist in this world, but there was a hole in that logic.

A hole, or rather, an opening. The fact that I, my vampiric nature deleted, existed here was already the answer. If the same phenomenon had visited Shinobu, she too could exist.

No, putting it that way was misleading. The Shinobu Oshino I knew, or the former Heartunderblade as Ononoki called her, had indeed been left behind in the other world—but that didn't mean she didn't exist in this one.

Just as there was no big Karen in this world, while a small Karen existed, *it had its own Shinobu Oshino.*

Now I understood Ononoki's puzzling line—about why she called me kind monster sir, monstieur, and so on.

The reason was clear in the other world. Though it wasn't exactly polite, calling a one-time vampire thrall a monster made sense.

Miss Hachikuji and Miss Serpent saw me in the same way, but if vampires couldn't exist in this world, a vampire thrall shouldn't either. There was an inconsistency—they knew I'd fallen victim to a vampire but also weren't aware of any vampires, a contradiction.

Vampires indeed didn't exist in this world, so there was no need to call me a monster, but no vampires didn't mean no Shinobu Oshino. I'd forgotten until just now, but according to what I'd heard over spring break a year ago, the iron-blooded, hot-blooded, yet cold-blooded vampire, the Aberration Slayer Kissshot Acerola-orion Heartunderblade, was once human.

Six hundred years ago, she was human.

Of the highest stock—yes, the kind of princess who might live in a castle, who'd see her castle as her extension. That—was her other side.

The flip side of Shinobu Oshino.

"Please, there's no cause to feel so tense. Lift your head, Sir Araragi."

Lift my head.

I finally noticed that I'd been having these thoughts on bent knee—I couldn't believe it. I'd genuflected reflexively, not to the vampiric but human aura of nobility emanating from beyond the curtain.

I was no master of etiquette, but the pressure had prevented me from even standing up... No, pressure was too coarse a word. Frighteningly, it was something kinder—she'd soothed me to my knee from across the curtain.

Was this charisma? Magnetism?

I could raise my head after hearing her words, but awe filled my chest.

Meanwhile, Ononoki stood straight as a ruler next to me, which didn't surprise me. Still, some sort of barrier seemed to prevent her from drawing any closer to the bed.

This was no aberration but a human. A human being.

This was Kissshot Acerolaorion Heartunderblade, the human being, on the other side of the curtain—forget her golden age as a vampire, in terms of sheer power she was possibly weaker now than in her little-girl form. And yet.

As a human, she was nobler, more unapproachable than I'd ever experienced her. You couldn't help but pay your respects, almost by fiat, as if a spell had been cast.

"Allow me to remain beyond these curtains like so. Forgive my rudeness, conversing thus without showing my face," she said. If anything, though, it must've been out of consideration for me—of course it was. If I was feeling this way with a curtain between us, speaking face to face was too much for me. Unable to endure my own worthlessness, we couldn't carry on any conversation—even on one knee, I was managing to be myself only because I knew Shinobu Oshino, knew Kissshot Acerolaorion Heartunderblade as a vampire.

Who knew what I might be doing in the moment otherwise? Obviously, as a human, she didn't live in my shadow, but I saw why she lived alone on the outskirts of town. Exuding this kind of nobility just anywhere simply wouldn't do. No wonder she resided in quiet seclusion in this world, even if this grand castle belied that expression.

This explained why Miss Hachikuji and Miss Serpent weren't familiar with her... Did Ononoki know simply because she was an expert? No, maybe her investigation turned it up—I'd ask her about that later. I bet she was already plenty satisfied seeing me kneel the moment we met; she'd probably let me know.

For now, I needed to talk to Shinobu. As intimidating as the prospect was—

"It seems as though you have come from another world. Sir Araragi, from another world... To wit, you are the same, yet different from the personage I've come to know. Is that correct?"

"Y-Yes."

It took everything I had just to nod. There wasn't even a mirror around, but my stomach was turning inside out.

She'd called this world's Koyomi Araragi a personage… Between this, trying to take off Ononoki's pants, and heeding Oikura's pleas, I couldn't get any read on what he was like.

That's who I was inside? Not Ogi?

"Fate has brought us together, and I interact with another world. I would love for us to speak at length over tea but fear that there is no time—Sir Araragi. Pray describe your predicament in a fashion that even I may understand. Though you see me as an untrusted stranger, met for but the first time, put your faith in me. I offer no guarantee but would yet be of use."

"O-Okay," I nodded without a second thought.

I'd obliged a dying vampire last spring break, but felt even more coerced now—no, that's not the right word.

I wanted to serve her of my own free will.

How unbelievably dangerous.

This actually seemed to surpass being flipped or turned inside out, she felt like an altogether different person… That little girl carried this inside of her?

Her self-image was way too exalted.

This was no time for jabs, though, and the woman before me wasn't to blame. I did as she requested and described the chain of events since the morning, in even more precise detail than I'd just done for Ononoki. I also took the opportunity to sketch out the other world—I fought off the urge to convey everything about it to her noble presence, and instead kept it to a sketch, but that wasn't thanks to any feat of self-restraint. I simply didn't dare tell her that in this other world, she was a little girl who seemed happy spending her life eating donuts and lazing around all day.

Her being a vampire in that other world, though. I couldn't hide that one.

But even as I talked, a cooler part of my head determined that this Shinobu Oshino—milady Kissshot Acerolaorion Heartunderblade could never aid my lowly self. Noble or grand, a human is still a human. She was hardly a "fellow" human, but human all the same.

Shinobu could open a gate to another dimension even as a little girl because she was a vampire—the person before me, a human, wouldn't have that skill.

When Ononoki offered to take me to Shinobu, I didn't assume it meant an immediate solution, and my prediction seemed to have hit the mark... I could converse like this and seek her advice, but how could she, nothing but a human, succeed where not one but two gods had failed?

Well... That was no reason to cast aside someone's good favor, and simply speaking to her might make me feel better.

Though I wondered—princess had slipped something in about there being no time. What could that mean? I'd prepared myself for a long and drawn-out struggle... Was it just that she had plans after this?

Wondering, and kneeling the whole time, I finished my story.

"Thank you kindly. You have come from a very interesting world," princess shared her thoughts. She really did seem pleased, and perhaps wasn't just being polite.

I felt like some kind of adventurer returning from a long journey to report his experiences to a noblewoman—maybe I'd be sent back with a few gold pieces as a reward.

Still. An interesting world, huh?

Miss Hachikuji and Miss Serpent had what you might call the composure that came with being a god and showed close to no interest in my world, but yes, it was "another world" for this one's inhabitants. Endlessly interesting to a human, especially if you lived all alone in a castle.

"Our world must seem counterfeit to one such as you—still, to hear that I am a vampire. Truly, how interesting it would be, to be a demon."

"..."

It felt rude not to respond, but what was I to say? I couldn't reply with a casual *Yup, it's nice being a vampire.*

"Yet, to me, that is the counterfeit—each of us must be a fake to the other," princess echoed Ononoki's sentiment on the way here. Or maybe this was deeper, weightier.

If you told me what's on the surface, not underneath, is the counterfeit, an illusion that doesn't really exist, I'd concede the point—while always being your natural self isn't necessarily good, we live our lives falsifying so much about ourselves.

"Like the moon reflected on water," princess remarked poetically.

Our Shinobu would never say such a thing. But a reflection on water was an apt comparison—it was what I was after when I tried to sneak into Kanbaru's place.

Of course, I couldn't say for sure that it was the ticket back to my world...but it was the only guide I had.

"Alas, with but a human body, unlike myself in your world, this feat of opening a portal to another world is not for me to perform," princess lamented with what sounded like genuine regret. Please, I was not worthy—making such a princess feel bad was making me regretful. Should I take responsibility and crush my own throat?

...What the hell? Why was I even thinking about crushing my own throat?

"But I do believe I can provide some insight, if you would kindly lend your ear to the nonsense of one as naïve to the world as myself."

"Y-Yes. I would be most grateful."

Most grateful—that was part of my vocabulary?

"Heartunderblade," Ononoki jumped in. "He's holding on better than I thought, but can you hurry it up? Monstieur is gonna be in pretty bad shape soon. Your influence is growing in proportion to his resistance."

What did that even mean? A terribly impudent tone to take with milady, but unusually for Ononoki, she was concerned about my health.

"Sure, Ononoki," princess replied, using a more casual register with the shikigami—and just her name.

The versions I knew got along horribly, ignoring each other when they crossed paths at home, but surprisingly, that wasn't the case here... So Ononoki wasn't lying earlier—in which case, maybe there was mutual recognition in their heart of hearts. While that seemed like a good thing, I wished I'd found out some other way...

"Sir Araragi. It would seem wise for you to return to your own world as soon as possible—I understand Miss Hachikuji suggested you take a relaxed attitude, but she spoke from the perspective of a god. It would not be in line with human nature," princess confirmed what I'd thought after her earlier aside that there was no time. What an honor that my thoughts were in line with milady's—or no, daring to read them was so lacking in decency that I deserved death, many times over.

...Yikes, what was with my mindset here? I wasn't part of her retinue or anything. I wasn't so servile even as Shinobu's vampire thrall.

"To wit, your existence in this world is exerting a massive influence. An influence...perhaps I ought to say, a negative influence. If you would excuse my rude choice of words, Sir Araragi, you are a calamity inflicted upon this weak world."

Negative influence? Calamity? Inflicted?

Unconsidered, abusive words, ill-befitting milady's pretty and polite language, but somehow, they didn't shock me—and just seemed strange.

I mean, I felt like the victim, wrapped up here in some kind of massive calamity—but I was suddenly reminded of Mèmè Oshino.

—*I can't stand you playing the victim.*

A line he uttered often.

That expert hated people going around blaming aberrations as soon as anything happened and shunting responsibility—it isn't what I meant to do, but had I started to think that way at some point this time?

Was milady nudging me towards such an understanding?

What a blessing!

"This world may be counterfeit in your eyes, a place filled with contradictions that does not follow reason, but it exists by way of its own balance. You are threatening that balance. In truth… Ononoki may look to you as though she has returned to normal, but to me, she has transformed into something unusual."

"!"

I reflexively looked over at Ononoki—who flashed a sideway peace sign.

Why?

But princess was right—even if the shikigami *knew this day would come.* And from the way milady was speaking, was I going to make not just Ononoki but others *transform?*

"I shan't go so far, but it will inevitably cause strain. Sir Araragi, you are and are not Sir Araragi—yet we accept and understand you as him. For you and he are the same. The pending strain could very well undo our world entire."

"…"

The world? The scale was starting to get pretty huge. Well, I guess we were talking about worlds from the start. I needed to be more aware of that.

I'd interacted with Karen, Tsukihi, and Oikura in a way that wouldn't give away that I was from another world, but I couldn't have lined up exactly with their image of Koyomi Araragi (I doubt

152

I'm one-faced like Tsukihi)—they had to be finding me odd, just as Ononoki thought something was off.

In fact, Oikura had said as much. It could be responsible for that line of hers, *This all seems like a lie.*

Yet the girls recognized me as Koyomi Araragi regardless—because I was none other than Koyomi Araragi. Just like the person in front of me was Shinobu Oshino, however far removed her appearance...

"You must return to your world before this world suffers from *cognitive dissonance*—we would not survive that unharmed, nor would you, of course. Surely, it would be an alarming state of events. In fact, I have already started to be affected—my understanding of who Koyomi Araragi is *already grows dim.*"

"I..."

I want to know what kind of person I was in this world, I asked milady a question for the first time—more because it seemed like bad news if I didn't than out of curiosity.

I felt so guilty I might off with my own head if I didn't stay strong—but why? Yes, I was causing harm to this world, but that harm could still be rectified. Why was I turning so soon to the idea of atoning with my life?

Did I think it was that much of a sin to destroy her image of Koyomi Araragi?

"That—is something I will not tell you," she answered.

"I-Is it because...you've forgotten so much already that you can't?"

"No, it is not yet to that stage—though I fear it may come to that at this rate. I will not tell you because the knowledge may, perchance, have a negative influence on you. Ononoki, be sure not to say anything uncalled for yourself."

"Of course. I haven't said a word," the shikigami blatantly lied.

She told me all that stuff about pantsing girls...or was she kidding? What a malicious joke. Of course, it'd be more malicious if it wasn't a lie.

"B-But...I too wish to return as soon as I may."

What was with my language? Had I come to beg for forgiveness for not making my yearly tribute?

"As I intimated, we lack a means," princess noted. "We might near our lone prospect, the bathing tub at the Kanbaru manse, yet fail to contact the other side."

True. We were clinging onto the legend about their cypress bath as our one hope when it was nothing more than a silly magic charm. It involved Toé Kanbaru, but the legend itself originated with the Kanbarus, not the Gaens. Seriously, should we be relying on it?

How dare I bother milady with such a tale, I promptly ought to end my life right—wait, why did I want to die so much?!

"No good. He's at his limit, Shinobu."

Ononoki grabbed me by the scruff of my neck from beside and forced me to stand.

Huh? What?

"Time's up. I'm bringing him back with me. Wrap whatever you need to say up."

What an unreasonable request to make of milady!

By my own death, this impudence ought—no, the sin was truly my lowly self's for standing without princess' permission, I would die, I would die, I needed to die—

"All right. Sorry for the trouble, Ononoki."

"I don't mind. Same old, same old."

Ononoki sounded kind of cool. Her role here seemed downright unfair.

"Sir Araragi. You are not mistaken in proceeding down your path. But that will not suffice. Do not endeavor to carry this out alone, rather seek support. Be another's light in this world, just as you became mine—"

"Unlimited Rulebook," Ononoki said.

Before jumping—teal, don't mink.

154

020

"It seems that Shinobu is different in your world, kind monster sir…but it's dangerous to talk for too long to the noble you just met. To put it simply, being exposed to her grandeur *makes you want to die*. She told you at the beginning that you don't have much time, right? That there was no time to sit around and chat."

She did.

I assumed she was urging me to return to my world soon, but that's what she meant when she cautioned me.

Putting that aside, Ononoki's Unlimited Rulebook was just as potent in this world—well, honestly, she seemed far more effective with it here.

Exiting Shinobu's castle by smashing through multiple roofs, she landed on a nearby road, all while holding onto the scruff of my neck. Despite the decisive launch and landing, my brain wasn't as badly shaken as you might think.

Accompanying her Unlimited Rulebook as a "regular human" had been awful in the past. I'd gotten altitude sickness, and blacked out, and more—but it seemed she could control its speed in this world. She hadn't used it for our trip here just to milk me for info as we traveled.

Don't get me wrong, maybe she could in the other world too, but I doubt she had that kind of precision—though the real issue here might have been personality.

The Ononoki in this world had modified it to attain peak performance, but that was ultimately a quick fix. She couldn't be a carbon copy... In fact, maybe this Ononoki couldn't wield her strength with the same kind of reckless abandon.

Everything has its advantages and disadvantages.

And that's what saved me here.

"Being exposed to her grandeur makes you want to die? Well, okay, I admit I knelt automatically, but if it's that bad then it's no laughing matter. Is that why she also stayed behind a curtain?"

"Yup. If your eyes beheld her full beauty, you'd claw out your entrails on the spot."

"Why choose that gruesome a suicide method? Let me die easy."

I feel bad saying this, but getting away from that bedchamber brought me a profound sense of relief, which was why I could riff off of Ononoki. Given what I'd heard, though, I shouldn't even be engaging in banter.

I was destroying the balance of the world. Ononoki would cease to be Ononoki, and a chain reaction would ripple out, flipping everything around like a Reversi piece placed in just the right square.

"For a better understanding of the details," advised Ononoki, "you might want to read the fairy tale called 'Beautiful Princess' in the anime adaptation's fan book."

"I might, but don't say that when I'm trying to be serious. I don't want to play the straight man with you anymore, so could you not bait me?"

"I told you, don't mind. When you act self-conscious, it makes things harder for me. Stop reacting like a boy who just realized that a girl he's known since elementary school has started wearing a bra."

"What kind of example is that?"

"I'm just doing my job. In my case, if I try hard enough, I can even fix my changed personality—since it lacked a set form in the first place, once I send you back to the other side, I can take my sweet time."

"Fine, then."

"Getting back on track. If you can't find the fan book, go to your nearest bookstore and have them order it for you."

"Enough with the promo, what kind of track are you getting us back on? I couldn't read it anyway because all the characters would be flipped around... So that's what Shinobu was like when she was a human. A real princess." Sure, she'd told me, but frankly I'd had my doubts.

"Not necessarily. According to your hypothesis, that's just her *inner self*, not a reflection of the truth. The moon reflected on water, as she put it."

"..."

"But yeah, in this world, she has too strong an effect on people, so she's chosen to live the solitary life of seclusion you just saw. Nobility so great it kills anyone who's granted an audience might spark a revolution—though she's human, she doesn't fit into that category."

So just as the noble vampire Kissshot Acerolaorion Heartunderblade exceeded vampiredom, as a human she exceeded humanity. I realized once again just how preposterous she was.

Someone I genuinely was no match for—I'd nearly killed myself in another world. Well, maybe my fate was to die for Shinobu no matter where I was.

Putting that aside.

I'd gotten out of a tight spot thanks to Ononoki (I might have made better use of our limited time together if she'd given me a proper explanation in advance, but what can we say, she wanted

157

to see me react to our meeting by kneeling—I needed to be glad it wasn't watching me kill myself), but the counsel bestowed upon me by milady (I was still feeling the effect) had been truncated as a result. Um, what had she told me again?

"My path isn't mistaken...so I'm not wrong to think that the Kanbarus' wood bath offers an opening?"

"That must be what she meant. But she also said to seek support, remember? You wouldn't be able to do anything on your own."

Hm, the opposite of what Oshino used to say.

To be sure, it did line up with Black Hanekawa's advice about finding a partner...but hearing it from Shinobu, my foremost partner, actually made it harder for me to take action.

"Like if the girl you're after told you, 'Hurry up and find a girlfriend, I'm sure there's someone you like'?"

"Um, why do you keep on going back to grade school romances for your examples?"

"Given the way Miss Mayoi and Shinobu are this time, we're kind of low on the child factor."

"Stop being weirdly considerate, and just carry that weight as you are."

If Black Hanekawa meant Shinobu, there was no way I could work alongside that noblewoman—those suicidal impulses posed a greater danger than your average aberration.

She'd called me a calamity and negative influence, but maybe it owed to the way she thought about herself. She did have the power to destroy the world all by herself.

She knew how fragile it all was.

"Still," I said, "it's not like we can go back to the castle and ask her what she meant."

"Right. You're already at your limit of suicide points. You shouldn't see her until things have settled down—not that you can wait until they have."

"Excuse me, suicide points? The everyday phrasing isn't making me feel any better... But yeah, this isn't a situation where I can wait for things to cool off."

Support, huh?

True, it'd be great if someone could distract Kanbaru as I tried to sneak into her home. If she—the Rainy Devil—got drawn away for even five minutes, I could use the time to check out that wood bath and see if it served as a route to the outside world.

This, it goes without saying, was a challenge.

Finding such a collaborator in this foreign land... Even if I succeeded, the Rainy Devil's brutality was nearly unmatched among the aberrations I knew. Forget five minutes, no ordinary human could keep that aberration engaged for one—I'd only escaped to safety thanks to Black Hanekawa's help.

I couldn't tell how much of milady's advice to take at face value...but were I to look for support, who would it even be?

Asking Miss Hachikuji and Miss Serpent was out of the question. I couldn't call upon gods to fight for me.

"What do you think, Ononoki? Any ideas as far as what kind of character could distract the Rainy Devil?"

"Well, hmm," she folded her arms. "Let's see. As destructive and capable in battle as the Rainy Devil, also knows the details about your situation, understands and supports your position, recognizes the danger at hand and hence is motivated to work toward a solution, naturally possesses at least some expert knowledge, must have a method of fleeing if it comes down to it... I don't know if anyone like that exists."

"It's you!"

It was Ononoki.

021

After that, I went home (just one leap with the Unlimited Rule-book, easy as pie) and snuck under the sheets of the bottom bunk so Oikura wouldn't notice, while Ononoki slipped back into my sisters' room.

I treated it like a joke without meaning to, but leaning on Ononoki to revisit Kanbaru's home probably wasn't what Black Hanekawa and Shinobu were recommending at all.

We'd formed a common front a number of times in the other world, and she'd saved me a few times too, but *partner* didn't describe Ononoki's relationship to me—she has a master she serves as a shikigami.

A more partnerly partner—a violent onmyoji fighting polar bears at my world's North Pole right about now. I had no idea what she was doing in this one (maybe she fought penguins at the South Pole, I hear they're pretty tough), but it didn't seem right to ignore her and make Ononoki my partner.

Ononoki and I were already allied to some degree during my audience with Shinobu—if milady was suggesting that I turn to the shikigami, why advise me to *seek support* in that scene?

Who the heck were they talking about? I pondered the question but got nowhere because this time, I managed to go to sleep. I had the faint hope that this was one of those stories where you woke up to learn it was all just a dream, but my expectations were for naught.

"Koyomiiii! It's morning, it's morning! Wake up, you big old sleepyhead!"

I had to wonder if it was a dream after all, a convenient and far-too-embarrassing delusion, when Oikura woke me up with a cheerful flying splash.

Ah, so Oikura, not Karen and Tsukihi, roused Araragi awake every morning in this world... My earnest wish had come true of having a childhood friend who would do just that.

Moreover, the custom persisted even after I graduated, a fact that didn't apply to my cruel little sisters.

"C'mon, get out, I need to change! Or do you want to see me changing? Oooh, such a dirty mind, but I wouldn't mind if it's you. Look!"

"S-Stop it, you idiot. You're gonna make me sick," I said, leaving the room in a flurry—*make me sick* might come off as overly harsh, even with family, but I seriously didn't need that from Oikura, who'd drawn the shortest straw of all in this otherwise lukewarm setup.

Really? This was another side of her?

But when I turned around for an instant to close the door, Oikura had her back to me and both hands on her head.

As if her actions were making her wonder: *Is this really who I am?*

A negative influence brought on by me, as Shinobu put it—as someone who lived under the same roof, in the same room, Oikura would have spent the greatest amount of time with me. Perhaps that influence was felt most strongly by her.

Yikes, I needed to hurry if that was the case. As cringeworthy as she was, I didn't want to ruin her bright, cheery life as part of a happy family. Ruining her life three times was enough already.

"Oh, Koyomi! Good morning!"

I crossed paths with Karen on the stairs.

Seeing my already-short sister down them made her look even littler.

She seemed to have gotten out of the bath but wore outdoor clothes—was she planning to go out so early?

"Yep. I'm gonna have fun with Sodachi today!"

"Oh… Well, show her a good time, will you?"

"Excuse me? And who exactly are you to her?" Karen gave a sarcastic chuckle, but seeing her now, I almost wanted to do the same—no, that'd be rude.

She'd always worn a tracksuit when not in her school uniform, but sure, she was free to wear a skirt—wait, was this yet another aspect of her inner self?

A rough girl like her wishing she could look cute was like something out of a manga… I swore to myself that once I made it back to my world safe and sound, I'd be a tad kinder to her.

"See ya," I said, then walked down the stairs and passed her. Well, even if her appearance and fashion choices had changed, her core personality had stayed more or less the same. In that sense, she seemed to be in better shape than Oikura.

It made me wonder just how much of her emotions my childhood friend had been suppressing, just how much of everything she was keeping bottled up inside.

Where was she now, and what was she up to? All of a sudden, I was worrying if she was okay—and realized that I seriously needed to ask myself why Oikura, who'd left for another town, and Hanekawa, who'd gone overseas, were still here.

My vague, initial thought was that if this world was flipped around, then the girls who'd left were flipped around into still being here. That interpretation fell short if we took Miss Serpent's inside-out theory, though.

What exactly did you need to turn inside out for Black Hanekawa and my housemate, Sodachi, to stay in town? Thinking, I entered the bathroom.

It was to wash my face, and of course to check the bathroom mirror, but there stood Tsukihi, naked.

Was someone always naked in our house? What kind of home did I live in?

Sadly, it was a question I needed to ask not just in this world but in my original one too... Tsukihi seemed about to take a morning bath after Karen.

"Oh my. Good day to you, my brother," she greeted, and for a moment I suspected she'd undergone a change as well. But this little sister of mine could never be so refined on the inside. I figured she was only messing around as usual.

"Don't you good-day me."

"What, need to brush your teeth?"

"No, I'm washing my face..."

I checked the mirror as I spoke. Standing at an angle meant seeing Tsukihi reflected in it in nothing but her panties, so it felt like a joke, but in any case, it was just a regular old mirror.

I remembered what Oikura said about reflectivity—and indeed I could tell the nude Tsukihi in the mirror and the actual nude Tsukihi weren't identical.

They say that the ink stands out more in manga e-books, clearer than in print, but was it that kind of a difference?

Reflectivity... I got oddly hung up on the word—but maybe I only felt partial and lingered on it because it came from Oikura's lips.

It was just simple trivia about mirrors, right? She said standard mirrors are about eighty percent reflective, but what about non-standard ones? Were there hundred-percent-reflective mirrors too?

Would this world be different if I'd passed through one of

those? Maybe I only thought this thanks to how inconsistent and sloppy around the edges, how eighty-percent-finished this world seemed…

"What's wrong, Koyomi? Aren't you gonna wash your face? I can't take my bath until you do."

"Why not? You can, either way. Actually, it'd be easier for me to wash my face if you went in."

"Fine, I get it. Say no more. You want your adorable little sister to wash your face, don't you? Okay, then get ready."

"For what? I'm washing my own face, obviously." I pushed her aside to stand in front of the sink—only for her to reach over my shoulders from behind me like in some skit.

"I'm not good enough for you, huh?" she said.

"Why are you turning this into a shojo manga? With me as the heroine, too."

"Bellyflop!"

Gluing herself to my back like a baby koala, she hooked both of my arms as if she'd be attempting a backbreaker next. She wasn't Karen, though, and didn't know the first thing about martial arts. All she did was work the faucet.

With such force that a good amount of water came rushing out… She sure lived in this world the way she turned the correct handle, unlike me.

"Now let's get you all nice and clean!" she said, scooping warm water into both hands and washing my face—doing a surprisingly proper job of it despite her comedic posture.

A very versatile young lady.

It felt strange to have hands, or rather fingers that weren't my own touching my face. She repeatedly squished and squashed the meat and flesh that clung to my skull—hmm.

"Your hair's really in the way. Why don't you cut it?" she asked.

"Like you're one to talk. I bet we look like a yokai from behind."

Or from any angle.

"Gah, big brother, get outta my way. I can't see the soap. Could you use your mouth to take it from the dish and drop it into my hands?"

"Why should I after being treated like an obstacle? And with my mouth?"

In spite of my retort, I, the ever-kind older brother, grabbed the soap with my mouth. Tsukihi made a lather with it in her hands, then returned it to my mouth.

Don't use my mouth as a soap dish.

When I spat it out, it fell into the sink, so the pooled water naturally turned soapy even as it swirled towards the drain.

"Close your eyes, okay? You could go blind."

"Maybe if you got bleach in them, but that kind of warning is unwarranted over face soap."

"No, it's because this is my first time washing someone's face. I might poke your eyeballs with my fingernails."

"It's a little late for that warning."

"Eat lather!" yelled Tsukihi, covering my face in soapy bubbles—as powerful as her scream was, her hands were gentler than before. She seemed pretty good at this for her first time, but apparently wasn't satisfied. "Hmm, I don't know... Maybe I'll go ahead and borrow Sodachi's foam cleanser."

"No, you shouldn't—glurp! Glorp!"

She really made me eat lather.

You mustn't try to talk when your little sister is washing your face, but it was my first time too, you see.

"Well, I guess I'll let you off with this for today. I wash your face of you!" she said, starting to wash the soap off my face. The water had been running this entire time, and when I opened my eyes a crack, the sink was full and on the verge of overflowing.

I'd have shut it off with my hand if I could, but Tsukihi had tied up my arms with her own—fine, I just had to use my mouth again.

As I did…

"Grrf?!"

The foam was mostly gone from my face, but I still made that noise—actually having eaten lather.

I opened my eyes.

Right below—was a pool of water.

Closing the faucet calmed its surface, but it was soapy thanks to the bar I'd dropped, and opaque—increasing its reflectivity.

In other words, I saw my own face reflected there, albeit imperfectly, as my little sister washed it. And that face looked at me.

With a smirk.

022

What's happening, what's going on here, why on water and not a mirror—I thought as I opened my eyes wide, only to have Tsukihi actually stick her fingernails in them.

No surprise there, but she really knew how to mess up a clutch moment.

"You can't put it on me, I did warn you. Why can't you ever do as you're told, big brother?"

Ditching the final steps of washing my face, Tsukihi scurried away into the bath.

I wished I could be like her. Seriously, I felt jealous.

When I looked back down into the sink, all the soapy water had been sucked down the drain. I felt like I'd lost my chance to seize a hint that had appeared out of the blue, but maybe, against my own will, my face had been beaming thanks to the heavenly experience that was having someone wash it. I shouldn't feel too dejected...

I wanted to curse Tsukihi for interfering, but I wouldn't have seen anything at all if she hadn't had the bright idea to wash my face—so par for the course. After waiting for her, Karen, and Oikura to leave, I brought Ononoki out from my sisters' room and headed to Kanbaru's.

We traveled by BMX, not the Unlimited Rulebook, because there were people around during the day to see us—yes, riding two to a bike was against the rules, but strictly speaking, Ononoki is a doll. Legally, if we interpreted it as riding around with a doll on my shoulders, it was just fine.

"I gotta say, it's still pretty abnormal to be riding around with a doll on your shoulders," the shikigami took her turn to quip at me—Ogi hadn't lent me her bike's foot-rest accessory, so there was nothing I could do. "Monstieur, you give all kinds of characters shoulder rides. Who's left?"

"You're making it sound like I've given them to a majority of the cast. Going down the list, it's only about four people long, counting you."

"Me, Shinobu, the bigger little sister, and who else?"

I exercised my right to silence.

Since Ononoki wore pants in this world, nothing too wonderful happened during the ride. Thanks to her experience supporting Miss Kagenui with one finger (?), she did have an excellent sense of balance, and operating the bicycle wasn't the slightest bit harder—in fact, I felt like I was the one being steered because she held onto my hair like a pair of handlebars (making me look like I had pigtails).

We'd discussed what we would do at Kanbaru's the previous night, and I didn't imagine there'd be any changes to our plan, but I still saw fit to report the little incident.

"Huh, is that so," Ononoki said. "Well, it's not your fault that the water went down the drain. It doesn't seem too relevant, so don't worry about it—wait a sec," she pulled off a double-take from her double-decker perch. "Isn't that really important? Could the gate to the other world be in our bathroom after all, and not in the monkey girl's home?"

"*Our* bathroom, my ass."

"I'll be sure to tell Big Sis Sodachi the same."

"No, she's suffered enough! Anyway, it was only for a moment, and maybe I was just seeing things—I couldn't make it happen again, either. I'm not even sure what caused it."

"Right. A mirror the first time, and a reflection in the sink the second time... The location was the same, but the meaning seems different. I guess the constant is that you were washing your face? The necessary condition for reflective surfaces opening to another world: washing your face."

"What kinda condition is that? If that's all, I washed my face in the bath too... Either way, my reflection laughing, or not moving the way I do, isn't that important—if going back home is my goal, I need to see Shinobu, or someone who can contact Shinobu, in the reflection."

"Hm, true. Which makes today's mission quite important."

"Yeah, if possible, I'd like to end this today—I didn't want this to take more than a day. Like I was saying, Oikura, for example, is starting to feel my negative influence."

"..."

Huh? Why stay silent there? Ononoki suddenly going quiet worried me—was she angry? I suppose missing my opportunity earlier in the bathroom deserved a scolding.

"Monsieur. Have you noticed there's a simple solution to this disturbance?"

"A simple solution."

"Yes. A super-simple super-solution."

"I'm fine with super-simple, but a super-solution sounds a little scary." The wording suggested something along the lines of *die and you'll never worry again*—but if she was saying a solution existed, I had to hear her out. Coolly, trying to come across as not one bit afraid or anything about this proposal of hers, I prodded, "What is it?"

"It's a sort of Copenhagen interpretation."

"Copenhagen interpretation? That's some complicated stuff... Quantum mechanics, was it?" Since we can't fully grasp the present, predicting the future with perfect accuracy is impossible—but how did my current situation relate to that line of thinking?

"Aren't you supposed to be the straight man? I obviously meant Copernican revolution."

"How should I know?! They're practically the same thing!"

"Uh, the Copenhagen interpretation and Copernican revolutions aren't that similar," Ononoki criticized me for her own misstatement—but that aside, she restated, "It's a sort of Copernican revolution. Simply give up on returning to your original world and resign yourself to settling down in this one."

"Oh! I guess I could! You're a sharp one, Ononoki, now there's no need to sneak into Kanbaru's bath. Why don't we head straight to the Häagen-Dazs shop, I'll treat you to whatever you—hold on," I attempted a clumsy double-take, as the other half of the double-decker arrangement.

Ononoki just said, "Häagen-Dazs stores don't exist in Japan anymore."

Right. Seriously, though? It wasn't just this world...but we digress.

"How is that a solution? Even if it's some super-solution, it doesn't solve anything. If I continue to exist in this world—"

"That's only because you're trying to go back to yours and refusing to grow accustomed to this one. You're like a transfer student who just won't stop bragging about his hometown and speaking in his local dialect, souring the mood for the whole class."

"What's with the mean example?"

"If I may, I'm the kind protagonist who reaches out to the kid who's sticking out like a sore thumb."

"Oh, so this was another one of your grade-school rom-com metaphors..."

"Surrender and open your heart to this world, be influenced

and pressured by it instead, and you might go back to normal—from our point of view. Actually, it might never be more than a compromise...but I don't think you'd overpower our influence when we hold the majority."

"..."

This seemed to be an honest proposal, not some kind of joke—and looking at it objectively, Ononoki could be right.

If I gave up.

If I abandoned my world and decided to live here—I guess, in the vein of Ononoki's analogy, it'd be like getting lost at sea, drifting off to a distant land, and hunkering down there?

"I don't think it's a bad suggestion, monsieur. Not just because it'd maintain this world's balance, but for you too. I mean, you might not have realized this yet, but you aren't in any danger as long as you don't try to go back, you know?" Thanks to her usual monotone, Ononoki didn't sound like she was trying particularly hard to convince me, but she certainly was nudging me in a certain direction. "So long as you don't try to get near Kanbaru's home, the monkey shouldn't decide to attack you on her part. All it takes is a resolution to start living the hanky-panky life with Big Sis Sodachi from tomorrow."

"Like that's my goal here. As if I'm going to stay just so I can be all lovey-dovey with Oikura... Phew."

Perhaps the proposal was worth considering? It might end up being my only option—but I still only considered it through an objective lens. It wasn't yet worth so much as a moment's thought.

I felt bad toward Ononoki, who'd gone out of her way to come up with it, but settling down in this world meant leaving far too much behind in mine. As long as there was hope, I'd pursue it, even if it put my life in danger.

"You know you're putting my life in danger too, right?"

"W-Well, I..."

"It's fine, I'm already dead. I just had to ask—just wanted to ask. And it's not as if this plan is airtight," Ononoki said. "Even if you settled right in to your current position, there's no guarantee the real Koyomi Araragi isn't coming back."

"The real? Well, the real one to you guys, but don't make me sound like a fake."

"A double of the same person, the doppelganger phenomenon, is probably enough to destabilize the world on its own... I wonder, where did Koyomi Araragi go? Maybe you two did switch places, and he went to that other world."

"..."

Then my fear that there were now two Ogi Oshinos in that world might not be idle—assuming the Koyomi Araragi in this world took her form. But it'd explain why Oikura and I lived in the same room. No matter how close, a high school-aged boy and girl sharing a room was irregular.

Couldn't that be why she was second only to Ononoki, a professional and expert, in sensing that something was wrong? Koyomi Araragi's gender was different from Koyomi Araragi's... For my part, our closeness seemed wrong when I already had a girlfriend.

"Hmm..."

I just hoped things in the other world weren't hopeless, like Ogi and Ogi trying to kill each other—she embodied my feelings of self-negation, after all.

I guess I also needed to figure out what kind of relationship I had with Hitagi Senjogahara in this world, but that concern could wait until our mission today ended in failure. For now, I would focus on evading the Rainy Devil—a fainthearted approach, as opposed to eliminating her, but putting aside the Monkey's Paw, it wasn't as if I could eliminate Kanbaru herself.

I told myself that my sights were set just right—and just as I did.

"We're here," Ononoki said, pointing ahead in the direction

of a wall smashed into dust.

The result of Kanbaru running along it a day ago—even if consistency didn't matter in this world, destroyed objects didn't seem to repair themselves, and the gate to the Kanbaru estate past it was a shambles as well.

"All right, monstieur, let's follow the plan. I'll do what I can to buy you time, so don't rush your investigation. Feel free to take a dip in the tub while you're there."

"As if I'm in such a state of mind."

"Maybe not, but you do have plenty of time. Forget five minutes, I could buy you five hours."

I'd feel woozy if I took a bath for that long.

I wondered how I might reply, but couldn't at all—having spotted beyond the pulverized wall, on the grounds of the Kanbaru estate, a raincoat kicking up a cloud of rubble as it dashed straight toward us.

So far away just a second ago, it was now *this* close—the day before, I'd found it strange that she'd run along the wall for no apparent reason, but I understood as she sped through the grand, or formerly grand, Japanese garden.

She ran *splitting the ground with each step*—wrecking a wall sure beat destroying our planet. It implied that she had some degree of judgment and reason, but I wasn't in a place to be giving it any more thought.

"Just go, kind monster sir. Unlimited Rulebook—"

Ononoki leapt off of my shoulders, and the finger she'd used to indicate the demolished wall grew massive and destructive. It now pointed at Suruga Kanbaru, who was coming at us head-on, ready to collide.

A finger of havoc pointed at legs of havoc—Ononoki had been riding on my shoulder in part so her hands would be free. And so, the battle between the monkey and the corpse began.

023

I stepped aside and snuck away once this battle to the death commenced, successfully completing the first stage of my mission to infiltrate Kanbaru's home. The Rainy Devil tried to chase after me, of course, but Ononoki did a beautiful job getting in her way.

I should be fine, given the state the two were in as I left—five hours had to be an exaggeration, but if Ononoki focused on defense, she'd never succumb to the Rainy Devil.

If anything, she might accidentally beat the Rainy Devil, in other words eliminate her without meaning to, but the shikigami seemed to understand the meaning of moderation in this world, perhaps in contrast to her counterpart in my world. Unless the situation took an extreme turn, I didn't think it'd happen.

Which is to say it could, if the situation took an extreme turn—I was in no position to order Ononoki to risk her own demise and avoid delivering a fatal blow to Rainy Devil. This was no time to be relaxing, I needed to hurry up and investigate that bath.

In spite of my resolve, I immediately got lost. Kanbaru's place is just too big—not to mention, I'd forgotten that left and right were switched around. What sounded like an extensive construction project on the lawn as my background music, I ran this way and that (that way and this?) until I discovered the bath at last.

"Phew…" I caught my breath for a moment.

Ten hours after I first got the idea of coming here on Kita-Shi-rahebi's grounds, I'd pulled it off… It felt like some kind of accomplishment, but I still hadn't done anything. Everything so far was like getting tips from all around on how to run a marathon, and only now was I hearing the starter gun's bang.

By the way, where were Kanbaru's grandparents, who lived here with her? We did come when they might be out—was that paying off? Not that it mattered who I met so long as it wasn't the Rainy Devil, but it was better if our paths didn't cross.

I traversed the dressing room, which was larger than my bedroom, and opened the sliding wood door to the space that contained the bath—fortunately, it was already filled. A stroke of luck, since it'd take more than just fifteen or thirty minutes to fill one of this scale from zero. Could the Rainy Devil have taken a morning bath like Karen and Tsukihi?

Staring at the bathwater of one of my juniors felt a little immoral…but I moved straight to studying the surface—at a slant, to see as much reflected light as possible.

"…"

I don't know, I felt incredibly stupid accomplishing my goal here… What the hell I was up to, going so far as to involve a corpse doll? Nor was anything showing up on the surface, which almost felt like a forgone conclusion. Sure, the water did reflect the ceiling, but that was all—what was I gonna say to Ononoki?

No, I hadn't expected this to work, and yes, I was grasping at straws, but faced with this outcome, I had to wonder why I'd bothered grasping at them at all. Did I think I was some sort of alchemist who turned straw into gold?

I splashed around with my hand to make a few waves but only created ripples. I was already searching for deft explanations

I might give to keep Ononoki from making fun of me, but as I played around...

"Ah!" I remembered—the precise wording of the story I'd heard from Kanbaru. Right, the image of your future spouse appeared on the surface as you bathed. It was only a slight difference, but maybe standing outside the bath and looking at it, while clothed, diverged from the legend—hmm.

If this was a case of in for a penny, in for a pound, I was already in for that pound, but did I need to put up my whole wallet, or even my bank account? I couldn't return empty-handed after coming this far... Well, I might have to, but that was no reason not to try everything.

Ononoki was battling the Rainy Devil, that brutal aberration, for my sake. Not only was there risk, she'd see very little return. This was for her, too—I had to strip nude! And take a nice little bath!

Fortunately, having tested it with my hand, the water was still warm. The culprit couldn't have gone far—sorry, no, there was no need to reheat the bath.

I went back to the dressing room, threw off my clothes, and returned. Being naked in someone else's home never felt quite right, but even if I needed to hurry, I couldn't forget my manners. You don't enter a bath without washing yourself down first—though if we're talking about manners, using another family's bath without permission was a massive breach of them.

When I listened closely, unmistakable destruction pierced the air every now and then—the battle seemed to rage on. I couldn't give up when Ononoki was still fighting, I thought, and fought my own battle, lathering my body and showering it down... Preparations complete.

I entered the cypress tub. To take a bath.

Ooh, feels nice.

No, I needed to hurry.

To cut to the chase, after stripping, dipping in, and examining the water from an angle, nothing in particular happened—and honestly, I wasn't expecting anything to.

Yeah. Things never go that well.

Why did I ever think this was a brilliant plan? How embarrassing... There was something wrong with me, that was the only explanation.

Fine, time for a new plan—maybe I should start by looking for the other Koyomi Araragi who lived in this world? Probably Ogi, but if it wasn't Ogi...and then.

This was the quickest of dips, let alone counting to a hundred, but I stood up. That was when.

Rattle.

The wooden door to the bath slid open—what, how? Was the Rainy Devil here after defeating Ononoki? Impossible.

I was pretty sure the shikigami wouldn't lose so easily, but more to the point, Suruga Kanbaru as the Rainy Devil didn't open doors like a reasonable person. As she'd proved with the gate out front, she saw them as something to destroy, not use.

And indeed, it wasn't Suruga Kanbaru, the Rainy Devil, standing on the other side of the door—but nor was it Ononoki after accidentally defeating her opponent.

Nor either of Kanbaru's grandparents who'd been home the entire time. As roundabout as my description is, I have no surprise punch line.

Because I didn't know this person.

Someone I was meeting for the first time—stood there completely naked.

Someone I'd never seen, nude like I'd never seen.

"Huh? Who the hell are you?" the stranger asked, making no effort whatsoever to cover up. Grasping in one hand a towel that stayed slung against her shoulder—unfazed.

The nude stranger was demanding to know who my nude self

was.

"Hah, if you want to know someone's name, you ought to introduce yourself first," I summoned up everything I had to put up this front—as fazed as could be, desperate to hide my body, goading my stark naked and desperate self.

In any case, I couldn't run away, couldn't exit the bath without shoving aside this stranger who stood in the doorway. Since I didn't dare to identify myself, my only real option was to turn the question around.

"I'm Toé Gaen."

But she answered it, just like that.

"And now, who the hell are you? Better answer me this time, or else you're not long for this world."

024

Toé Gaen.

A name that has come up many times—but not someone I ever imagined popping up, which is why I hadn't introduced her properly.

Suruga Kanbaru's mother.

Izuko Gaen's older sister.

The individual who left Kanbaru the Monkey's Paw, the only person in this world for whom Izuko Gaen, the woman who knows everything, feels any awe and fear.

And—she's deceased.

Deceased... Right, she ought to have died in a traffic accident along with her husband, Kanbaru's grandparents' eldest son... So why was she here?

Why was she here now, bathing with me?

"Ah, sorry about that, sorry about threatening you. I never thought you'd be Suruga's senior, is all. You should've just told me in that case," Ms. Toé said in a laidback tone, with a hearty laugh—was *laidback* even the right word? She still wasn't making any attempt to hide her body...

She knew her breasts were hanging out in the open, didn't she?

Unable to leave due to this turn of events, I sat back down in the bath—sinking down to my shoulders, hiding as much of my body as I could, in contrast to Ms. Toé.

Call it unmanly, but I can't say I'm positive about my body.

"Araragi, was it? So, how's Suruga at school? I bet that idiot's getting into nothing but a bunch of stupid trouble."

"U-Um…"

Forget school, she was fighting an idiotically savage battle out on the front lawn—did Ms. Toé not know?

Maybe I shouldn't be surprised that people in this world acted in inconsistent ways, but then I was a confused mess—not having prepared myself emotionally for a hot-tub experience with my junior's mom.

And wait, wasn't she way too young?

I couldn't be sure because she lacked the surprisingly important factor in determining someone's age, namely, clothes…but how old was she, again? Was I told at some point that she was several years older than Miss Gaen?

Hard to say when she was fully au naturel, both in attire and makeup, but Miss Gaen had such a babyface she didn't look above thirty, and maybe the same went for her older sister? Either way, I suck at guessing women's ages even when they aren't naked. Or perhaps—

Perhaps I was seeing her as she was when she passed away in the accident. Like with Hachikuji in my world… Possible if this lady was a ghost.

Damn, I couldn't think straight.

My thoughts were all jumbled up—you couldn't blame me, with a naked lady right in front of me, but I needed to get ahold of myself.

"…"

I decided to approach the situation like a test and begin with the questions I did know the answers to. With the easiest bits—

first off, was this person really Toé Gaen, Kanbaru's mother?

Given the illogic and inconsistency of this world, trusting her self-reported info seemed to be my only choice, really.

But well, if you asked…I guess she looked similar?

To Miss Gaen, and to Kanbaru.

Personality-wise, she was definitively bolder, or less sensitive, but her build was similar: short and slim. She looked closer to Miss Gaen, if I had to pick one—didn't that make genetic sense for sisters? At the same time, Kanbaru had inherited her intense, driven eyes, her eyebrows, and more…

"Wow. You've got some nerve, ogling me like that. Just how thirsty are you?"

"Huh? N-No, I wasn't. Your face…" She'd misinterpreted my gaze (really, it was a misinterpretation), but her understandable reaction made me stammer. "I was looking at your face. I-I was just thinking how much you and Kanbaru look alike."

"Oh, she looks like me? Keheheh. I see, so her breasts have gotten this big."

"Er, no, like I said, your face…"

Come on, I've never seen Kanbaru's boobs. Just barely, but I haven't.

Hm? Hold on, something was off about this last exchange— she didn't know about Kanbaru's breasts getting bigger?

"…"

"Mm. Ha. Does it really matter if I didn't know?" Ms. Toé seemed to intuit my doubts. I suppose she and her little sister, Miss Gaen, had different values.

Well, maybe *values* overstated her lackadaisical attitude, but the big sis of a little sis who knew everything laughing that what you knew didn't really matter was…unfortunate.

Actually, I was remembering some stuff now, and this lady seemed pretty different from the image Miss Gaen had given me of her older sister…an extremely self-critical, austere person if I recalled correctly. I didn't see a hint of that.

She was an approachable mom—well, okay, even an approachable mom didn't normally bathe with her daughter's senior from school. Of course, I couldn't fault her or say there was anything wrong with her since I was a trespasser who could easily be handed over to the cops otherwise.

Family members don't always see one another as others do—and come to think of it, Miss Gaen's characterization of me was off the mark too. She thought I was stoic and no different from her big sister.

Maybe knowing everything didn't necessarily make you a good judge of character.

"Oh, no, I only calmed down after I got married—after I found myself a man, in other words," Ms. Toé answered before I could speak, seeming to anticipate my queries again.

No, hold on. Wasn't she a little too good at it? I wasn't planning on asking her anything that personal... If she'd seen it in my expression, then my face was far too eloquent.

"While I say I calmed down, I never got as lukewarm as this setup, so give a girl a pass—things happen once you become an adult, okay? Being told that I haven't changed one bit since the old days might make me happy, but it isn't true."

"Okay... Hm?"

A lukewarm setup—a silly line I'd used with Miss Hachikuji. Why would Ms. Toé know it? Hello...

It felt like she was seeing straight into my mind.

Yes, we were quite literally baring all, but did it really include my thoughts and feelings? I mean, I couldn't begin to read her intentions, for my part.

What was she, the mind-reading yokai *satori*?

"Wh-What—do you know?"

"Like. I. Said. Knowing, not knowing, none of it matters. What's important is understanding. You can know something, but it'll only go to waste if you can't use that knowledge, and half-assed knowledge can keep you from understanding by way of intuition." Ms. Toé smirked, running her fingers through her wet hair. "I'm telling you, even if you don't know something, you begin to get it just from seeing it."

"…"

The brilliant type.

I'd thought she might be like Oshino, or maybe her sister Miss Gaen, but these remarks made her seem completely different… In other words, did she not know anything when she stepped into the bath but manage to put together a rough guess as to my predicament? Just from my demeanor, speech, and behavior, even though I hadn't told her anything in particular?

Hard to say.

Maybe I was overestimating her. Maybe she'd only meant to describe our bathing together as a lukewarm setup. As far as hot-spring travelogues went, this was pretty tepid, after all…

"Of course, back in my day, suspense dramas always had a steamy little bath scene right in the middle. Keheheh. Are there restrictions on that kind of thing nowadays? You don't see too many tops on television lately."

"Tops? Er, no, um…"

Our conversation risked getting dangerously off-track, so I did my best to correct its course—or rather, the question here was how to get myself out of this.

I needed to escape this suspense drama.

No, hold on a second.

As Miss Gaen's sister, and having bequeathed the Monkey's Paw to Kanbaru, she was, if not an expert on aberrations, at least a pro…or I guess a wild card.

I didn't know if it applied in this one, but in my original world, I often came across her influence—the responsibility for Ogi's birth lay squarely on my shoulders, but it was also a fact that this lady was involved.

In which case… I had no idea why she was here now, but Kanbaru's mom or not, she was on bad terms with the Kanbarus and shouldn't be allowed on these premises—didn't I need to welcome this encounter? My idea of trying to communicate via the water's surface had been a bust, but if that failure meant getting to meet Ms. Toé, it turned my moonshot into an *all's well that ends well* scenario…

"Hm? You're staring at me again," she reacted sharply to my gaze for the second time—my assessing gaze. Ms. Toé then put both her hands behind her head, as if in resignation, and said, "Okay, I get it. We'll do it later, so just come to my room. You'd better keep this a secret from Suruga, though."

"No, that's not it!"

There was nothing okay about it!

Seeing it didn't always mean getting it, even for her—well, I suppose she was just kidding, but it was in pretty bad taste.

What kind of person was she?

Even if the lady didn't necessarily equal my mental image of Toé Gaen, this did seem to banish the notion that the land of mirrors was all my delusion or a dream. If you told me that somewhere inside of me, I wanted to see an energetic Sengoku or a playful Oikura, I couldn't argue with you, but even I didn't yearn to take a bath with the mom of one of my juniors.

What kind of unconscious was that?

"Ha… Seems like this has been an interesting development, I'm glad for you. A lot happens once you become an adult, but also when you're a kid, I guess? Hang in there, young man."

"And what am I to do with such easy advice?"

"Oh, you wanted advice? Well, I suppose you might—but you see, Araragi. I'm not anyone's idea of a life coach."

"…"

"I mean that in all sorts of ways. Considering your situation and given what you've done for Suruga, I want to help you, but I don't know about butting into this story when no one's asked me to."

She was being awfully mystifying for someone so laidback. How was I to interpret that? What I'd done for Kanbaru…in this world, or in the other world? I had no idea, and couldn't even tell if I should. As much as I wanted to bombard her with questions, I needed to be careful, as a potential negative influence on this world.

In her case, though, she proactively—or rather, spontaneously figured out the situation just by looking at me. If I didn't want to influence this world, my best course of action was to hurry up and get out of the bath and retreat to Ononoki's position.

Yet escaping from this place meant running away naked. Without so much as a towel, I'd be baring my ass to Ms. Toé.

How embarrassing!

Putting aside my own shame, turning and showing my butt to the mom of a junior I felt indebted to was beyond rude.

I hoped that she might get out first, but Ms. Toé, her scrub towel folded atop her head, looked poised for a long soak. If only I could act so unconcerned.

"…"

"About what I was saying about knowing and not knowing—things aren't that simple here, Araragi."

"E-Excuse me?"

I'd gone silent, only for her to start speaking. I wasn't asking her any questions, but the result was the same if she was going to talk to me—and still short of a course of action, I was barely able to react. My hesitation must've been one of those things that didn't matter to Ms. Toé, who continued, "Knowing and not knowing aren't dualistic. My little sister has pursued knowing by removing any traces of not knowing, and your friend Miss Hanekawa has kept both knowing and not knowing as close parts of herself, but both of them are overlooking a crucial fact. Which is that a lot of knowledge is wrongly known—you think you know but have gotten it wrong. That's why understanding is so important in matters."

"...You know Hanekawa?"

Did she mean this world's Black Hanekawa, or the Tsubasa Hanekawa I knew who'd left the country? Also, she didn't mention Ogi, who professed not to know anything, but was that because Ms. Toé didn't know her or—dammit, the more I tried to think, the more I was spinning my wheels.

I was getting too heated and about to blow my top, and not because I was sitting in a bath.

"Can't say I know her. I understand her a little, that's all—how about you, Araragi? How well do you understand your friend? Maybe you don't get a thing about the thinking of your friend who decided to go overseas."

"..."

That word *overseas* meant she was talking about the Hanekawa I knew. Okay, so now this lady who shouldn't have known anything about me when she'd entered the bath grasped my situation perfectly. At what point had she started asking leading questions and gauging my reactions? She was on an altogether different level.

It was counterproductive to act awkward and reserved around her, and I found myself in a state of resignation, which is to say, I decided to stop trying to hide things—my inner thoughts, I mean, not the details of my anatomy. Nor would she be particularly surprised whatever I confessed now.

I shared why I now sat in this bath, what had compelled me to do so. I hadn't forgotten about the influence I might have—it had forced Ononoki to "change"—but felt like it didn't really apply to her.

This was only instinct, but she didn't seem the type to be

influenced by me. She wouldn't come under anyone's influence, was above influence. She just digested it all.

"Hmm...so you came here believing in this magic charm? What a pure-hearted maiden you are," Ms. Toé said with a be-mused nod after hearing me out. "Reminds me of a student of mine. Liked magic charms, or maybe I should say curses... But you might as well give up on that approach. This bath—"

Splash, she slapped the water's surface.

"—is nothing but a bath. If anyone ever saw something on its surface, it's on the person who saw it."

"Is that so."

Yeah. I mean, I knew that. Still, I'd been hopeful because I'd heard the story as an episode involving Toé Gaen. Having it de-nied in person made it sound all the more ridiculous.

"Oh, no, don't be embarrassed. I feel kind of bad that I was the reason you got your hopes up," she consoled me, but when I thought about how excited I'd gotten, how Ononoki was locked in battle, my shame wasn't so easily wiped away.

Also, I was naked. How could I not be embarrassed?

"It sounds like my little sister and Oshino have gone around saying all kinds of things about me, but this is what happens when you meet a legend for yourself. It's like reading about a great his-torical figure only to find a slew of scandals or learning about someone else who was a lot greater. Sorry for being such a plain old lady," Ms. Toé said all too candidly—but the very fact that she could hinted that she wasn't just anybody.

I had to wonder. She'd declared her lack of interest in butting into this story, so I wasn't coming clean to get her advice—but having told her everything, I felt like that process had been nec-essary here. Until now, I'd been explaining stuff so others would understand, but this time it seemed to be for my own sake: a way of straightening out my own thoughts.

"Well, there's not much I have to say," Ms. Toé cushioned our conversation. "After having you tell me all that, I'd be terribly cold to do nothing in return, though. All right, Araragi, let me wash your back."

She stood.

With a sploosh.

Even as I was feeling embarrassed every which way, Ms. Toé continued to show no modesty whatsoever—and walked right over to the shower area.

"C'mon, hurry up. It's not every day that you get to have your back washed by a Gaen."

It's not every day that you get to have your back washed by anyone, a Gaen or not. Still, and even though Ms. Toé was losing no time working up a lather with her towel, I answered, "N-No, I'm fine. I've already washed myself down."

"Hey, it's fine," she said, not taking no for an answer. "You can't do a proper job of washing your own back. Not that you can count on me to do any better. I've never even washed my husband's back."

"Ma'am, maybe don't share anything that heavy when we're meeting for the first time?"

"But we're not meeting for the first time," she casually informed me. "My left hand—has met you, hasn't it?"

"…"

"You haven't heard about that yet, have you, Araragi—aren't you curious? About why I gave that wish-granting Monkey's Paw to my daughter…to Suruga."

025

Right.

Mirrors reversed right and left, flipped front and back, turned everything inside out—it was probably the same no matter how you described it, but from my point of view, it was all very *through a glass, darkly.*

I thought this facing the mirror right in front of where I sat outside the tub as Ms. Toé washed my back—yeah, I had that realization because staring into the mirror was all I could do. A practical stranger was washing my back, even if I'd heard her name before, and I was nervous.

You see, I could place my palm against the mirror to high-five my reflected self, but upon closer inspection, there was a looking glass-deep gap between our hands.

We could never come into contact. The reflected me, on the mirror's surface or not, existed on the other side of that glass—you might even say the mirror image was reflected on its reverse face.

Was the true essence of a mirror just its silver coating and the rest nothing more than a transparent sheet of glass? Was I looking at a mirror, a piece of glass, or myself? What is it that we see when we face a mirror?

Reflected light? Really?

Pondering these ideas wasn't going to let me escape my predicament, but at least it helped me escape reality, which is to say ignore it, for the time being.

"You've got a nice, muscular back. That's a young man for you."

"Um, I have no idea what kind of back I have... Plus, the one simple trick behind my physique is that I was a vampire..."

"A vampire? Oh, okay, you did tell me about that just now. What a convenient fitness regimen. You wouldn't believe how much work I put in to maintain this figure," Ms. Toé said, scrubbing my back with her towel—it felt more like she was shaving my back than washing it.

Was she really using a towel? Wasn't it a rough sponge?

What a world I'd gotten myself into—my little sister washing my face in the morning, my junior's mom washing my back in the afternoon... Who was going to wash what part of me tonight? My instincts told me to be on the lookout for Oikura...

I needed to solve this before night fell.

To protect Sodachi Oikura!

From myself...

"Washing your back almost makes me feel like you're my grandpa, but I guess the paw you wanted to talk about was a monkey's."

"U-Uh huh."

Of course. That's why I was submitting myself to this bizarre exercise—but in that case, there was another thing I wanted to ask: yes, I was letting her wash my back so I could hear more about the Monkey's Paw, a vital item to us, but why was she so eager to wash it that it was what she got out of the bargain? If I were to believe her, it wasn't because she enjoyed washing young men's backs... I admit I've had my fun playing with the young, little, and tween girls that were Hachikuji, Shinobu, and Onono-

194

ki, but it was dawning on me that I too, legally speaking, would be classified as a minor.

"Right, I don't want to sound out of line," I said, "but from my perspective...speaking only based on my own values and about the world I came from, I'm not sure leaving Kanbaru the Monkey's Paw was the best thing for her."

In fact, that wasn't limited to my world. Whatever happened—or didn't happen—beforehand, the ill effects of the Monkey's Paw had to be responsible for Kanbaru becoming the Rainy Devil here as well...

"Oh, it's not like I had any clear intention in mind when I gifted it to her. I wasn't trying to help her, nor was I trying to spite her—I think? The other me, too."

"..."

A subtle reply. It was unclear whether the Ms. Toé with me now was alive or dead—but one thing was certain.

The mirror embedded in the Kanbarus' bath wall, the mirror that had occasioned me to ponder its *thickness*, reflected me and only me.

Ms. Toé—wasn't behind me.

It didn't reflect her nude body. How to interpret the unexpected but clear fact facing me now.

Once, when I took a bath with my little sister, I was the one who didn't appear in the mirror as we washed each other's hair. That's how I learned that my transformation into a vampire was progressing past a certain threshold... If Ms. Toé had no reflection either, did it mean she was a vampire?

No, I could rule that out. Vampires didn't exist in this world—"here" was inside a mirror, and I needed to flip around my interpretation.

This was probably how her absence in what I saw as my original world, what this side saw as the other world, manifested itself—so then, was Toé Gaen dead in the other world but alive in this one?

Maybe she was a ghost who only existed in a mirror. I could imagine that sort of scary story, and if anything, the idea helped calm me down. It was a lot less stressful than my junior's mom being here in the flesh, alive, and washing my back.

"The Monkey's Paw, or rather its source the Rainy Devil, is actually my avatar, as you already know—it was my flip side, a flip side attacking myself. That's the kind of family we Gaens have been for generations...experts at *creating monsters.*"

"Creating—monsters."

"You know that my sorry excuse for a sister worked with some of her friends to create a corpse aberration, right? It was a variation on this theme—she'd deny it, but in the end, she's the true inheritor of the gifts of our lineage. Even if the path she chose, for whatever reason, is to rid the world of monsters."

On your side too, Ms. Toé added.

Too—so Miss Gaen was an expert yokai exterminator, the big boss of them all, on this side as well?

That was sort of comforting...being one of the few things this world and the other had in common—though it was hardly a feel-good moment when you analyzed Miss Gaen's reasons for choosing such a path.

"It's a question of how you face your other side," Ms. Toé went on. "It might be your flip side, but you shouldn't stand back to back with it—that's what I think. How you see your own back."

She began scrubbing my back even harder, with her bare hands. I didn't know when, but at some point, she'd stopped using her towel.

A far cry from Tsukihi's gentle touch, this was more like being scratched—hard. At this rate, I was going to end up as a scratchboard.

"Your own back? Unless you've got a real long neck, you'll need a mirror," I said.

"Right. Mirrors make you face yourself from various angles—that's its function as a device, after all, and the Rainy Devil was my mirror."

"But didn't you get rid of it by giving it that name? You didn't just face it, you defeated it..."

"While the Kanbarus took Suruga in, there's no question that she has Gaen blood in her. She'll end up facing herself just like my sister and I—maybe I did hope the paw would help. That left hand is just one part of the Rainy Devil, and it'll simply vanish if there's no use for it."

"Now that you mention it, I forget when, but Oshino—Mèmè Oshino was wondering where the rest of the Rainy Devil was. Um, at least in my world, Kanbaru only inherited that left hand..."

"I scattered them all around. They're safe as long as they're not together, but it might be dangerous if someone collects them. It's my avatar, you see."

"What a casually scary remark."

"Oh, no. I say that, but they're mummified. It's the corpse of an aberration, really—neither poison nor medicine, just a corpse. Don't be too worried, but if you happen across them, could you dispose of them for me? The sins of the mother are visited upon the daughter, but they also say that kids grow with or without parents... Tell Suruga for me when the time seems right, will you? Tell her there's no need to cherish it for life, that I really only wanted to tell her one thing—don't turn out like me."

"I could never. Not that. As a mother's words to her daughter?"

"Listen to yourself, an eighteen-year-old boy preaching about motherhood? What exactly do you think you know about being a mother?" Ms. Toé teased me, and I had no reply—I'd never been a mother, I'd never be a mother, I even had a strained relationship with my mother.

"..."

"Keheheh, sorry. You're right, it's a heavy message to ask some-one else to deliver. I take it back…but if Suruga ends up facing herself and seems stuck, do lend her a hand, will you?"

At this point, Ms. Toé was speaking purely about the other side—what a mysterious person. I was beginning to see why even someone like Miss Gaen chose her words carefully when (and only when) it came to her big sister.

Reaching past my head to grab the showerhead, Ms. Toé be-gan rinsing my back—torture time must've come to an end.

My back had been going numb, but now it burned—the hot water stung. Was I bleeding?

"If you can't be medicine, be poison. Otherwise you're noth-ing but water," Ms. Toé said over the noise the water was making. "That's what I told her, raising her—I wonder how much of my point got through? Maybe I just thought I was speaking to her, but was actually trying to get through to myself. She saw me as her parent, and my sister saw me as her big sister, but looking back—I was just a crybaby and a devil."

A weakling, she said. She sounded her usual self, so maybe it was just my impression, but was she whining?

"The best I could manage was to defeat that devil, while you, Araragi—protected your double. In which case, stick to your path. Darkness or light, that's your partner for sure."

"Partner?"

I looked behind me at that word.

Partner.

Find one, Black Hanekawa had told me—maybe it was sheer coincidence, but if Ms. Toé was using that word now, I had to ask what she meant.

I had to but didn't get the chance.

Because when I looked, I found no one there. Just as the mir-ror had shown, I was alone in this room with a cypress bath.

Since when? Or was it from the beginning?

Toé Gaen was gone, leaving behind just her towel—the showerhead lying on the floor.

"…"

I quietly placed it back on its hook, shut off the running water, and picked up the towel.

Well, at least the towel proved that our conversation wasn't just a fantasy I concocted once it became clear that Koyomi Araragi wasn't going to establish comms via any cypress bath—an excuse to give to Ononoki, but hey, while we're at it, I guess my smarting back was also proof?

It tingled and throbbed to the point that I honestly wondered if I was bleeding… Not to underscore my dialogue with Ms. Toé and needing a mirror to face my back, but I stood up to do just that. Then—

I gasped.

In the reflection I'd twisted my neck to see, my back wasn't bleeding, but there were welts all across it as if I'd been sentenced to a lashing—and they formed words.

In proper, mirrored characters.

There in the looking glass, they were easy to make out.

"NAOETSUHIGH"

It seemed I had my next destination.

026

"You think it's funny, shit-for-brains? I ought to kill you."

When I recounted the whole business to Ononoki, she abused me with some filthy language—she'd never gone on such a tirade against me, in this world or the other.

She did maintain her expressionless face and affectless tone, but had she been this world's original Ononoki, I imagine her look would have been anything but dashing.

"Who actually agrees to take a bath in that situation? With a married woman, at that. Who's yet to follow her husband in death."

"Um, I don't know about that last part…"

If she was a ghost, she already was dead along with her husband. Ononoki also needed to be careful about her sexist assumptions—though among men, the same concept was called a pledge of eternal friendship, say, or the Oath of the Peach Garden.

We'd left the Kanbaru estate by now and moved to Shirohebi Park—not that we needed to be there, but I'd evaded the Rainy Devil the day before by coming here, so we rehashed the same pattern.

After getting out of the bath, I'd exited out to the yard, gotten on my bike, and jumped into Kanbaru and Ononoki's battle, and the shikigami had taken that as her cue.

"Unlimited Rulebook—"

We'd shot into the sky.

As far as I could tell, the Rainy Devil hadn't taken any significant damage, with just a few scraps missing from her raincoat.

Ononoki had managed to accomplish her mission, fighting to buy me time but holding back and not injuring her opponent—what a professional.

I wanted her to know that I, an amateur, had also done good work, so once we arrived at the park's plaza, I related the ghost story I'd experienced in the wood bath—only to trigger the above verbal abuse.

"Sheesh... I feel like a kitty who caught a mouse and brought it to his master to be praised but who got yelled at instead."

"What you did wasn't so good."

"The simile is, though." I thought comparing myself to a feline when I didn't care for cats expressed the depth of my shock.

"Also, casting me as your master? It violates good-faith principles. You'd be Big Sis' sub-shikigami."

"A sub-shikigami? Is that a real concept? Wouldn't want to be under Miss Kagenui's umbrella..."

I looked around the park as I said this—fortunately, there were no witnesses, or rather no one had overheard my exchange with Ononoki.

Anyway, I'd ended up taking a rather long bath, and it was already past noon. My plan was to visit Kita-Shirahebi Shrine again at night, and we still had the time for one other action.

"So, Ononoki. I was thinking of going to NAOETSUHIGH... er, Naoetsu High, but what do you say?"

"Hmm... Well, I guess that's our only option if we don't have any other leads. Meanwhile, if you want to know how I feel, I'm not terribly excited about following Miss Gaen's sister's advice."

Feel, excited—words that didn't quite suit Ononoki.

"Advice, it probably isn't," I said. "She told me she wouldn't give me any—I think it's a suggestion, or maybe a screening process…something like a hint that we're free to discard."

That just might be where she drew the line, I thought—just as Oshino had one when it came to saving others, she might be limiting her assistance on account of her cheat-grade skills, intentionally or not.

That was my impression.

"You keep on talking about these stigmata, monstieur, but you still haven't shown them to me."

"What? You wanna look? You're telling me to strip here? I'm feeling a little shy…"

"You're acting legitimately self-conscious when your story's so phony that I can't believe it without some kind of proof. Aren't you just making stuff up to cover for the fact that you found nothing?"

"D-Don't be ridiculous. I'd never cover up a blunder."

I'd tried to come up with something, yes, but my dithering had led to getting my back washed by a married woman.

"Okay, turn around," Ononoki said like a doctor—how funny, a doll was playing doctor with a guy.

I pulled up my shirt.

"Are you kidding me?"

"Huh? What? Why that tone? And why those words?"

"There's not a thing there. Just a well-toned back."

"I'm not sure how to respond to that compliment…but seriously?"

"Seriously."

"No…"

I twisted my neck but naturally couldn't see my own back. Still, how could Ononoki not see those impressive welts?

Yet now that she said so, the pain had vanished at some

point… In the bath mirror, those nail marks had made me wonder if they'd ever disappear, but I suppose Ms. Toé had shown me some consideration. In that case, however, they'd gone away a little too soon…

"N-No, they were there until just now. NAOETSUHIGH, it said right on my back, in mirrored characters."

"Wow. Desperate, aren't you? A boy who gets trapped in his own lies about having a cute pen pal level of desperate."

"No elementary school rom-com metaphors please, this isn't a joke. I'm serious, Ononoki, look at my eyes! Are these the eyes of a liar?!"

"It's the first time anyone tried that line on me. This isn't a manga, looking at your eyes won't tell me anything. That's just called a staring contest. Want me to make a funny face while we're at it?"

"Look at my pupils!"

"Are they dilated or something? A whole other kind of suspicious. Anyway, I'm not an ophthalmologist. But I wish the lady had gone for a nice, full sentence."

"You're traumatizing me!"

Like I'd let her scar me in essay form!

Capital letters were bad enough!

"…Um, Ononoki, are you saying you believe it now? My tale of adventure that unfolded as you were busy fighting the Rainy Devil?"

"Not sure if you should be calling it that, but…if you're going to lie, try and tell a more believable lie."

"Wait, are you criticizing me now?"

"Sorry. I meant to say that if you were lying, you'd try and tell a more believable lie… I'm afraid I blurted out my creed."

"Your rephrasing was empty cant, then."

"Whatever the case, it's not like we have any other course of action. Right now I'm hung up on the fact that it was Miss Gaen's big sister who gave you that advice…or hint, as you put it."

Just like in my world, the name Toé Gaen carried *that kind* of connotation. Having met her, I could see why… Even apart from that, I didn't particularly want to visit Naoetsu High.

I preferred not to, in fact. A place I thought I was done with— what sort of face was I going to wear walking into my alma mater when I'd gotten down on all fours and apologized in the teachers' room on graduation day?

But at this hour, maybe school was out…and there weren't too many people. Sure, a good opportunity to sneak in, but alumnus or not, I was an outsider now, and they might get really mad at me (I'd be lucky if it ended there).

"Let's see… I'm one thing, but you'd stand out, Ononoki…"

"True, my cuteness attracts a lot of attention, wherever I go."

"…"

No, I was saying that a tween girl couldn't avoid standing out at a high school… If she was joking, it wasn't really her brand of humor—there was somewhat of a deviation between this Ononoki and the one I knew after all.

Berating me earlier felt like another variant of that, but just as I was thinking about what to do—

"That's it. Why don't we split up?" she proposed. "If there's no risk of the Rainy Devil coming into the picture, which is to say, of a battle erupting, I don't need to be with you. I'll try a different route while you head to Naoetsu High."

"A different route? Like?"

"Well, I only thought of it just now… Searching for a good excuse not to go there, because I really don't want to do as Miss Gaen's sister says, I had an idea."

"Are you being cautious, or do you just hate her? How unwilling can you be to visit Naoetsu High?"

"Let me try checking with Black Hanekawa—checking with her, or maybe finding her… Why she decided to save you is still a big question for me. I'm going to clear that up."

"Any idea where she might be?"

"No, but it'd be negligence if I used that as an excuse and didn't even try. Nothing wrong with looking for a lost cat now and then. I feel like a P.I."

"Well..."

It did seem like a good enough reason to reject Ms. Toé's hint—while I didn't know what I might find at Naoetsu High, contacting Black Hanekawa would undoubtedly represent significant progress.

Even if Ononoki located her, it'd be no walk in the park getting anything out of Black Hanekawa. Still, I wanted to know who had asked her to save me.

"Also," said Ononoki, "I probably won't get anywhere with it, but I'd like to see Shinobu again first."

"What? That's kind of worrisome... Will you be okay?"

"Heh. Never thought you'd worry yourself over the likes of me."

"There you go again, like we're in some buddy-cop movie... It's either that or a grade school romance, huh? Your repertoire's way too narrow."

"Don't worry, you saw for yourself how Shinobu's aura doesn't really work on me. I'm not saying it doesn't affect me at all, but it's still better than you going. I might get to hear the final bit of a conversation that got cut short... Of course, that selfish princess is more stubborn than you'd expect, and she might not talk unless it's directly to you, which is why I woke you up in the middle of the night, but I'll figure something out. I'll try reverse-prostrating myself and asking her."

"Okay. Thanks for begging on my behalf—hold on, reverse-prostrating?"

"The esoteric technique known as a back bridge. Primarily, bending your body backwards."

"Who do you think you are to assume such a cocky pose before milady... But how well do you think that'll all go? You said you have no idea where Black Hanekawa is, and you might not get anywhere with Shinobu, but if it's more promising than going to Naoetsu High, I could also—"

"Keep in mind that I only came up with these ideas because I don't want to go to Naoetsu High... If you came with me, I'd have to accompany you to Naoetsu High as a show of thanks."

She was telling me this to my face—did she hate Ms. Toé that much?

"Hence a plan you'd specifically have trouble coming along on. Your lack of mobility would only get in the way of chasing after Black Hanekawa, and you'd shrivel up and wither if you visited Shinobu—so. Give up yet?"

"I give up."

Well argued on her part.

It was educational, the way she weaved logical reasons for not doing something she didn't want to do. I hadn't been making excuses, but in contrast, how nonsensical my account of seeing nothing on the bathwater surface, meeting Kanbaru's mom instead, taking a soak with her, and receiving a message on my back must have sounded to Ononoki.

"In that case," she said, "let's meet back here in about three hours and then head to Kita-Shirahebi Shrine. We'll squeeze the most out of our time if we join up at the last second and jump over with my Unlimited Rulebook, instead of meeting up there. You go gather firewood at Naoetsu High, and I'll wash our laundry with Black Hanekawa and Shinobu."

"Did you just try to broaden your analogy repertoire and fail miserably? Your folktale reference even managed to muddy your point... Well, I don't think I'll be in any danger, but you be careful. Shinobu's one thing, but Black Hanekawa seems plenty dangerous in this world, too. I mean, she can drain your energy."

"Her energy drain doesn't mean much to me. I'm a corpse, okay?"

"Oh yeah? I didn't know."

"If we're talking about danger, I think you'll be in more of it, monsieur. You may not get in any battles, but doing exactly as Miss Gaen's sister says? It's bound to be costly—I think something is going to happen."

"…"

To be honest, I wasn't sensing any danger. What about Ms. Toé was making Ononoki this wary?

Of course, depending on how you looked at it, her intense caution was an expression of high esteem—if there wouldn't be any battles, it seemed worth going there just on my own.

"Should I drop by my house first and change into my school uniform, in that case?" I asked Ononoki. "Would it be better if I pretended to be a high schooler?"

I hadn't thought I'd ever wear my uniform again, but it looked like I had to one last time… Oikura should be out with my little sisters, so there was no risk of running into her even if I went back to my room.

"I think so. I'll escort you. I feel bad about abandoning you, it's the least I can do."

"Maybe don't abandon me and don't feel bad in the first place?"

That said, her relationship with Miss Gaen was probably at play here. To begin with, Ononoki didn't need to be helping me at all.

"Fine, please just take me home then. But you be careful too and don't try anything reckless," I warned her, knowing just how terrifying Black Hanekawa could be, and concluded our briefing…giving the matter no further thought.

But I ought to have given far more weight to Ononoki's misgivings—I'd yet to see just how terrifying Toé Gaen could be.

208

At her guidance, I was heading to Naoetsu High—and while I'd lived to tell numerous tales of aberrations, just barely making it through, I'd be coming face to face with a hair-raising, supreme terror like none other.

027

Or so I say, but it wasn't the destination Ms. Toé gave me, Naoetsu High, where I faced this terror.

It happened at an earlier stage.

After Ononoki transported me back to the Araragi residence
so I could drop in, I bumped into this dreadful situation in my, or
rather, Koyomi and Sodachi's room.

It felt like trying to pick the right gear and stocking back
up on recovery items before a big boss fight but instead getting
attacked by the arms shop owner and getting a game over. Now,
let me tell you this in advance: If you're one of those Oikura fans
who loves to see terrible things happen to her, sorry but she wasn't
there.

Fortunately, she was out shopping with Karen and Tsukihi—
the Araragi residence was empty, and it was going well at first.

Smooth sailing.

The problem occurred when I opened my room closet to
change into the outfit that my stealth mission at Naoetsu High
demanded—my second in a row after infiltrating the Kanbaru
estate. In other words, when I tried to get my school uniform.

It wasn't there.

Hm, had it already been thrown out? That seemed impossible...

Maybe it was in Oikura's closet? We were family living in the same room, but I couldn't open it without even asking...so I checked every piece of clothing hanging in my own, one at a time, until at last—I found it.

No, not my school uniform.

Well—when I use that term, I picture the outfit I wore for three years, that tight-collared jacket and trousers, and maybe I just wasn't accustomed to describing it as such, but it was one in its own way. At least, it was a uniform you wore to school, and calling it a school uniform was totally proper.

A sailor-style blouse. A skirt.

What a girl calls a school uniform—the hard problem that arose here wasn't one of nomenclature.

"Oh. Oh. Oh."

I see.

You see?

If this world was inside out rather than flipped around sideways—if Koyomi Araragi lived here as Ogi Oshino, just as Tsubasa Hanekawa had become Black Hanekawa, this made sense. My school uniform would be a girl's rather than a boy's.

I've heard about new major leaguers finding cosplay outfits in their lockers as a form of hazing, and I guess this was the land of mirrors doing the same to me, an outsider. I hadn't noticed because I'd been wearing jeans, a t-shirt, and a hoodie, which is to say my usual outfit, but now it seemed certain that in this world Koyomi Araragi was Ogi Oshino.

Perhaps sharing a room with Oikura, and Ms. Toé not hesitating to bathe with me, were manifestations of the same inconsistency, or maybe incoherency... Okay, in Ms. Toé's case, I guess it was just a matter of personality, but Oikura's overfriendly openness made a little more sense if she'd been interacting with another girl.

She did chase me out of the room to get changed, but also jokingly invited me to take a bath with her on the first day.

"Nkk..."

I gritted my teeth.

Did I have no choice? The one thing I'd managed to avoid the entire series...the red line that I drew. There might've been little girls and mature ladies and the brushing of teeth, all sorts of stuff, but had I gotten carried away? I wasn't the type, it just wasn't me, and I'd thought I was all talk. That I was different from those other protagonists, the nonsense-users, the sister-obsessed middle schoolers, the swordless swordsmen, and the legendary heroes...

But I, too, was on team comic relief.

Okay, then, best not to brood over this.

Let's hurry up and get this on. Let's hurry up and get this going. We're already eating pretty far into our page count. At times like these, the greatest form of resistance is not resisting at all.

I began putting on the Naoetsu High girl's uniform—I really didn't get how consistency worked in this instance because Ogi and I should've worn completely different sizes, even if I'm on the small side. Yet the uniform fit so well it seemed tailor-made for me.

Maybe it had been.

Having come into contact with girls' clothes more than once during my adventures, fortuitously, I wasn't clueless about how you put them on. Since dressing someone else was indeed flipped left-right compared to wearing them yourself, after some effort it came together.

I was lucky that Ogi preferred to wear stockings—I lacked the fashion sense to care too much, but going out with bare legs was one of my few hang-ups. Nothing more undignified in a man.

All right, changed and ready to go. My plan had been to hop into my uniform and turn right back, but I'd ended up spending more time than I expected—I skipped down the steps two at a time and exited our house.

I hadn't looked in the mirror. Why would I?

Thanks to having let my hair grow out, I'd seem way too earnest about this.

Once outside, I realized just how anxious girls' clothes made me feel—and not just because this was my first time. I was left speechless by how defenseless a skirt left you.

A mere breeze could deal some damage to me. I had to respect girls if they went through high school in this kind of armor—and felt like apologizing to Hanekawa in particular.

But this was no time to be understanding Scottish culture. I straddled the BMX (and learned just how risky even getting on a bike seat was. I'd have never known otherwise—Ms. Toé was right about how knowing or not knowing wasn't what mattered, the point was to understand), then started pedaling toward Naoetsu High.

I thought I wouldn't ever, not anymore—would be an overstatement, but I didn't think I'd be rushing my way to school like this anytime soon, certainly not after just one day. In a girl's uniform was even more unexpected, but actually, this was no longer even my way to school.

That thought did make me a little melancholic. Whether I wore a boy's uniform or a girl's, whether I biked or walked—in any case, I was no longer a high school student.

I had no title. You might say I was therefore in another world, wherever I was, but getting lost in thought like this while I was biking wasn't safe, so I focused on focusing.

Once I did, it felt a little strange—yes, strange. Not a little, quite strange.

It was odd. I'd accepted my uniform being a girl's without much unease because if Koyomi Araragi existed in this world, he'd be Ogi. According to that logic, though, all of my clothes should've been feminine. Jeans, t-shirts, hoodies, pajamas, and the like are unisex—that had been my earlier rationalization, but I'd been overlooking the issue of underwear.

If all of my clothes really had changed, I should've noticed last night when I got out of the bath. As I put on Ogi's panties, or when I wore a bra—how do you explain that?

Of course, you couldn't expect too much logic out of this world. Why try to make honest sense out of it when I couldn't be taking Ogi's place to begin with? Still, this was intriguing.

Because—it was the other way around. Backwards.

The true nature of my odd feeling became clear when I considered the examples of Ononoki, Oikura, and Shinobu.

Ononoki thought something was off when I appeared before her from another world, and she modified herself to cope with it—yeah, the tween was just preposterous, but in any case, by doing so, she grew closer to the Ononoki I knew.

Oikura didn't know I was a visitor from another world and treated me the same. The issues it caused seemed to torment her, and she could be inching toward the truth given her smarts.

Shinobu, too, said her memories of this world's Koyomi Araragi were growing dim—her common sense was being replaced by mine.

That was the negative influence I had here, my effect on this world as an alien element—but wasn't it strange, then, that a closet full of my clothes yesterday contained Ogi's today?

Wasn't the vector pointing the other way around? The direction of the change made sense if I'd worn Ogi's underwear yesterday and my school jacket today, but when a jacket turned into a skirt—

"…"

It was too strange to overlook. Or so it seemed, but I also felt like contradictions on that level didn't matter anymore.

Didn't one way or the other.

I admit, a guy taking a bath with his junior's mom and then fussing over these details has hardly any authority—I'd been failing to behave in a reasonable manner for some time now.

Yes, that.

In other words—at the same time as I was influencing this world, was it influencing me? Was I *becoming* Ogi?

Beyond just my clothes, was I, myself, turning into a... mean-spirited, or let's say awful to deal with girl like her? It seemed ridiculous, but also completely possible—even the far more legitimate outcome.

Heat moves from hot to cold. Even if I had a strong influence on this world, just how much could a single drop of hot water affect an entire pool?

It'd get leveled out in no time. I'd turn into just another scoop of cold water.

Nothing but water.

I needed to do as Shinobu said and return to my world as soon as possible, literally asap.

Otherwise—I'd be lost.

I'd vanish.

Losing the part of me that should stay me no matter what.

I would go away.

Just as I lost my title when I graduated.

Koyomi Araragi would be erased.

And that—was the supreme, hair-raising terror.

028

Around this time, Yotsugi Ononoki, who was now acting independently, had gone to Shinobu Oshino—or Keepshot Castleorion Fortunderblade, that's to say Kissshot Acerolaorion Heartunderblade in her peak form, but in her peak form as a human—and finished her audience and exited the palace. An impressive show of initiative when my own drama had been to wear or not to wear, her actions conformed to our expectations of an expert.

More than enough talent to make up for a nasty personality—and yet, she would regret to report that she'd gained nothing from the audience.

According to her subsequent explanation: "Well, she might make herself out to be important, but she's no monster. The only unique thing about her is her charisma—it's not as if she's omniscient or omnipotent."

Being a corpse made it harder for Kissshot Acerolaorion Heartunderblade's grandeur to affect her, but it still did to some extent. Perhaps having no choice but to keep their conversation brief, she'd left empty-handed—unfortunate, but then her solo quest's main purpose was not having to heed Miss Gaen's sister's instructions, so perhaps it was all the same to Ononoki.

As much as that pissed me off, nothing would be more futile than to comment on it. She hadn't exactly strayed from her path and slacked off, and had done her job properly. Far be it from me to complain—in fact, it wasn't her job in the first place.

All right, Yotsugi Ononoki said, wiping her memory of her fruitless audience and moving on to her next item—in other words, finding Black Hanekawa.

Who knew *something*. Maybe just what she knew—but she did know.

In which case, we needed to ask her. Lacking a single clue as to her location, the only option was to comb through our town—well, no, I wouldn't say we didn't have any idea.

Like we said, Miss Serpent—this world's Nadeko Sengoku spoke as though she knew Black Hanekawa, and that might be considered a clue. Miss Serpent wasn't interested in discussing the matter, and since I couldn't bring myself to be assertive with Nadeko Sengoku, I'd had trouble digging into the topic. Yotsugi Ononoki, on the other hand, had no such qualms.

She could dive head-first if she wanted.

While we weren't sure that Miss Serpent would answer—not to mention the obscurity of her own whereabouts—we couldn't be any more certain about the location of her "friend"…or should we say successor.

A place Ononoki knew quite well herself, one she'd visited a number of times—Kita-Shirahebi Shrine. No need even to set any coordinates.

Unlimited Rulebook, was all it took. Uttering the words with no emotion, no expression—she flew.

Soaring at top speed now that she had no cargo, namely me getting in the way and weighing her down, she arrived at Kita-Shirahebi a dozen or so seconds later. Her body, her dead body, absorbed the impact so as not to destroy her destination—an impressive, environmentally-friendly landing that surprised no one, coming from her. But then…

Hm?

Yotsugi Ononoki's expressionless face wavered.

She didn't smile, nor did she put on a dashing look, but the expressionless one she'd settled on, so seemingly fixed, now cracked the tiniest bit.

Her current personality may have been a rush job, but what really surprised her was feeling perturbed at all while in full work mode. Well, chalk that up to this being another world and remaking herself to belong to *the other side*—she looked at what lay before her again.

In her defense, the sight would've surprised anyone, not just Ononoki.

The great god Mayoi Hachikuji and Miss Serpent—just the fact that those two people, or gods, were there was providential, as it meant skipping the preliminary step of talking to Miss Hachikuji to find Miss Serpent. Wary as Ononoki might be of such a convenient development, she'd take it.

But there, drinking hard with the duo, was a third individual—or rather, a little girl.

Who wouldn't be stunned to see an elementary schooler with braided hair and glasses—scratch that, an elementary schooler joining in on a drunken revel?

Unbelievable, I thought the little-girl factor rested entirely on me this time, Ononoki muttered in a solemn (rather than flat) tone, appraising the little girl—whose cheeks were flushed but not out of bashfulness.

"Hnm? Mrowww?" the little girl slurred with a sloppy smile on her face. "Tsubasa Hanyekawa here. Myahaha."

"…"

This actually allowed Ononoki to regain her composure.

It goes without saying that she didn't know Hanekawa at six years old. In fact, the shikigami barely knew Tsubasa Hanekawa, and even her familiarity with Black Hanekawa was limited to what I'd told her.

But if anything, this scene was easier to accept if the drunken little girl claimed to be Tsubasa Hanekawa—it was at least less scandalous than a regular little girl getting drunk.

"Miss Hachikuji. What's going on here?" the shikigami asked the lone individual present old enough to legally consume alcohol, who seemed to have a nice buzz going on too.

"Hm? Oh," she replied, sounding surprisingly sober. She was sitting there cross-legged on the ground, but perhaps gods were best when they weren't too uptight. "What's going on here is that Tsubasa Hanekawa's got more than one other side to her, though you still have her beat. Her early childhood is certainly one of her inner selves, while on the outside—well, since we haven't seen that little tiger of ours yet, maybe it all got settled."

"…"

Ononoki tilted her head in confusion at what purported to be an explanation. An outsider to the incidents involving Hanekawa, it didn't mean a thing to her.

She didn't know what was being said.

But ignoring what she didn't understand was Ononoki's specialty—her special move, even. She didn't expect any correct information from a drunk, anyway, and decided to just go over the important points one more time.

"So Black Hanekawa—is another pattern of Tsubasa Hanekawa, yes? Of course, thanks to kind monster sir breaking me in, I can't grasp this world properly anymore…"

Breaking in sounded a little too violent, but this was a real issue for her—she could no longer accept what was "obvious" in this world as such.

She'd modified her own personality into one that stressed logic and reason.

"Yep, you got it—hsshh hsshh!"

This of course was Miss Serpent, wasted too, nodding in reply. Ononoki enjoyed no real familiarity with Nadeko Sengoku either, but their ties were far from shallow. At least, in the world I knew—but those memories both existed and didn't. How did that work in this case?

"Because Tsubasa Hanekawa's an honest-to-god case of multiple personalities, unlike me. Hsshh hsshh hsshh."

"I see…"

Though Ononoki nodded, she calmly determined that this trip was fruitless in its own way—Miss Serpent aside, leaping straight to discovering Hanekawa, the very person she was looking for, went beyond convenient and into too-good-to-be-true territory. Finding them all drunk here almost made it feel like her trail had been cut short.

She might have managed to extract info from the six-year-old Hanekawa, something like a double of Black Hanekawa, a double herself, if she weren't inebriated—or maybe not. Talking to a six-year-old girl, whether or not she was drunk, wasn't much better, she thought.

Ononoki was being a little naive, or as someone who didn't know Hanekawa, committing an unavoidable error. (Six or not, drunk or not, Hanekawa was still Hanekawa. Asking her a question would still get you a response). Unwilling to return empty-handed, however, she chose to join the three-person ring and sat herself down. Not to take part in the booze-soaked revelry, of course—alcohol was nothing more than a preservative to a corpse like her.

A third party objectively examining this scene and hypothesizing the appropriate course of action would, we imagine, have her conclude her solo quest and meet with me at Naoetsu High, where I now headed—but Ononoki, who'd rather be drawn and quartered, pretended not to notice this option.

Or really didn't notice. She just didn't want to that much.

221

"Well, aren't you all carefree, drinking like this when kind monster sir is in so much trouble," Ononoki scolded the three females, two of whom were gods. Humans have a tendency to attack others when they feel guilty, and the same seemed to go for corpses.

Perhaps, in terms of social standing, this didn't count as being disrespectful because as a shikigami, she was technically a god too.

"Oh, that stuff will be fine," Miss Hachikuji answered—now that she was drunk, her already reversed voice sounded even more falsetto, but her words had a strange sense of certainty at their core. "I just heard from little Tsubasa here… That's why we're drinking to celebrate."

"Celebration. Myahaha," the girl laughed, though Ononoki didn't know what was so funny.

"Hsshh hsshh hsshh hsshh," Miss Serpent joined in.

Ononoki, unable to blend into the already established mood, felt left out and uncomfortable (she actually did), but it wasn't enough for her to take a cue and leave.

Doing so meant going to Naoetsu High, which was out of the question.

"There've been various misconceptions, on my part, on everyone else's—Koyomi Araragi included, of course," Miss Hachikuji continued. "Maybe on your part too. No, that's not it—you could say this entire world is the product of a massive misconception."

"I'm not sure I get you…" Though wary about heeding the opinion of a drunk, Ononoki translated the remark and interpreted it as best she could. "Should I look at it like this? Judging by your calm…or loose demeanor, this situation, this case, has been settled."

"To be precise, it's heading toward a solution, mrow," responded the six-year-old Hanekawa, her tone anything but settled. "It's Araragi himself who's nyow heading toward it—mew could say it's always been that simple from the start. This is a tail of him coming to an understanding, and all we nyeeded to do was wait fur him to nyotice."

"Notice?"

"*Nyotice the existence of his partnyer*—though that partnyer *getting caged in* due to a mistake made things a little complicated... It would've all ended on the first day, nyotherwise. This is like a continyuation of the end. That's why I've had to run around everywhere, pouncing and pawing... Rolly-rolly."

"..."

If she was saying anything important, Ononoki couldn't quite figure it out. Still, she did get the vague nyoutline.

Or rather, outline—her job was over. It was an intuition that also sank into her. She could just stay here for the rest of this episode.

She understood—that she only had to wait with these three drunks for Koyomi Araragi to return via Naoetsu High.

This was far from the sense of accomplishment you felt after a job well done—in fact, the realization came with a sense of loss, like something had slipped out of her hands.

But never mind. She knew this day would come.

029

I arrived at Naoetsu High, parked the BMX in the bike lot, and entered its grounds. The air about this place felt completely different.

Not just because everything had been flipped around—there was a gentle sense of rejection, as though I were never meant to come here.

Maybe it had to do with my own mindset?

I started getting the sense that maybe this was what it meant to graduate. I'd felt refreshed in a way after graduating, but coming back here, it was almost like I'd been shoved through the place and extruded out the other end.

I'd had similar thoughts visiting my middle school with Ogi, but all it took was a day's time to feel this way. It wasn't sorrow, nor emptiness, but I think it did come down to my emotions.

Ruminating, I entered the school's halls—Ms. Toé had only written "NAOETSUHIGH" on my back.

Those coordinates were fairly specific, but the Naoetsu High campus was by no means small, so it was hard to decide where to go next—or so I say, but I knew I needed to head to my last classroom first. The one where I spent my days with Hitagi

Senjogahara and Tsubasa Hanekawa.

I didn't know what, or who, would be there, but I climbed the stairs until I arrived at the top floor.

Fortunately, I didn't run into anyone. Classes were done for the day, and the students had filed out. As for the Rainy Devil, or Suruga Kanbaru, she probably hadn't even been here—was she okay in this world? Did she ever come to school? Then again, according to Ms. Toé, those loose ends didn't necessarily have to meet.

This all ran through my mind as I opened the door to a classroom that was so fresh in my memory it didn't even feel nostalgic—and to cut to the chase, I found nothing. The tidied classroom's air just made me feel even more out of place, and naturally, no one else was there, either.

"…"

A swing and a miss? No, Ms. Toé had pointed this way, and it didn't make sense for there to be nothing—did I need to go somewhere else? To another classroom I'd used? How about the gym, or the teachers' room where I'd gotten on my hands and knees? Maybe the athletic field that had hosted more than one battle with an aberration… I could think of a number of places, but none of them stood out.

None of them fit. Ms. Toé never said it'd be a spot I knew well, of course, but given what she must've meant by finding my partner, she did seem to hint at some place connected to Koyomi Araragi… That said, the classrooms I'd used during my first and second years didn't seem likely—I had even less of a connection to them, a year or two having passed since I'd stopped using them to hand them down to my juniors. If this classroom wasn't it, it couldn't be those either…

Could it be the athletic field, after all? It was linked to aberrations.

Or maybe the P.E. shed. That was more linked to Hanekawa

than to aberrations, though…and I felt vaguely awkward about searching it so soon.

And then—I struck upon a different possibility altogether.

If we were talking about my connections to a place, there was a classroom with a deeper tie to me than the one where I spent my senior year. The cause of my time as a high schooler being not all too spectacular, a place where time stopped.

If that was it, I knew for certain who would be there—it felt like I'd just been slapped in the face with the answer.

That happened often with the math puzzles Oikura loved so much. They looked difficult, even impossible, but you figured them out the moment you realized the questioner's intent. That kind of feeling.

Of course.

That's all I could say.

I left the classroom—that was no longer mine.

030

I couldn't believe how casually she sat there.

"Hey, you're late—I've been waiting for ages, my dear senior," I was greeted by a line her uncle might use.

Ogi Oshino.

Ogi. My junior, a first-year at Naoetsu High.

Her impression of her uncle, Mèmè Oshino, may have been her way of getting back at me for the other day. She'd done a pretty good job of it, too.

Yeah, you could tell they were related.

"But wait, what's with that getup? Are you seriously cosplaying me?"

"You say that, but aren't you cosplaying me right back?" I asked in return. Ogi wore a Naoetsu High uniform, which is to say a high-collared jacket, there where she sat on one of the classroom's desks.

A Year 1, Class 3 desk.

But not the *current* Year 1, Class 3, nor an *extant* Year 1, Class 3. It wasn't the classroom once used by me, or later by any of my juniors—no.

The ghost of a classroom that never should have existed, that

Ogi and I wandered into and *got trapped in* not long after she transferred to my school, a room that shouldn't exist at Naoetsu High going by its blueprint—the apparitional Year 1, Class 3.

The place where it all began for Koyomi Araragi and Ogi Oshino, as it were.

"Well, *this* is just a joke. Though *that* was just a joke, too," Ogi said, bemused, her cheeks puffed out like she was trying not to laugh—I guess I looked that funny cosplaying her. "No one told you? Or was everyone just playing along? You absolutely didn't need to wear my uniform just because yours had been swapped out for it."

"Oh."

"Is that all you have to say? 'Oh'? You really are such a fool—but I suppose that's also one of your virtues. Don't worry, nothing too terrible is happening here."

Was that meant to be reassuring?

I had to wonder as I took my seat, finding the chair I'd used at the time. I looked at the clock, and while it was flipped around, its hands were moving, unlike before. After time had started to move back then, it hadn't stopped.

I was all alone with Ogi like before, though—or no, maybe I should say I was by myself?

She was my double, after all. My shadow, my copy, myself as reflected in a mirror.

Ogi Oshino, therefore—*was none other than my partner.*

"Wait, hm? Isn't that weird?"

"Huh? What is it, Araragi-senpai? There's nothing weird going on here." Ogi tilted her head—the way she always did to play dumb.

"Well...aren't you this world's Koyomi Araragi? Since you weren't in it, I was going to turn into you from the pressure this world exerted on me... But if you're here, why was my uniform replaced by a girl's?"

I had the vague notion that this world's Ogi—or this world's Araragi—had gone over to my original world and switched places with me, but if she was here, then maybe not?

Well, as rude as it might sound, she was even more anything-goes than this world, so maybe it was fine for there to be two, or even three of her... Did one go to my world, while another didn't?

"You've thought of all kinds of things, haven't you—you think too much. I'm pretty sure I told Black Hanekawa."

"Huh? You told her? Black Hanekawa? What do you mean..."

But there was only one thing it could mean.

Ogi had been the one to ask that cat to rescue me—she was me, after all, so it made perfect sense once I had the thought. I'd never considered it because Hanekawa and Ogi were on worse than bad terms, but maybe a partnership between them was possible in an inside-out world.

"Thinking too much... Maybe you're right. But I can't be thoughtless here, can I? Without an adequate amount of thinking, and adequate understanding—"

"Is that Ms. Toé's view of things? In the end, though, reason can only get you so far. As strange as that is for me to say." Ogi smirked—a bottomless smile. "No, don't worry, Araragi-senpai. You've reached your goal. You have no further destination after this. You know something?"

"What now?" I replied warily.

If she wanted to start comparing answers with me, how could I not be wary—how, when finding my partner, as everyone had urged me to do, actually meant finding the culprit?

I wasn't ruling out the chance that this was Ogi's all-too-speedy revenge. What she was about to deliver might not be her solution to the puzzle, but a confession.

"Did it never occur to you that this might all be a dream?" she asked me.

231

"Huh? Oh, uh…" The changeup of a question caught me off guard and took the wind out of my sails—what, was she going to hold out here? "I did think about that. More than once… I mean, who wouldn't in this situation? An illogical world full of contradictions where causes don't cause… A lucid dream, is that what you call it? I still think that this might be nothing more than a dream."

"Yes, you're right. It really is like a perfect dream, whether you're getting in a bath with Kanbaru's mom or putting on my school uniform."

"Um, could you not phrase it like I wanted to do those things?"

"Oikura, that hell-sent girl, is here leading such a joyful life. Didn't you want to see that, at least?"

"Oikura? Hell-sent…" I'd never met someone who used that phrase before. Well, I guess it was technically me using it, but it suited that girl to a t. "How do I put it, though. It wouldn't quite make sense if this was a dream. Things that I don't wish for happen here, and the place is teeming with things I don't know."

"Heheheh, I wonder. This idea that what you don't know can't appear in a dream is actually baseless. And nightmares are a thing, aren't they?"

"I considered that, but…are you saying this world is something that I dreamed up? Am I sleeping at home in my bed, still unable to wake up? Do I have this much trouble waking up if my sisters don't do it for me?"

"That, or you got in a traffic accident like Hachikuji or Ms. Toé as you headed back from graduation, riding happily along on my BMX, and you're in a hospital, wandering the border between life and death—it's a vision you're having on the brink of death."

"…"

"No, Shinobu would surely save you in that situation. That's what I'd call overthinking."

It's an illustration, Ogi said. She was as mysterious as ever, with her clear words and murky intent—hard to accept in a partner and double.

"Then what about this?" she went on. "I personally would call it a pretty convincing hypothesis."

"What is it this time? Give it to me, at this point I'm ready to hear whatever you've got."

"Relax, this is my last hypothesis—no need to brace yourself. Everything broke down between you and Sodachi Oikura two years ago in this classroom, right?"

"...Yeah." Sure, things had broken down between me and my former childhood friend long before then—but that day, that time, was decisive.

"Right, right. And you met Kissshot Acerolaorion Heartunderblade during spring break a year ago—so much has happened since then. You got to know Tsubasa Hanekawa, you fell in love with Hitagi Senjogahara, you became pals with Mayoi Hachikuji, you played around with Suruga Kanbaru, you were reacquainted with Nadeko Sengoku—you came across many names in many places, whether it was my uncle, Yozuru Kagenui, Deishu Kaiki, Yotsugi Ononoki, Tadatsuru Teori, or Seishiro Shishirui."

"So? A recap, like now? Are you trying to get your yearbook signed when graduation is already over?"

"Say," Ogi ignored my awkward attempt at a dismissal to continue—to present me with her final hypothesis. *"Say it was all a dream—then what?"*

Not just this tale.

Every tale until now—what if it was all just a dream.

031

Battling on the precipice of death against Kissshot Acerolaorion Heartunderblade.

Being saved by Mèmè Oshino.

Facing Tsubasa Hanekawa—Black Hanekawa.

Catching Hitagi Senjogahara at the bottom of the stairs.

Walking Mayoi Hachikuji home.

Competing for a girl's heart with Suruga Kanbaru.

Freeing Nadeko Sengoku from a charm.

Facing Black Hanekawa again.

Reconciling with Shinobu Oshino.

Banishing Deishu Kaiki.

Fighting Yotsugi Ononoki.

Getting spared by Yozuru Kagenui.

Having Tsubasa Hanekawa confess to me.

Failing to save Mayoi Hachikuji and parting ways.

Confronting Seishiro Shishirui.

Getting reintroduced to Sodachi Oikura.

Failing to save Nadeko Sengoku after all.

Sitting in Tadatsuru Teori's sights.

And settling it all with Ogi Oshino.

An entire year—our year-long tale, all just a dream? I hadn't wandered into another world—but only woken up?

Just as many people do every morning.

I simply woke up? All that sorrow, joy, loneliness, frustration, pain, and fun, all the smiles, tears, words, and strength, all the life and death—was all just something I dreamed? This inconsistent, contradictory world was in fact real, was the original world that I always existed in?

Both sides see the other as the counterfeit—Shinobu had told me, but only my world was the counterfeit?

Only I was the counterfeit. The world had always been universal.

Next morning—I'd wake up as always.

"If you're saying all of it is a dream…" I—Koyomi Araragi, answered. "I'd say I had a wonderful dream, stretch my arms—and know with a smile on my face that an incredible day awaits me."

"An answer you could only dream of."

In that case, let me retract my hypothesis, Ogi said with a shrug—excuse me, what?

"I said I take back my hypothetical. It can't be true. So, why don't we cut out the small talk and get to the topic at hand?"

"Small talk?!"

Hold on, hold on, hold on! It all seemed pretty serious to me!

We neatly summed up all the previous installments and drummed up a crisis that threatened to turn everything on its head, ruining it all!

"Ha haa. Even I don't have the courage."

"I'd say faking me out with something that malicious is pretty brave… Wait, so it's not true? The entire series of tales so far wasn't just a dream?"

"I guarantee it. I mean, just how long would you have to be dreaming for that to be true? Speaking of which, did we discuss it the other day—the butterfly dream? Where you can't tell if you're a human being dreaming of having become a butterfly, or a butterfly dreaming of having become a human being—which would be just a dream when you wake up?"

"Oh…if you put it that way, I guess the idea of experiences all being a dream is thought-provoking."

"But, Araragi-senpai. However thought-provoking, don't you think there's an innegligible hole in it?"

"A hole?" Was she claiming to have found one in a famous anecdote that people have been telling for thousands of years? Now, this was big.

"Challenging historical fact is a part of period mysteries. Just because something is written down in an ancient text doesn't make it indisputable—for example, did the Honnoji Incident really happen?"

"You're saying the butterfly dream isn't real? Is that it?"

"My conclusion is that it never happened—it was just a type of thought experiment by an ancient philosopher. That it, if anything, is a hypothesis. A metaphor. In other words, it's saying, 'I was dreaming. In my dream, I was a butterfly, floating from flower to flower—and then I woke up. I was a human. But then the thought struck me, could I simply be a butterfly dreaming that I'd become human…'"

"I don't see that as contradictory. At least, you can't disprove it in theory."

"But for an entirely emotional argument against it, I'd say, *Who the hell dreams of becoming a butterfly?!*"

There's my double for you. She delivered the quip exactly as I would, in an identical tone—then, a beat later…

"No matter how fantastical a dream, *you're never going to not be you*. Or—has that ever happened to you? Have you ever dreamed of being a butterfly? It doesn't have to be a butterfly. A dream where you're a dog, say, or a bird."

No, I couldn't say I had.

I was pretty sure, too... I'd had a lot of dreams in my life, but they were always from my own point of view—I'd never been anyone other than myself. Even if I budged and pretended that I'd dreamed of being a butterfly, that'd still be a dream about nothing more than *me as a butterfly*. Plus, I didn't imagine a butterfly had the mental capacity in the first place to dream of becoming human.

"Indeed. Dreams are always had from the dreamer's perspective. Butterflies must not be able to recognize themselves in mirrors—but anyway, that's why it's a kind of metaphor. He used the example of a butterfly for ease of understanding. In other words, nothing but-a-flight of fancy," Ogi punned. "*It was all just a dream* endings are considered off-limits not because they're cowardly and unfair, but because they aren't realistic. They aren't convincing— you couldn't possibly accept everything so far being a dream, could you?"

"True, but..."

As her senior, and as her partner, I wanted to respond to her big lie, which had felt a little too true-to-life—but I wasn't going to let Ogi's mean tricks get to me at this point. Sheesh, what was it that this girl wanted to do? Don't confuse me as a prank.

"In that case, what *is* happening to me? You're saying that this isn't a dream either, right? This world, that world. Inside a mirror, the land of mirrors—left and right being flipped around, everything being inside out, it's all so incoherent that my brain can barely handle it. If there's something you know, tell me, I'd really appreciate it. Ogi, what exactly do you know?"

"I don't know anything—you're the one who knows. And the work of understanding falls on you too," she said. "It's because you're so slow to understand that you end up having to cosplay me in an unsightly display."

"Oh...right." Calling me unsightly was going too far, but having nothing to say in return, I asked a question to shift the topic, to hide my embarrassment so to speak. "Whatever this world is, if you exist in it, I don't see any reason for the school uniform in my closet to change into a girl's uniform—could you start by explaining that?"

"I don't think that's where I should begin...and didn't I explain that already?"

"What? No, I don't remember ever getting an explanation?"

"I told you *that* was just a joke too, right at the outset."

"..."

Had she? Ah, yes, but I hadn't taken her meaning. Though I certainly remembered thinking that me cosplaying her as she cosplayed me was some sort of sick joke...

"It should go without saying," averred Ogi, "but let me play the boor and give you the details. You were taking too long sitting back and enjoying your time here flirting with Miss Oikura, so I got annoyed and thought to tease you by swapping my uniform with yours."

"How does that go without saying?!"

Like I'd ever figure out from a single line that she'd been so proactive!

What was the point of this costume change, then?!

"Please don't get so upset. Listen, I wasn't expecting this either. I thought maybe you'd get a little flustered if you saw that your uniform had changed. But you went so far past flustered that you even put on a pair of stockings... I don't think that's normal."

In fact, I ended up being the flustered one, Ogi noted. *I panicked and put a barrier around the whole school.*

So not encountering anyone or being spotted on campus wasn't just dumb luck...

In the end, the change in my school uniform—the idea of changes coming from the opposite vector—was only a prank on Ogi's part.

"Also, while I'm confessing here," she said, "the smirking face you saw in the bathroom mirror when Tsukihi washed your face was also me."

"Not the kind of thing you just tack on to a confession... Seriously? You can do that?"

"Yes. It's hardly impressive, you and I are the same person. Or rather, that was about all I could do, trapped here in this classroom. To fan your sense of crisis, of course."

"..."

Oh. While I was furious, this gave me some respite. For the time being, the idea of me no longer being me, the loss of Koyomi Araragi, was ruled out. But it only meant that the world exerted no pressure on me, and didn't do away with the pressure I put on the world.

Ogi trying to make me fret implied that I needed to hurry up and go home. It was a sort of request on her part, in which case I shouldn't be mad at her—nor would I be awarded any injury time at the end here.

"But even if you're telling me to go home, I don't know how," I grumbled. "Unless you're able to create a gate to the other world like Shinobu? Actually, which are you anyway? The Ogi who's my double, or Ogi, this world's Koyomi Araragi? You could even be both..."

"I'm your double," she answered with unexpected candor—Ogi never answered a simple question with a simple answer, so I was a bit stunned.

Was she being so forthcoming because of how much laid ahead of us? She'd said no more small talk, but were we already on the main topic? Or were we still on the runup—I did hope this was at least the prologue.

"I'm your Ogi Oshino."

"Could you not phrase it that way? Our distance is already awkward enough now that I've learned your true identity."

"How cold—you might be surprised to hear this, but I'm grateful to you in my own way, okay? You risked your life to save me from the Darkness' judgment, and I'd like to pay you back for what you did."

Her tone was far too hollow for me to believe her, but I couldn't ignore her if she put it that way. I was surprised though, I'll admit.

"My double... Does that mean you came into this land of mirrors along with me? I guess you could come to this side as yourself, unlike Shinobu, a vampire... But that does bring back another problem that I thought was solved. In that case, where did the inside-out Koyomi Araragi that should exist in this world go?"

"..."

Oh? Even if it was standard operating procedure for Ogi not to give a straight answer, going silent was unusual—she loved running her mouth just as much as her uncle, or maybe even more than him.

"Ogi?"

"Has anyone talked to you yet...about the reflectivity of mirrors?" she asked, fixing her eyes on me after I called her name—with those black orbs that sucked you in.

"Has anyone... As my double, aren't you aware of my every deed? Oikura told me."

"You're misunderstanding something. It's not as if I grasped everything about you—there'd be no point in my existence. Overlapping and failing to at the same time is what allows me to be my own critic."

Miss Oikura, you say? Just the kind of role she'd play, Ogi laughed. "Yes, the reflectivity of the average mirror is about eighty percent—you could say the rest is blurred, but also that the twenty-or-so percent is whittled away in reflection, and sentenced to death."

"Sentenced to death..."

Right.

We always tend to focus on the larger proportion, on the eighty percent, but if we looked to the remaining twenty percent—well, no, we can't see it.

Because there's no light there. It's absorbed, never reflected back.

"So...Koyomi Araragi never existed in this world to begin with?"

I belonged to the twenty percent that didn't exist? No wonder I couldn't find him no matter how hard I looked. Searching for something that exists is simple compared to searching for something that doesn't—you can seek something that is, but how do you find something that isn't? I was part of the light absorbed by a mirror and not reflected—no, wait.

That couldn't be it—I'd seen myself in the mirror before being sucked into it yesterday, and that's where this whole story began. When I was more vampiric and mirrors didn't reflect me, you might've said that, but not anymore. Even if you ignored that line of reasoning and accepted that I was part of the twenty percent that was left un-reflected, you could still ask, *So what?*

It wasn't as if I'd been sucked into the mirror because I was the light it didn't absorb—because then a lot more than just me would have been sucked in.

"...Is this another hypothesis of yours, Ogi?"

"No, no, you're jumping to the wrong conclusion. I'm not trying to dredge up hypotheses, nor your emotions for that matter... Well, how should I put it. You've jumped to the wrong conclusion, that really is the best way to phrase it."

Hearing this was vexing—jumping to conclusions. Yes, doing so one too many times might be to blame for my predicament. Hadn't I jumped from one conclusion to the next throughout high school?

"But it's not as if I dislike that impatience of yours," Ogi said. "And your kindness, I suppose, how you sympathize with the excised twenty percent."

"…"

She then beckoned me over—what a presumptuous girl, summoning her senior, but I couldn't complain when I was used to Kanbaru doing just that. I stood up and moved over—only now noticing that the seat my double had taken was Oikura's.

God, she really did like staging every last detail.

"Heyyy!" she called out as I approached, motioning for a high five—what the heck?

"Heyyy," I complied.

A nice *smack* filled the room.

"So, what's this about?"

"Well, you know," Ogi said. "You and I are mirror images of the same person—flip sides of each other, yes, but we can't put our hands together like this with a mirror between us, right?"

"…"

I'd had that thought before. When and where?

Strictly speaking, when we talk about a mirror's face, we're referring to the silver coating applied to its backside, so there's always going to be a gap equal to the depth of the glass between your hand and your reflection's, even if you try to make them touch—

"It was when Ms. Toé washed your back. Could you not pretend something that shocking never happened?"

"Oh, was it? It totally slipped my mind since it was nothing to me… Anyway, is that important?"

"We're talking about a mirror's thickness, stop playing thick yourself. What I'm saying is that if you want to enter a mirror—if you want to travel to the land of mirrors—you first need to *physically pass through the glass.*"

You first need a portable portal like a pass loop, Ogi used one of Doraemon's secret tools as an example.

I wasn't so sure about minding physical phenomena in the

context of a feat as fantasyish as entering a mirror, though...

"Fine," I said, "it'd be one thing if I was reflected on water or on polished iron, but with a mirror, the glass acts as a gate I need to pass through first. I get what you're saying, but...so what?"

"So what? So that's the answer—don't you remember what I told you when we were stuck here before?"

"Hm? You told me a whole lot of things. To be specific?"

"Vampires."

Vampires can't enter a room without permission.

Right, she'd said that—which is why we'd been trapped, or why we couldn't get out. And the characteristic meant that as someone with a vampiric aspect, passing through the glass in the first place was much harder than entering a mirror... Even if I could leave my vampiric aspect on the other side in order to do so, it's not like humans can pass through glass. Then again, that rendered everything moot.

In which case, what was this girl trying to say? It felt like she was still toying around with hypotheses...or were we in fact closing in on the solution?

"It's not good to overthink things, but you shouldn't be thoughtless, either—you're right about that, Araragi-senpai. Also, you're thinking about this the wrong way around."

"Hm?"

"You may not be able to pass to the other side of a sheet of glass, but even a vampire can be *pulled into it* from this side."

"Hm?"

"You know how we just discussed all of it being a dream? Well—that's not the case, but what about this? I don't think you can disprove the idea that *this* isn't the real world yet."

I didn't follow. Was she switching topics again without me noticing, maybe going back to an old one? "No, Ogi... If this were the real world, the other side would be the counterfeit. Whether I'm in a dream or in a mirror."

"Don't think of that side as inside a mirror, think of this one as outside it—now do you understand?"

"I don't. You're only making this more confusing—inside, outside, isn't it all the same?"

If we were *outside a mirror*, didn't that place my previous world *inside a mirror*, after all? Actually, no—there was one last possibility I had to consider.

It would never come from me, but had been prompted by Ogi—*the opposite of it all being a dream*.

If I'd always lived in this land of mirrors but been expelled from it—but no, wasn't that only a matter of perspective? It wouldn't change the fact of me being me and barely functioned as an answer to Ogi's question.

So long as I couldn't pass through a sheet of glass, I couldn't enter or exit any land of mirrors—pulled into it? Like *pulling up* a drowning man grasping at straws?

Sure, I couldn't swim, but splashing around in bathwater and checking its temperature wasn't beyond me—no.

Even if you could pull something in through its surface, or that of a mirror across a pane of glass, from the other side—what exactly had I offered a hand to?

"The twenty percent, that's what," Ogi said. "The light that should've been absorbed *and never reflected*—you scooped it up and rescued it. *You opened the gate* and brought it to this side for safety. You ended up *making* this world into the land of mirrors. You haven't come to it—*you pulled it in*. Almost like they say the ancient gods pulled all of Japan together as one."

032

That, of course, was another joke.

I expected Ogi to follow up with a line like that, but she didn't. *Honestly, one wrong step there and it would've been a disaster*, she said instead, as if to frighten me.

She seemed to be having fun.

"You didn't get caught up in this land of mirrors, Araragi-senpai, you got it caught up with you."

"…"

"Of course, this town is the only thing being affected, in spite of all the talk of worlds and lands—but please do be careful going forward. I'm not sure how much you realize this, but you've subdued a legendary vampire, built amicable relationships with gods, and are one and the same as me, someone with all kinds of elements from all kinds of aberrations. You suggested earlier that anything goes with me, but I'd say you're pretty anything-goes yourself."

Then the culprit wasn't Ogi.

It was me—okay, it was Koyomi Araragi either way. But it didn't change the fact that I was playing solitaire. It didn't, but…

"Isn't this already a disaster? You could put me on the same level as Shinobu when she destroyed the world in another time-line. Messing up an entire town—"

"Oh, no. This is still just a counterfeit. I said you pulled this land together, but it's not like you did that physically. It's only a question of how you feel about it. If that side is a counterfeit, then so is this one—just like Miss Shinobu said. All you did was bring a sense of *maybe it's all my imagination* to the entire town. It's not as if anything you did stopped being history, right? You only modestly rescued the light that was lost, the light that had gone out of sight—you only gave everyone a tiny little reminder of the forgotten ones, those feelings that had been left behind."

Though you did put us in a dangerous spot, she said consolingly—well, no, I was sure it was just mean-spirited nagging.

"It won't be a problem if you act appropriately from here. Yes, to put it as you might, it'll just seem like you had a wonderful little dream."

"Appropriately..." I sat down, all the strength instantly draining from my body. "It seems to me like there's a lot you're going to have to tell me if I want to do that."

"Yes, and that's why I'm here—we couldn't bother any experts over something like this. I was impressed by Yotsugi Ononoki's emergency response, but this story of aberrations is compact enough that we can handle it between you and me... Do be careful going forward, though. Don't forget that we're marked by those experts for observation."

"..."

True. A chilling thought.

If Miss Gaen got word of this—fine, she knew everything, so maybe she already did. I could imagine how pissed she was at me for stirring up trouble all over again, after we'd pacified the town by settling that whole series of incidents... In fact, she might more than just scold me.

"No," disagreed Ogi, "while she might know about this affair, she hasn't the right to blow her top. She was the one who *left behind* Toé Gaen's existence, after all, here in this town—and while it turned out for the best, I doubt it had been on purpose. It sure would've taken you longer to arrive at this classroom, though, without Ms. Toé."

"I don't get it… If you want to hurry me up so badly, why not come meet me at my house instead of sitting cooped up in this classroom?"

"Like I said, I was locked in—because this classroom was established as where I belong. *This* is my own lingering regret—or mistake, or stroke of bad luck… I failed to secure a good place for myself. That's why messing with you in a roundabout way was the best I could do—anything may go when it comes to me, but I'm not omnipotent."

"…"

"Miss Gaen must have left Ms. Toé behind due to some bitter memories, but I bet it was a simple case of lingering regret for Miss Hanekawa. Saying goodbye to everyone must've been very difficult. Almost like a six-year-old child, don't you think? Then again, that might be why we could work in tandem…"

And yet she left with a big smile on her face. That big-breasted girl is as foolish as they come, Ogi laughed—apparently disliking Hanekawa as always.

Still, she'd allied herself with the class president among class presidents when this wasn't even the land of mirrors. Did that mean there'd been a change in her nevertheless?

Just as I'd changed—perhaps Ogi could, too?

"Hanekawa…felt that way when she left? She's my friend, but I didn't do anything to show her I understood that at all."

"That large-chested senior of mine would only hate it if someone saw straight through her, friend or not. She's the kind of person who hides many things and has lots of secrets—you don't believe Miss Oikura wanted you to know that she hoped to be better friends with you when she left this town, do you?"

"…"

"Then there's Kissshot Acerolaorion Heartunderblade when she was a human, and those vestiges of the living Yotsugi Ononoki—and Karen Araragi's complex about not being girly. Mayoi Hachikuji, who could never become an adult—and the savagery lurking in Nadeko Sengoku and Suruga Kanbaru. These were all forgotten, or were things they wish they could forget. You took *all those things* that were left behind and brought them to this side. That's how you created—the so-called land of mirrors."

It's like some sort of light-based magic trick, Ogi quipped—and also that if she used black magic, I must use white magic.

That made sense. If she belonged to the element of darkness, my element was light, in contrast to her—though it sounds like bragging to assign yourself light as an element. I was buying myself shoes I could never fill.

"The mirror was nothing more than a catalyst—or maybe a detonator, but in any case, it only provided the chance. Of course, a mirror being the cue for all this did cause everything in the world to be flipped around."

"If I didn't get caught up in the land of mirrors but got it caught up with me—then I guess this was far from a lukewarm setup. Hm? In that case, did Ononoki and Oikura feel that something about the world was off not because of the negative effects that I had on it as an outsider, but rather because of its shortcomings?"

"I'd call them excesses, not shortcomings. You dragged another twenty percent from the land of mirrors, giving this place a hundred and twenty percent—it's going to run over, beyond capacity like that. Either way, it doesn't have much to do with them interacting with you. So if you feel like it, you're welcome to fool around with Miss Oikura."

Just as with Ms. Toé and Black Hanekawa, she's not the real thing, though—Ogi said. That was a relief, or rather, I needed to straighten out the situation before the real Oikura came back to this town by some mistake.

"I need to figure something out...or wait...can we return things back to the way they were? Can we make this inconsistent world into a consistent one again?"

"I wouldn't call it going back to the way things were. It might be more like moving forward—with an extra twenty percent in tow. Everyone regained what they'd lost, if only temporarily, so there will of course be some effect. That would be the influence you exert, if anything—for example, I imagine Miss Kanbaru is going to dream about Ms. Toé for a little while. Nothing more serious than that."

"Can I really think of this as not having done anything serious?"

I couldn't tell if Ogi was trying to be considerate, or if she was trying to bully me... Still, it was a load off my chest to know that despite inconveniencing everyone, I hadn't done them any harm.

How would I ever forgive myself if Shinobu, who'd even taken the form of a little girl, could no longer be certified as harmless?

"Ha haa. You know, I think this turned out to be a good test case."

"A test case? Of what?"

"You foolishly saved me when I should've been sucked up by the Darkness. My uncle may have supported your intentions there, but it's not as if all those experts wholeheartedly approve of what you did. I think it's clear as day that no small number of ungenerous characters would have rather seen a dangerous element like myself disappear."

I count myself among them by the way, said a self-flagellating Ogi—while she often said these kinds of things to feign humility, I could tell she really meant it now.

"Yet this time, I acted as your safety valve—letting me live had some meaning. Forget being certified as harmless, I think this confirms it as fact. The surveillance level on you could rise a bit, though."

"..."

The surveillance level? I didn't need any more freeloaders. Ononoki was plenty on her own.

"Of course, walking away from this situation as it stands will have them swooping in and crushing it with all their might. Miss Gaen will get ready to face off against her sister, I'm sure—would you like that? I do think it's a valid option. We could live in this inconsistent world forever."

"Don't make me weird offers. Why would I ever want that? I just want to hurry up and go home...or I guess that's not how I should put it. I'm already home. Um..."

How should I word it?

Release the twenty percent of light I pulled into this world back through the mirror? How would I go about doing that? I didn't even know how I pulled it here in the first place...

"I do want—to hurry up and proceed."

"Ha haa. And again, that's why I'm here—I take care of your mess-ups. Just as you take care of mine."

"Kind of feels like an unfair peace treaty to me..."

No, I couldn't say that as a fact. This could have turned into a genuine calamity—both Ogi and Shinobu called it a counterfeit, but when a screen is exposed to light for too long, that light can burn itself in. If I'd accepted Ogi's offer just now—this world would be permanent.

She'd put a stop to it at the last second, and I sincerely owed her. I'd thought this might be her all-too-speedy revenge, but in fact it had been her payback that was speedy.

Her payback in a backwards world.

Though I wish I could come up with a better line than that.

"Um, could you please wait a second? I'm going to bring something out," Ogi said, sticking her hand in her school jacket and fishing around before pulling out a bare Blu-ray—why stick it uncased in your uniform, I wondered, what if you scratched the disc, but no, it was no Blu-ray.

Because it was pure black.

Black like darkness.

A Blu-ray was a reflective silver on at least one side—while on both sides of the palm-sized, disc-shaped object Ogi held by the edges, as if to keep any fingerprints from getting on it, was a shade of black that felt like it could suck you in.

"Um...was that how PlayStation 1 games were?"

"Bingo. But this isn't a PlayStation 1 game—I do have a PSX at home and would be happy to play with you, just not this. Because..."

Ogi threw it at me side-armed, like a frisbee—why make it so hard to catch when we were so close, I wasn't a dog, I thought, but I somehow grabbed it, using my torso as a net.

"Look," she urged.

And all I needed to do was look—because you couldn't play this on a console when it had no donut hole.

A perfectly disc-shaped object, the kind you might expect to see in a math textbook—even a jet-black game disk might reflect something, but this one didn't.

It reflected nothing to an excessive degree.

A flat, total black, like it had been painted.

Almost seeming to absorb any and all light that hit it—darkness.

"..."

I returned the black object to Ogi with trepidation, as if I were handling a bomb. "Don't act so scared," she said, taking it and raising it overhead before continuing, "Zero percent reflectivity—a mirror that's a hundred percent absorbent."

A mirror...that black?

Well, like she said—it was zero percent reflective.

"I was bored, stuck here in this classroom. Crafting something like this was about all I could do—using the blackboard."

"The blackboard?"

I glanced over...and looking closely, found a chip missing from the corner. I had no idea what kind of tools and technology she'd used to create a disc out of it, though... That was some impressive DIY work.

I never imagined a piece of Year 1, Class 3 classroom's ghost, which I'd fixed in place, could take such a form... Was it like plucking a four-leaf clover to keep with you?

"I guess," affirmed Ogi. "It carries just as much supernatural power, if not more. You're planning on visiting Kita-Shirahebi after this, right? In that case, I want you to offer it to the shrine there—it's what you might call a votive object."

"A votive object..."

This reminded me—as items that reflected the truth, mirrors were seen as holy since ancient times. Forget votive objects, they could even be treated like dwellings for the divine. Could Ogi's handmade mirror, this black mirror, be one?

"Call it a gift to congratulate Hachikuji on her new post as god—it seems like she wasn't able to fully deal with this situation, which is no surprise given that she only became a deity thanks to a sophistic technicality, but in reality, as the god meant to protect this town, she's the one who needs to settle this all peacefully, not me. I suppose I'll let her take the credit."

"That shrine is the heart of this town. What's going to happen when I place it there? If it has zero reflectivity, it doesn't just show you nothing...it can even suck light into itself, right?"

"Well, it's going to suck up that twenty percent of light that would have been lost if you hadn't guided it here—lingering regrets and remnants that ought to have faded into obscurity. Part of a shrine's job to accept those, right? Kita-Shirahebi is also an air pocket that attracts the stuff that aberrations are made of, and now that Mister Shishirui is no longer with us, it requires a tool to help it absorb wayward thoughts."

True. It was asking too much of Hachikuji, who only happened to become a god due to the way everything progressed, to keep the town tranquil and pacified all on her own. We might have tied up those loose ends, all too neatly, but if there were any remaining openings, or maybe concerns, it was this.

Miss Gaen would surely continue to follow up on the situation, but it wasn't as if she could spend all her time worrying about one town... I didn't see the harm in bringing over one of these votive objects, or a cheat item.

"Okay. I'll offer it to the shrine."

"I appreciate it. By the way, you'll know it's time to swap it out once it's turned completely white."

"So it's like a filter? How long does it last?"

"A few centuries, under normal circumstances...but then we're talking about this town. A town once attacked by a legendary vampire, a town that you now grace with your presence—who knows, it might only last a few months."

"You really know how to scare me."

This time, Ogi offered the black mirror to me with care, and I took it with reverence—if what she said was true, offering it to the shrine wouldn't fix everything. I needed to keep on frequenting Kita-Shirahebi, I thought—hm?

"What's the matter, Araragi-senpai?"

Just as Ogi handed me the mirror and we both held it, together.

Just as Ogi and I faced each other, with what was still a mirror between us, even if it was zero percent reflective—a black mirror between us, its front side indistinguishable from its back, I thought, *Hold on.*

My doubts were reignited.

Ogi's flowing delivery made me think that all the mysteries

had been solved, that we even had countermeasures—but one vital point remained vague.

I got that I'd scooped up this lost twenty percent from the other side of the mirror at that moment—but still didn't know why.

Rescuing these poor little regrets left lingering behind to fade away and giving them form sounded nice, but I hadn't meant to do anything so noble.

In fact, I hadn't known anything about reflectivity and the like until Oikura ('s residual thoughts?) bothered to school me.

Yes, I'd reached out to the mirror yesterday morning because something seemed wrong with the me I saw in it—my reflected self in the mirror. It had stopped.

"Unlike the reflection I saw in the sink, that wasn't you, right? Then what exactly—"

"Come up with the answer to that one on your own, at least. Think about it, reflect on it."

"You mean it requires self-reflection?"

"Yes, I suppose. Really, consider what you've done…or so I say, but we'd be back at square one if you started overthinking things again. I'll borrow a page from my predecessors and just give you a hint."

Ogi let go of the black mirror.

And said: "Who exactly are you?"

What, she wanted me to say it? My expression turned sober and austere, but I couldn't reply to her question any other way. Even a lukewarm setup needed a reasonably serious conclusion.

So I answered her, looking into the dark black mirror.

"Koyomi Araragi here. Just the man you see."

And then I understood.

Of course.

My own lingering regrets.

033

The epilogue, or maybe just a log in this case?

Either way, I was the one to rouse myself the next day, not my little sisters Karen and Tsukihi—I did have some help from an alarm clock if we're splitting hairs, but I think it still counts.

I was alone in my room, of course, with no childhood friend sharing it with me. Getting ready to leave the house, I saw my tall little sister, and my other little sister who was the exact same; I flipped the skirt of an expressionless doll, then headed to the bathroom mirror to straighten out my hair, when the doorbell rang.

It was Hitagi Senjogahara.

Not a second off our agreed-upon time. Did she wear a stopwatch for a wristwatch, or what? Either way, I stepped outside with a *see ya later*—

"Good morning, Koyomi," she waved at me from the other side of the gate, her hair in pigtails.

I nearly lost my balance.

To go into more detail before I regain my balance, Hitagi Senjogahara had on pigtails, a miniskirt, a smaller t-shirt that emphasized her figure ever so slightly, and a shawl draped over her.

She looked like a nymph who'd fallen from heaven.

Oh no. I froze, afraid this entire dimension had been twisted in some way again, but…

"Just trying to imitate Miss Hanekawa is only going to leave me depressed. I thought I'd go big and went for a makeover. What do you think? Am I on point?" she explained.

If I had to pick one or the other, she was off point. I couldn't figure out why her style was regressing the moment she graduated, but when I asked her, she replied:

"*Mature* isn't such a compliment now that I'm not a high school student anymore, so I thought I'd go for a youthful look."

It seemed Hitagi had her own thoughts about graduating from high school. What in the world was she thinking, though? Maybe it was a serious problem for a girl.

"Still, Hitagi. Isn't your skirt too short? Your legs are extra-long to begin with, so it's a pretty overboard look. You're going to make your boyfriend worry."

"Overboard? How rude. It's fine, it might look like a skirt, but these are actually shorts where the fabric around the outside is designed to look like a skirt. It's a marvelous garment that fulfills a lady's desire to wear a cute skirt without showing off her underwear."

"They make clothes like that?" The world was full of things I didn't know—I shouldn't have been satisfied simply wearing Ogi's skirt… "Is it like a running skirt? Anyway, this is a big makeover for you."

"Heh. Well, I wouldn't have minded showing off even more skin when I consider the peaks of excitement I'll be feeling when we find out you got into college."

"Doesn't that mean it'll be hell on earth if I got rejected?"

Anyway, warming up to each other from having this conversation right off the bat, we left—to visit none other than my first-choice school, which had already accepted Hitagi Senjogahara.

Actually, that description is the other way around. The college was Hitagi Senjogahara's first-choice school, and I'd done my best to get in so I could attend the same school as my girlfriend... But it's easy for the order of things to get flipped around, and if I found myself on the wrong side of the school's gates, I'd be the one turned inside out.

"So," Hitagi fished for info as we walked to the bus stop, "how did it go this time around? I'd be happy to hear all about it, if you want to tell me. I think you might feel better if you did."

"...I wouldn't say an envious position, but you've certainly settled into a delicious one."

In terms of resourcefulness, she was on a different level from the likes of Oikura. I wished I could be like Hitagi someday and just get to listen to stories of other people's adventures from a safe distance.

"Well, you know," she said. "If this were *Columbo*, my goal is to be the missus."

"That's as delicious as it gets." A hall-of-fame role as far as never being in danger—though even Mrs. Columbo was once targeted by a killer.

"In other words, I may have allowed Hachikuji to be this town's lord, but there's no way I'd let anyone else be your lady."

"I'm happy to hear that, but are you really telling me there was a time you were angling to become a god?"

No fact could raise more hairs.

In any case, I gave Hitagi an outline of the last couple of days—naturally, she'd experienced them as well, but when I'd surveyed Karen, Tsukihi, and Ononoki about the topic, their recollection of what had happened seemed vague.

Light had flooded the entire town, creating enough confusion to make you think you were in another world, and yet no one found it strange. They just went along with their lives, facing today as another day—looking to the future just a little bit more than yesterday.

I guess I shouldn't expect anything else from a logical world?

Consistency worked itself out when it came to this kind of thing, it seemed—maybe Ogi was right and it was all just an issue of mindset, but at the same time, I couldn't shake the feeling that it was all very slipshod.

This left me with some thoughts I hadn't sorted through as a first party in the matter, but Hitagi turned out to be right. I did feel a little better telling her about it all.

"You did a good job," she said with a smile, applauding after she'd finished hearing me out—well, she clapped twice above her head and a little to the left, so it seemed more like a flamenco move than applause.

Or maybe she'd summoned ninjas?

"That was quite the satisfying story. I would say its message comes off a little too strong, though. Were you too fired up over your first case since graduating high school?"

"There's no message. I'd be happy if it earned the label of a slapstick comedy now that it's over."

"You know, Koyomi, I actually kind of like the way you're so aggressive about toeing the line between cheating on me and not. Keep on keeping me on pins and needles, okay?"

"What kind of woman are you? Hearing you say that puts me on pins and needles, if anything. And that wasn't the point... Were you even listening?"

"Of course. I'd never fail to, Koyomi. You really have grown over the last year. You might require support, and from so many women too, but it's as if you solved everything on your own."

"On my own, no..."

I wasn't sure how to count Ogi. She was a partner, but she was me.

Either way, though, I had everyone to thank.

"Oh, you're always so modest. Look at how you've matured. Can I start calling you Daddy?"

260

"That's not even funny. Who matures that much in a couple of days?"

"You know how people wonder why mirrors reverse left and right, but not up and down?"

If we were talking about lines, she shifted lines of conversation as smoothly as ever. "Oh, yeah… That's like a trick question, right? Where if you put a mirror on the floor and stand on top of it, it does reverse up and down."

"Yes. In other words, up, down, left, and right are all about perspective—but aren't there facets of it that you're still missing? I doubt you've forgotten everything you learned about science already—so you know how when we see things through our eyes, the eyeball acts as a lens that reflects the image it receives from light on the retina, reversing it?"

"Oh, yeah…" That was something I learned in human anatomy class during elementary or middle school, not while studying for college entrance exams, but I did recall—that while mirrors were mirrors, there was also the question of the lens. "And?"

"Well, it was just such a mystery to me as a child. Why don't we see the world in reverse, even though it looks that way on the retina?"

"Oh, umm."

Umm, what was the answer to that?

I felt like I'd read about it in a trivia book, not any textbook… That because up and down are relative just like left and right, our brains adjust what we see even if it's upside down—or something?

"It's a matter of practice, in other words," Hitagi said. "Just like how you were so in love with the idea of being left-handed that you wore your watch on your right wrist and practiced writing with your left hand."

"You aren't going to let that one go, are you…"

Personally, I wished that my actions then belonged to the twenty percent—though I did continue to wear my watch on my right wrist.

It was a habit by now.

But she'd said practice, not habit.

"How did it all start in the first place?" she asked me. "It was a little abstract and hard to understand, but why did your mirror image stop in the mirror, again?"

"Like I said—it was regret that lingered there. A symbol of it all. Now that I've graduated, lost my title as student, and am trying to move on, it was the part of Koyomi Araragi that I'm trying to leave behind."

"…"

"In other words, those were the regrets I tried to put behind me yesterday, and leave there—but I missed it all so much that I ended up reaching out for them. The stuff about me rescuing the lost twenty percent was a consequence of that—nothing but a byproduct. All I tried to do when I saw myself in the mirror for the first time in so long was to remember something I was close to forgetting."

Everything else had only gotten wrapped up in it.

Entangled in an act I performed for my own sake.

Ogi was right, I needed to think about what I'd done.

I'd forced the entire town to partake in my own sentimentality, in my meddling with a mirrored world…

"True, but it must've been fun for everyone, no? It's not as if you put anyone's life in danger," Hitagi said offhandedly.

She hardly understood the gravity of it—that's an irresponsible spectator for you.

"People influence the world around them just by passing someone on the street. You shouldn't worry about it too much. I've caused a lot of folks trouble over the course of my life, but I believe they grew as people by overcoming those troubles."

"That's the most selfish excuse I've ever heard."

"Someday, they'll say they're the individuals they are now

thanks to the trouble I caused them."

"They wouldn't be complimenting you…"

"People are tougher than you'd expect. A world where everything is inside out—I have to admit, I'd be interested to know how I was in that world," Hitagi brought up a topic that interested me very much as well, to be honest.

"Hmm, well, I never got a chance to meet you. I think it's one of those things better left to the imagination."

"Why? You should've gone and met me. I appreciate your consideration, but I wish you'd be a little rougher with me. But maybe that's only the kind of thing a spoiled girl asks for. Still, what were they, anyway? These lingering regrets of yours, Koyomi—were you able to address them?"

"It was because I did, according to Ogi, that we managed to regain control. And that's why she could create the black mirror, or something. I actually don't know what they are myself."

"What? Really?"

"Yeah…but that's what makes it something I've forgotten and left behind. Of all my experiences in the virtual land of mirrors, I don't know which was my own regret—maybe there was more than one."

While they were the lingering regrets of all the girls—they were mine as well, according to Ogi. Their twenty percent, and my twenty percent too.

Feelings forgotten and left behind.

Maybe I wanted to apologize about the time I saw Karen in a skirt and laughed. Maybe Ononoki being a doll didn't allay my remorse for making her attack Tadatsuru Teori. I couldn't save Hachikuji and had her deified. I could never do anything about Kanbaru's left arm as a student. I couldn't come to Oikura's aid sooner. As far as Sengoku, that one goes without saying—and I continued to bind Shinobu to my shadow.

Year 1, Class 3—and so much more.

I had a mountain of regrets.

I couldn't claim that I'd graduated with a clear conscience—even if I did, I could never say for certain.

I merely remembered it and faced it.

That was probably enough.

I wouldn't be able to shoulder it all, nor could I carry it with me.

I wasn't Hanekawa or Oikura, but I still needed to pack as light as possible for my journey—I only had so much space in my suitcase.

Still, there was nothing wrong with thinking back on it every now and then, yes?

"Yes…you're right. I suppose your regrets linger because you leave them behind. Leaving little bits of your heart along the path, à la Hansel and Gretel, might be kind of convenient—for fondly looking back on it."

"I'm not sure that's how it works, but yeah, that'd be neat."

"If you don't know, though, that makes me wonder. Which of those regrets were yours? I feel like everyone's slightly skewed image of you might be a hint. The ideal Koyomi Araragi—and the mirrored Koyomi Araragi. I'm just being silly… I wouldn't keep wearing my hair in these childish pigtails if your regret was not getting to bathe with Kanbaru's mom, though."

"Don't worry, I'm pretty sure that wasn't it… Also, there's one thing I can say for certain."

Then—putting my arm around Hitagi's shoulder as she walked beside me, I tugged her close.

"I didn't have any regrets when it comes to you. Because we're always going to be together from now on."

"Let's wait until we see your exam results. We're going to be far apart if you don't get in."

Her words were more ruthless than realistic, but she didn't try to brush off my arm—a relief, given all the courage it took to put it there.

We'd managed to walk quite a distance while we chatted. One more pedestrian crossing and we'd be at our bus stop—not our final destination, of course, just a checkpoint. We needed to get on a train, keep on walking, climb some stairs, cross a pedestrian bridge, get on an elevator, get on an escalator, and walk some more.

"By the way," Hitagi said as we stood side by side at a red light. "Remember what we said about *sansukumi*, the original form of rock-paper-scissors—one of the reasons Hachikuji became a god? I heard that the slug in that game used to be a centipede."

"A centipede? Really?"

"Yes, I don't remember why, but what started out as a game of frog, snake, and centipede turned into frog-snake-slug over the years... I guess if you think of which one a snake would hate more, the hundred-legged centipede makes more sense."

Hm, no legs at all versus a hundred. That did make sense.

"Of course, I'd flinch if I saw any of them. Frog, snake, slug, or centipede."

"Seriously? My impression was that you didn't mind that sort of thing."

"I'm a girl, okay," teased Hitagi, grabbing both of her pigtails and flapping them around.

What? So cute...

Speaking of flinching, though. And centipedes.

"It only happens every once in a while," I said, "but I've always had this problem. Waiting for a pedestrian light to change, I suddenly can't figure out which foot I should start with when it turns green. Do I take the first step with my right foot, or with my left? I should probably just make a rule about it, like some kind of superstition."

Thinking leads to hesitation.

Yes, you could call it overthinking and yell at me to hurry up

265

and take that step, but if it were that easy, it wouldn't be a problem in the first place. No conceptual leaps come from overthinking things, I've been told time and again, but it's not as if humans can stop thinking.

My mind might know that I need to move forward, but my legs just won't.

Like my body is flinching.

As if my feet are choking—I sit there, unable to take a single step, like the centipede who forgets how to walk.

Even if I know it's nothing major that could define my fate, it leaves me not knowing which way to go.

My body, rather than my thoughts, gets left behind.

"That's your problem?" asked Hitagi, guffawing. She never used to laugh with such hearty cheer—but she was a lively young woman now. "If you don't know which foot to start with, you just have to do this."

She made sure the light had turned green. Checking both ways to make sure it was safe—she crouched.

Hitagi Senjogahara lowered her center of gravity, and then...

"Hup!"

Jumped forward with both legs.

Teal, don't mink.

With my arm still wrapped around the former track runner's shoulder, her resilient legs pulled me along. I rushed to trail after her, not wanting to be left behind, moving forward—leaping towards the light, with an extra twenty percent.

Ending the tale that continued for so long.

Recalling my remembrances, leaving behind what lingered.

The margins open for notes, a note in the air.

We flew to our next tale.

Afterword

Taking my life until now and thinking about the proportion of *things I've done* and *things I haven't done*, the latter is overwhelmingly larger, which makes total sense, because when you're *doing something*, you're ultimately *not doing everything else*. Furthermore, *working at something* means *slacking off on everything else*. When I read about great historical figures, the absurd amount of effort geniuses spend for their goals often leaves me speechless, but on second thought, weren't they neglecting quite a large portion of the rest of their lives? Could it be that we can't do everything in the end, that we always have to give up on something? Choosing one form of happiness means sacrificing other forms—and the antonym of fortune is not misfortune, but other fortunes? Not infrequently, when you think "I did it!" you've lost much of whatever else is important to you, and as you keep on doing that, things proceed to a point where there's no turning back, or something like that. Still, it's unrealistic to do just a little bit of lots of things, or at least it wouldn't be very fruitful. Of course, they also say that mastery in one thing leads to all things, and what you learn by plumbing the depths of one field can in fact apply to others, so doing something is certainly better than doing nothing at all. But in that case, since the difference between *doing* and *being able to* is quite salient, it'd be pretty rough if *what you did* equaled *what you couldn't*. Just accumulating more regret and remorse the more you do something is depressing, but I also feel that thinking "if only I'd done it *so*" actually leads to more than you'd expect.

And so, here's a bonus installment of the *MONOGATARI* series. One last stubborn book. The actual final volume was the one before this, *End Tale Part 03*, so I wanted to go back to the roots of what it means to read a novel, which is to say I aimed for a book that you can read or just as well not. In that spirit, it's filled to the brim with unignorable contradictions. A worldview that doesn't require thinking about how to pay off foreshadowing is nice in its own way. It'd be a problem if I always did that, though. Anyway, this has been *End Tale (Cont.)*, "Final Chapter: Koyomi Reverse," or not knowing when to quit. Oh, speaking of which, it's a little late, but I changed the subtitle from "Koyomi Book" because that obviously deserved to be a *Calendar Tale* subtitle instead.

We see a happy Miss Sodachi Oikura on the cover here. So cute! I was asking for a lot when I pushed for the choice, but VOFAN did an incredible job. Thank you. I'd also like to give my deepest thanks to all of you who've read all of the installments of the *MONOGATARI* series. Even this one, which you could just as well not—I couldn't be happier.

Great work, everyone!

NISIOISIN

NISIOISIN

Art by
Kinako

The Dark St★r that Shines for You Alone

1 Pretty Boy Detective Club

JOIN THE CLUB

Ten years ago, Mayumi Dojima saw a star...and she's been searching for it ever since. The mysterious organization that solves (and causes?) all the problems at Yubiwa Academy—the *Pretty Boy Detective Club* is on the case! Five beautiful youths, each more eccentric than the last, united only by their devotion to the aesthetics of mystery-solving. Together they find much, much more than they bargained for.

AVAILABLE NOW!